"A STURDY, MEDIUM-SIZED DOG SAT UNDER THE TREES"

(See page 60)

BEAUTIFUL JOE'S PARADISE

OR

THE ISLAND OF BROTHERLY LOVE

A SEQUEL TO "BEAUTIFUL JOE"

BY

MARSHALL SAUNDERS

AUTHOR OF
BEAUTIFUL JOE
FOR HIS COUNTRY
TILDA JANE
&c.

ILLUSTRATED BY
CHARLES LIVINGSTON BULL

L. C. PAGE & COMPANY
·BOSTON· ·MASS· ·MCMII·

526b6

280300
29 · 11 · 32

preface

For a long time I have had in mind a story bearing on the immortality of animals. Some four years ago, while walking with my father, I sketched the outline of this paradise for animals that I so earnestly wished to write about. He was much interested, and said at once, " You should make your old favourite Joe the hero of this paradise." Almost shocked at the idea of trading, as it were, on the popularity of the dear old animal, I said, firmly, " I can not do that. I shall never bring Joe into another story."

However, last autumn, when in great grief over the death of a beloved dog, my mind turned strongly

to my animal story, old Joe was ever before me. He, and only he, was suited to preside over the happy republic where the animals found themselves after death.

Struggle against it as I would, Joe constantly confronted me, and as his death has occurred since the publication of the story of his life, I at first reluctantly, then gladly, introduced my former friend into a second story.

This is my apology for a sequel — an after-part — which in many cases is of doubtful discretion.

Marshall Saunders.

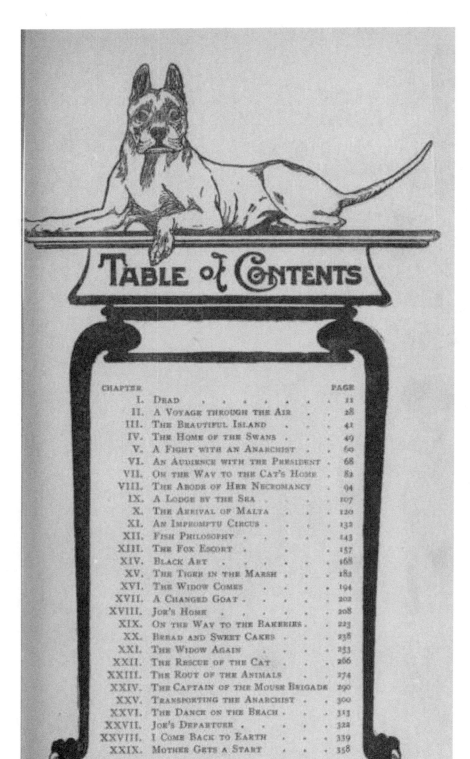

TABLE of CONTENTS

LIST OF ILLUSTRATIONS

BEAUTIFUL JOE"S PARADISE

CHAPTER I.

DEAD

I HAVE had some pretty queer adventures lately, and as I don't want to forget one of them, and as 1 also want old Joe's friends to hear about them, I am going to write them down.

I will start at the first. My name is Sam Emerson, and I live in San Francisco — used to live East, but came West for my mother's health. She is a widow, and I am her only child. People say she spoils me, but that is a mistake. I spoil her.

Well, one day a month ago, I came into the house with Ragtime under my arm.

Ragtime is my bull terrier, or was. He was wrapped up in me, and I — well, I guess I just liked Ragtime about as much as a boy ever liked a dog.

He was dead. — There was a fellow called Geoffrey Hillington living next door to us. He was a

Californian, and nearly six feet tall, as a good many Californian boys have a trick of getting when they are about sixteen.

Geoffrey was a perfect gentleman according to the gospel of his mamma, and he hated me.

I don't know why, for I never did a thing to him till he began to make faces at me. Maybe he was jealous because I was tough and could knock about, while he had to stay in the house a good deal and keep his legs on a chair because they grew so fast.

It was a very pretty hatred. We never tired of doing things to each other, and I never slacked up, even when an awful fear came over me that he would strike at me some day through Ragtime.

I kept the dog with me all the time, except when I was in school, and then he was shut up, but even a cat will be caught napping, and one day mother sent me on an errand across the street, and I forgot Ragtime.

I raced back when I remembered, but it was too late. My foe was ever watchful. He had been out in his garden. There was a ladder against the wall that his father's gardener had been using. He mounted it with his pocket full of stones.

I won't say that he intended to kill the dog. He only threw stones when Ragtime began to tell him in dog language that the wall was half ours, and not all his. A nasty sharp-pointed bit of rock hit

the dog on the head. There was just a little dent in Rag's velvet forehead when I picked him up, only that and nothing more, but he was as limp as a doll.

I held him in my arms. I didn't know there was

I such a difference between a dead dog and a live one. His legs hung loose. Then I took him in the house. I put him on my bed and sat down by him. Where was Ragtime? A few minutes ago he had been screaming, jumping, yelping — now he was only a warm heap of bones and flesh.

Ragtime was not here. I had lost him. The stupid feeling went away. Something awful came over me. Ragtime was dead, but his murderer was alive.

I pushed away the servants — mother had gone cut — and rushed down-stairs.

I didn't stop to ring the Hillingtons' bell. I tore into the garden. Geoffrey was lying in a hammock. He looked kind of white when he saw me coming, but his lip went up into its usual curl, and I could see the word " Baby! " coming out of his mouth.

It never got out. I gave a roar. I had never fought him because he was so large, but now there was a demon in each of my fists. I butted the hammock, and he went sprawling on the ground.

Then I called to him to get up. He did, and I ran at his legs and upset him again. Then I pounded him. I was going to make him suffer, and

I did, until, in the midst of my jellying, I thought of his mother.

" Ragtime! Ragtime! Ragtime! " I howled in his ears. Then I finished mashing and pounding him, and let him get in a few digs. They didn't hurt me, for my flesh was like iron, and they encouraged him.

Then I keeled him over once more. He went down like a gum-tree and I ran home.

If there was a God of justice surely he would let Ragtime come to life — no, he wouldn't. There lay my dog on the bed, getting cold and stiff now.

I shut the door, and pulled down the blinds. This was death. I had heard of it before, but hadn't had much acquaintance with it. In school, we used to sing about the old King reaper, who with his sickle keen, bearded the little children, but singing is nothing, talking is nothing, hearing is nothing, it's feeling that counts.

My father had died when I was a baby, too young to feel my loss. I had never lost an animal. I had never had a brother or sister to lose. I only stared when other people cried. Now I cried myself.

Then I walked the floor. Then I groaned. Where was my dog? I only had his body. There had been life inside him — that was Ragtime. Where was that life?

I went out to the balcony outside my windows, and looked up at the sky.

I

My mother said we all went to heaven when we died. Just then she came into the room.

*' Oh, Sam," she said, " I am so sorry for you."

" Mother," I said, " where is Ragtime ? He isn't there," and I pointed to the bed.

She looked troubled.

" Do dogs go to heaven ? " I asked.

She was quite shocked.

" Why not? " I said. " Wouldn't you rather meet that dear old dog in heaven than Hillington?"

" Yes," she said, she would, but Hillington had a soul, and Ragtime hadn't.

" But Ragtime made better use of his no-soul than Hillington does of his soul."

She said she didn't know — she would ask her clergyman, but she thought that when animals died they just turned to earth.

" But there was something alive inside Ragtime, Mother," I argued, " something that would never die."

" But all animals could not go to heaven, Sam," she said, " lions and tigers, and flies, and creatures that bite us."

"Mother," I said, "Hillington is a biter. Wouldn't he have to be made better to go to heaven? "

She said she thought he would. He was too malicious to go in his present state.

" Then if the God that made us, can improve Hill-ington, he can improve lions, and tigers, and even snakes," I said. " I don't believe he would create a dog as good as Ragtime just for a little bit of a time. He was made to live for ever. And if he isn't good enough now to live for ever, he will be made so."

My mother said again she didn't know. Then she was called away.

In a few minutes she came back. " Sam, you have got yourself into terrible trouble. The Hill-ingtons are threatening to have you arrested. Geoffrey's face is swollen enormously, and both his eyes are closed."

" Let them arrest me," I said, for I began to feel desperate again, " and I hope he will swell all over — feet, and hands, and joints, and ears, and every hole and corner of his body " — and I went in and threw myself on the bed. Nothing mattered now. I didn't care what became of me.

I've got the best mother in the world, and she sat down beside me and smoothed my head. " If you had only waited, Sam, I could have had Geoffrey arrested. There is a good society for the protection of animals in San Francisco, but you took the law into your own hands, and now the Hilling-tons can arrest you."

" I wish I could get at him again," I roared.

" Sam, you are no better than he is."

" Go away, Mother," I said, trying to push her from me.

But she would not go. She kept on smoothing my head, then she begged me to cry a Httle. It would make me feel better.

" I am not a girl," I said, " and there is a great, dark pit inside me."

" Have something to eat," she said.

Faugh! the mention of food made me sick. If I could see that dear old dog get up and crunch a bone! but he would never eat again!

Mother sat beside me all the evening. When bedtime came, she begged me to let the coachman take the dog away and bury him.

"Not to-night, Mother," I said. "He's slept with me every night for ten years. Ltt me have him once more."

Then I broke down. You would have thought I was a girl.

My mother begged me to compose myself, but I couldn't. Then I made her go to bed. I had to promise to leave my door open, so she could hear every groan I made. I promised, but there are so many ways of deceiving a good mother!

I took Rag in my arms and went out on the balcony, and shut the glass doors behind me.

I was alone now with my trouble. The sky was

like a great blue blanket wrapping up everything for me. The stars peeping down, and mocking me through their pin-holes, knew where Rag was. Whether he was gone to nothing, or whether he was still alive.

Perhaps he was away up there behind the blanket. Perhaps there was a heaven for animals, just as there is a heaven for us.

The stars would not tell me, and I let my eyes fall down from them to the sweet-smelling gardens back of our house and the Hillingtons'.

Beyond the gardens was the city, and beyond the city the grand old Bay.

Up to four o'clock this afternoon I used to feel comfortable when I took in this view. Now it was all dull and dead. Was this the way a fellow felt whenever he lost anybody belonging to him? Why, you might as well die yourself at once, and be done with it. Life wasn't worth living. I wished I could lie down beside Ragtime.

I couldn't cry now, but there was an awful feeling inside me — a kind of sinking, dreary, smothering feeling. I didn't want to sleep, I didn't want to eat, I didn't want to go anywhere, or do anything.

Then the dog side of the question came over me again. Where was Ragtime? If he were alive and in another world, he was looking for me. I would Jiave feet my life on Jtbat. Not all the angel dogs in

creation would make up to Ragtime for one minute with me. Why, that dog hardly ever took his eyes off my face. He was more brother than dog.

We'd go up Pine Street, and down California Street, and along Bush Street, and there wasn't a dog or a boy that dared to look cross-eyed at us when we were together. Not one — where was he now?

" Give me back my dog," I muttered, and I pounded my hands on the iron railing, but softly for fear of waking mother. " God, or Devil, or whatever has him, give me back my dog. It doesn't make a mite of difference to you, and it makes all the difference in the world to me."

Something seemed to burst inside me. There was a kind of fluttering and breathing under my breast-bone, as if there was a bellows or a wind-bag there. I couldn't control it. My breath came and went. Why, this must be sobbing. I had often read of it, but had never felt it.

Anyway, it kept itself up, till I was weak, and my eyes felt as if they had been boiled. That water pouring out of my head was very warm, but it couldn't heat poor Rag's cold head, and I doubled up in a heap beside him.

I sobbed like a baby or an idiot, till I was tired out. Then I fell asleep.

I was as sound as a log for about two hours,

and then something took me by the arm and woke me up.

I opened my eyes. A round soup-plate of a moon was just edging over the top of our house, and looking down at me. Then something got between me and the moon. Some hairy creature was trying to pull Ragtime from under my arm.

I felt ugly, and sprang up. A huge monkey with a face as round and big as the moon was staring down at me in the soft light.

I snarled at him, and tried to push him away. My one thought was to protect Ragtime.

" I want your dog's body," he said, mildly.

I looked all round. Was he speaking? Yes, he must be. There was no one else near.

Somehow or other, it didn't seem queer to me. It's wonderful how quickly we get used to things. However, I wasn't going to swallow him whole, so I said, " You sha'n't have it."

He grinned, and said, " Here, Gibbon."

Immediately another smaller monkey, and uglier than the first one, if that could be possible, came scrambling over the iron railing of the balcony.

I gave a kind of roar, and prepared to fight them both.

" Hush," said the big monkey, " you'll wake your mother."

" I don't care if I do," I said, trying to frighten them.

The old monkey grinned again, and stared at me ^ery kindly. Then he said to the young one, " Go >ring the air-ship." The young one disappeared round the corner of le house, and presently a very snug little white [balloon, with a wicker car below, floated beside my ^balcony. I was dumfounded, and stood with my ick against the wall, and Rag in my arms. There was a third monkey steering the air-ship, id curled up on one of the seats, on a folded bit of loth of gold, lay quite a common-looking black It.

The old monkey stepped up to the air-ship, and lid something to the Cat in a low voice. The Cat didn't seem to be listening, but right terward she sprang to the balcony railing. I was nearly staring my eyes out. I had never ;ard of anything as queer as this. It was a heap leerer in a minute, too, when the Cat just carelessly ived her paw at me, and my arms dropped to my [des as if they had been paralysed.

The old monkey caught Ragtime's body as it Fell to the floor, and was about to put it in the air-ship.

I caught hold of him. Now I was frightened, for he had beaten me.

" Don't take my dog away," I begged, like another dog. " Please don't do it. I want to bury him in the garden."

" To bury this ?" said the monkey, with a strange smile. " Go bury that," and he nodded over his shoulder.

I caught my breath. There was another Ragtime lying dead on the balcony, the very image of my own Ragtime, but I held on to the real one.

" This dog has his spirit in him," said the old monkey, softly; *'you must not bury him."

I caught hold of his hairy old arm again. " Will he come to life ? "

He nodded.

" And be just as he was here? "

" Exactly."

Something choked me. " Where? " I said.

" On the Island of Brotherly Love."

"What island is that?"

" Oh, 'way over yonder," and he waved his hand in the air.

The monkey looked queerly at me as he spoke. Like lightning it flashed into my mind that he wished I were going with him.

" Take me to that Island," I said, boldly. " I want to be with my dog."

"But your mother?"

"Could you take her, too?"

I was sorry as soon as I asked the question. I had lately been reading aloud from a boy's paper a good deal about air-ships and races that were being

leld in Paris. Ballooning was getting to be as safe railroading. No accidents out of five hundred jcensions. No need of accidents, if one had plenty (f nerve and common sense. Still, I was not willing take my mother, and anyway she wouldn't go. " Couldn't you take me with you for a visit? " I lid, "and then let me come back?"

Certainly," said the monkey, " but I must msult Her Necromancy." Her who?"

Her Necromancy, the Cat. I have but little)wer over mortals. She has a great deal. We)metimes have visitors to the Island, and it is well have her cooperation." *^ Did you plan to take me ? " I asked. He hesitated. " No, not exactly; but we all lew how you were suffering, and we were sorry)r you. You have a good name among the animals the Island."

' Are your animals all dead ? " I asked. " Oh, yes, what you call dead. We haven't a igle living one."

Are you dead ? " " " As a door-nail," he said.

I felt a kind of shock. Still there was nothing to be frightened of, unless they tried to kill me.

I think the old monkey guessed what I was thinking, for he said, kindly: " You will be perfectly safe

with me. You are under powerful protection from the moment you leave here till you come back — that is, if Her Necromancy doesn't turn stubborn," and he stepped toward the Cat.

I could not help overhearing their conversation, at least the monkey part of it. " The President won't mind," he said. " I have heard him speak favourably of the boy. He is mischievous, but he has been a brother to animals. He is in danger here. The next-door people will have him arrested in the morning. Can't your Necromancy make a false image ? "

The Cat as before scarcely seemed to hear him. However, when he finished speaking, she rose, stretched herself, and went leisurely into my bedroom.

The glass doors were shut, but I saw her go through them as plainly as I ever saw anything. She sprang on the bed, and stared as hard at the pillow as if there were a mouse under it.

"What is she doing?" I whispered to the old monkey.

" Wait and see."

I did wait, and in a few minutes I saw a shadow on my bed. The shadow deepened and strengthened, until at last there was I in a rumpled baseball suit, just as I was when my dog died.

I tried to rush in through the doors like the Cat,

but only broke the glass. I drew back, seized the handle, and tore in. I never before had such a chance to examine myself. This was better than any mirror.

This boy was asleep. First I stared at him. I fairly ate him up with my eyes — not very tall, chunky rather than graceful, pretty good limbs though — not every fellow has a chance to feel his own arms and legs with another set as I did — bullet head, short-cropped hair, never cared for football — pug nose, eyes shut, but I knew they were gray — boy sounder asleep than ever.

I grinned at the Cat, but as if not liking any familiarity, she immediately disappeared.

" Come back," said the monkey, running after her, " his mother heard the breaking glass and is coming." The Cat came back. She waved her paw at me, and though I felt myself standing there, I knew she had made me invisible — my mother could not see me.

The little woman was shading a candle with her hand. Going up to the bed, she bent over that mock boy, she kissed him, she said in a whisper, " He is sleeping, my poor darling."

I was in a rage. I ran up to her. I threw my arms about her. I tried to draw her to me, but she only clasped her white gown round her, and murmuring, " It is chilly here, he will get cold," went to the window.

I was in terror. She would discover the broken glass, she would be frightened.

She did not. The window had mended itself, or had been mended by that extraordinary Cat.

I stood paralysed till she went to her room. Then when the Cat waved her paw at me, and I felt myself growing visible, I turned sullenly to the monkey.

" Have you made me dead ? "

" Oh, no," he said, in a shocked voice. " It takes a higher power than ours to do that."

" Well, I don't like your magic tricks," I said, and I dropped into a chair. I felt weak and miserable. I suppose I wanted food.

" The most of our performances are natural," said the old monkey. " We only resort to magic when the natural won't work. It would have been an unkind thing to shock your good mother."

" Yes, it would," I muttered.

" We have made that image of you to save her feelings," he went on. " She would be frantic if you were missing. When you come back, that image will disappear. While you are away, it will lie in a trance — a good thing, for a warrant for your arrest has been made out. The officers of the law will not take a sick boy from his mother. Be easy on that score. Now, are you coming with us, or are you not ? "

The old monkey was a good fellow. No one

looking into his honest face could doubt it. My wrath was over. I slapped his hairy old back, and followed him. I wanted my dog. I would follow him to the clouds if necessary, for the sake of bringing my good Ragtime back to earth.

CHAPTER II.

A VOYAGE THROUGH THE AIR

The old monkey climbed into the wicker basket. He pushed aside some bags of ballast, made a place for me, then signalled to one of the young monkeys to lift the anchor that held us to the balcony railing.

I set my teeth hard. This was more or less of an adventure. Then we were off, — the three monkeys, the Cat curled up on the cloth of gold, and dear old Rag on the bags of sand at my feet.

I must not forget our escort. Just as we were starting, two large, beautiful birds flew down from the roof of the house, where they had been resting. They were two swans, — the handsomest I had ever seen, — and when we started, they placed themselves beside the car, one on each side.

I held my breath. We were going up and up, and I expected to gasp and have a catching in my throat as if I were in a swing. But there was nothing of the sort. It just seemed as if there was a sweet little breeze blowing by the balcony, that took us

WE WERE GOING UP AND UP

in its arms, and bore us right out over the Bay. In going with it we felt nothing, no rocking motion, nor rushing motion, nor any kind of motion, but just the sweeping away of things beneath us.

All my trouble was over now, and I could have thrown my cap up in the air for joy, only I was afraid I mightn't get it back again. Mother would not be worried. Rag was going to come to life — now if I only had something to eat, I would be as happy as a lord.

I edged up to the old monkey. He was still fussing about the car among instruments, blankets, bottles, ropes, and boxes.

I felt as free to speak to him as he were my father or brother, so I said, " Have you got anything to eat?"

" I was just looking for some seed-cakes," he said; " here they are."

He handed me a paper bag and a bottle.

The cakes were good, and the water was extraordinary. It livened one up like a tonic.

I ate, and while I ate, I looked down. What a scene! What would the fellows at school say if they could see that map? The teachers were always giving us things to draw; just suppose I could hand in a sketch of this!

San Francisco from the clouds : it was a diamond map spread over dull velvet sand-hills. The electric

lights ran away out like trailers, to bring the suburbs into line. And across from the city, Oakland, and Alameda, and Berkeley were sparkling like a necklace on the throat of the Bay. Away in the distance, little towns twinkled and winked at us, as if to say, " Come back to earth." All except lonely San Quentin prison off in a corner. Its lights seemed sad and dull.

Tamalpais, old Mount Tamalpais, was a beauty. It was queer to have the stone profile looking up at us, and not for us to be looking up at her. Clapped right on her head was the gay hotel, just like the bright things that ladies wear on their heads. I had looked at her a good many times from the valley, never from the air.

Zigzag down her sides went the track of the mountain railway. We could see the rails shining in the moonlight; and I could make out the faint line of trail in some places through the chaparral. Many a time I had gone stumbling down there with some of the boys.

Now we were sailing out over the Golden Gate. I threw a last glance at the solemn, old mountains standing round the Bay, and watching us go. The dear only knew when I should see them again.

" Good-bye, old Grizzly, and Diablo, and Hamilton," I said to myself. " I wonder whether the I^ick telescope is turned on us ? "

" Could they see us from the observatory ? " I asked the old monkey.

" No, we are invisible to mortals."

" And yet this seems an ordinary air-ship, and you are managing it in the usual fashion, aren't you?" I asked, trying to air some of the balloon knowledge I had picked up.

" Yes, the President of the Island has a great prejudice against magic, except for purposes of amusement. We have to do things by natural means, and obtain results by our own labour. Are you having any trouble in breathing?"

We were still going up, and I was beginning to feel queer.

" Here is an oxygen bag," said one of the young monkeys.

The old monkey shook his head, and pulled the valve rope. " Don't give it to him. We will descend."

A cloud bank sailed below us, soft and fleecy like cotton wool. I felt better now, and began to think over my situation. Was this I, myself, Sam Emerson, up here in the clouds with a car full of animals ? and I pinched my arm.

I hurt myself, and gave a kind of squeal. It sounded like the blast of a trumpet. I felt ashamed, for the animals were all laughing at me, even the Cat, and the gentle swans, who turned their long necks in amusement.

Now I remembered how plainly we had heard the earth sounds when we were over the city. Even though it was night, a kind of hum came up from it, and in the midst of the hum I could catch single noises, like the barking of a dog, the cry of a cat, and the hoot of the cunning, little, gray tufts of owls that came round the suburbs at night.

Just at present, there were some sailors bawling a song on a fishing-vessel down below us. I suppose they were in good spirits because they were going in through the Golden Gate. We could hear every word of the song:

" Nancy was a tom-boy, Sarah was a witch, But Polly was a dandy girl That carried every stitch

of sail that a sea-bird could carry, and here was a rover come home for to tarry, with a hey ho, jolly boys " — and so on, a long rigmarole that I couldn't catch, but I gathered that Polly was the name of their ship, and I laughed loudly.

My laugh sounded like the roar of a cannon, but the animals did not make fun of me this time, for they were all taken up with something in the water below us.

It was the Japanese mail steamer from San Francisco, bound for Honolulu, the old monkey told me,

M Togage gr<)tottgt| tjie ^Iv 33

id it was steaming along at a fine rate, bright with fhts, and looking very cheerful. I don't know why, but I am always crazy about leans of locomotion. Trains and ships stir me like everything, and I had often watched this jry steamer passing in and out the Golden Gate. I knew its name, I knew some of the people on)ard, and I screamed and waved my cap, and ie old monkey obligingly manipulated the valve >pe until we were just over the smoke-stacks of le steamer.

The people on it did not pay the slightest atten-)n to me, though the air fairly rang with the)ise I made, and the peals of laughter of the young mkeys, who seemed to think I was a pretty good >rt of a joke.

The old monkey scowled at them, then he looked >und for something for them to do. " Throw out le ballast," he said, shortly. They stopped laughing then, for each one had take a tin dipper and ladle out allowances of sand.

Some of it went on the steamer, but no one felt it, no one saw it. I stared in amazement at a lady who was lying in a deck chair gazing up at the moon. She got a dipperful fair in her lap, but she didn't notice it a particle. I was in the magic circle. I was cut off from human beings, and I groaned, and fell back, and held my tongue.

" You are frightened," said the old monkey, kindly, " but you will soon get over it. Should you like the Cat to make you visible and be dropped down on the deck there ? "

"Could Rag go?" I asked.

The monkey shook his head.

" Then I stay," I said, " I'm going to see this thing through."

The old monkey nodded approvingly, threw out half a bag of sand, and we flew up and away like a bird, beyond the slow old black tortoise in the water.

" Is this a dirigible balloon ? " I asked the old monkey.

" Yes, but we have been going directly with the wind. Now we shall mount. Gibbon, the oxygen. You won't need it long," he said to me.

" How far are we up now ? " I asked.

He looked at an instrument.

" About four miles."

My head felt light again, and to calm myself, I put out a hand and touched Ragtime. Here was something familiar. Then I slipped down, and threw my arm over him. There was no sign of life in him yet.

" You are cold," said the old monkey, and he gave me a blanket. I put it half over myself, and half | over Rag. It was fine to have something to curll

mder in that clear, cold, crystal air, and having no longer any nasty, biting kind of a trouble to keep [me awake, I fell asleep.

When I woke, it was day. I could not stand the sudden and awful glory of that sun looking [down at me as if it was my creator, so I dropped ly gaze to earth.

But there wasn't any earth. It was all water, rpon my word, I was frightened, and my eyes just ^lued themselves to the old monkey's face. Here was a lovely spot to drop a boy and a dog. Is — is it the P-p-pacific ? " I gasped, " or are ^e in — in another world ? " The old monkey chuckled. " Which do you think it is? " "" I — I don't know," I said. " Well, it is another world," he said. I stared and gasped for a few more minutes, 'hen I said, " But it is the same old sun, and I [eel just the same."

The old monkey laughed outright. " Why how lid you expect to feel ? "

" I don't know, but it sounds queer to say another rorld. Well, what world is this anyway ? "

" One of many," he said, gravely. " Surely you lidn't suppose that your little world was the only ^inhabited one in this vast universe ? *'

" I didn't know. I've heard of people having

been seen on MarvS, but I thought it was all guesswork."

" Well, don't puzzle too much about it now," he said, kindly. " I will talk to you again. I haven't time now, for we are nearly home. I will just say that this world consists of a system of large, floating islands. We are going to the Island of Brotherly Love, where all animals from the United States of North Amicrica come immediately after death. Gibbon, the cloth of gold."

One of the young monkeys respectfully approached the Cat. She got up, and taking the cloth of gold from under her, he unfolded it, and lifting the blanket, spread it over Ragtime's body.

" Now don't touch him for awhile," said the old monkey. " Just w^ait and see what will happen, now that he is in the reviving air of this world."

I drew back. For a long time there wasn't a movement. Just the shining yellow cloth spread over my dog's gamey outline. I did not watch our course any more. I had no eyes for the sky getting more and more glittering and beautiful above us, and the water getting more and more beautiful and glittering below, till our little white balloon seemed to be in the hollow of a magnificent cup.

No, I was thinking of a little dog spirit, and my head just ached from staring at the yellow cloth. I knew what was going to happen. I am not a

Remarkably smart chap naturally, but I was getting

larpened by contact with these clever animals.

Very soon I saw a tiny morsel of dangling gold [ringe quiver, just quiver, not shake nor move violently.

It was enough, though. I would have sprung to ly dog, as a cat springs on a mouse, if the old lonkey hadn't grabbed me.

Wait still longer, and look about you. We are)proaching the Island."

I just gave one hasty glance over my shoulder.

kyond us were a number of other balloons, sailing

)out in the air as if it were as common a thing

travel by air in this world, as it is to travel by ind and water in the one we had just left. Below

the sea was alive with leaping, gamboling fishes

bright colours, and in the distance a long shore ras in sight — a green shore with a fringe of white reakers and tall palms. There was also a sound

singing, and a joyful confusion of noises — a sort barnyard and circus chorus mixture, but I >uldn't pay attention to it.

All the mind I had was on my dog. I saw those impact feet kick out, that long flat head raise itself.

saw, saw — for I snatched the cloth of gold side. Not all the monkeys in creation could hold le. Then I had my dog in my arms, and I thought should die of joy.

Have I described Rag? No, not yet. Well, if you want to hear of a beauty, listen.

He was a dead white, thoroughbred animal, only I never sent him to shows, because they wouldn't let me in his box with him, and I couldn't have Rag stand the fuss and misery of a show for all the prizes in the world. Weight, thirty-five pounds, chest like a table, strong and broad. Coat, glossy, short, and stiff: nice little dent down face without a " stop " between the eyes. Eyes, small, and black as shoe-buttons, regular steel-trap jaws, tail long and low-set. Two rags of ears originally cut, and the rest chewed off in fights — Oh, he was a beauty!

Well, I thought I'd go crazy when I felt the heart beating in him again, and when that pink tongue went working over my face, round one ear, via forehead and cheeks, then to the other ear and back again.

" Rag! Rag! Rag! " I said, " you've been dead, but now you're alive. I'll never be mad at anything again, never in my life. I'm jam full of thanks."

" So am I, master," he said.

I nearly fell over the edge of the car into the sea.

So am I, master! Why, Rag was speaking, too! Somehow or other it had not seemed strange to me that the monkeys could speak, but that Rag had found a voice, was the biggest surprise in my life.

" Why, Rag," I gasped, when I recovered my

centre of gravity, " can you talk ? Do you know ^what I say ? "

I've always partly understood you," he said, [coolly, " now I know every word," and his dear [old eyes shone like black stars.

Rag! Rag! Rag! " and I choked and hugged [him till he scarcely had any breath left. Then he ^grunted, as he always did when I squeezed him, and looked round with a comical face. " Where are we at ? "

" You're resurrected, old fellow," I said, " and this is your paradise. I'm just calling on you, but I'm going to raise rebellion, if I don't get permission !to take you back to 'Frisco with me."

Rag didn't answer me. He was puzzled almost mt of his dog senses, and wrinkling his white Forehead in a comical way he had of doing, he was staring at the dark monkeys and the white swans. Those grand old birds were singing now — such [a beautiful song — and stretching out their necks md their wings, till I thought of the hymn we sing in church about the bird returning fondly home. After Rag got done inspecting them, he took in le Island, and now he was a more flabbergasted [dog than ever.

It was a gorgeous place, and if I shut my eyes tnow, I can see those palms and flowers, and hear those white breakers throwing themselves like big, powerful dogs along the golden sands.

But more wonderful than breakers and palms, for we had them in California, was the crowd of animals waiting our arrival.

It looked as if this animal heaven was all alive for the arrival of friends, and that, I found out, was the exact state of affairs.

Our air-ship had floated over a good-sized green hill, and the old monkey was throwing out an anchor. It bit the ground right on top of the hill, and without a single jar we were hooked and steady.

CHAPTER III.

THE BEAUTIFUL ISLAND

The Cat sprang out first, the monkeys followed, Rag bounded after them, and I came last.

" Me-ow, me-ow," said something close to my ankles, "don't you know me, Master Sam?"

I fell back a step. There was a thick fringe of animals round the hillock, — two elephants, goats, a camel or two, dogs, a royal Bengal tiger, cows, sheep, horses, hens, rats, mice, rabbits, weasels, and a lot of other animals sandwiched in between them.

They were nearly all motionless, and it flashed into my mind that it was etiquette for them all to stand still, except those animals who recognised friends on the air-ship.

This cat that pressed forward was an Angora kitten that my mother had lost from poison a month before.

" Oh, Rag, I'm glad to see you,'" she murmured, purring round him, and arching her back, with her tail held aloft, and looking as big as ten tails.

She was a daisy of a cat — pure white, longhaired, and blue-eyed.

" Why, puss, I'm happy to find you here,*' I said, and really it seemed just like meeting an old friend.

" Oh, you nice boy," she said, and she sprang on my shoulder, and ran her nutmeg-grater of a tongue over my face, till I laughed and put her down.

Then I just gazed at the other animals, and Rag gazed too.

" Ton my word, master," he said, in a queer way, " there's a lamb licking that Bengal tiger's skin. Wouldn't you think he'd nab the little creature ? "

" Oh, Rag," said Pussy, in her funny little voice, " you've got ever so much to learn. Animals don't tease each other here. You used to chase every cat but me. You won't want to chase any cat here. All the badness will fall away from you."

" I say. Pussy," I remarked, " Rag is a good dog."

" Yes, but he used to hunt cats. I've seen him. Look, Master Sam, there is another friend."

I haven't said anything about the birds. But they were there — flocks of them. Some perched away up on the palms, some in lower growing shrubs — pomegranates and little oaks, and fig-trees.

A tiny canary bird had left them, and was circling round my head — such a yellow morsel of a thing.

" Why, Taffy," I said, " are you here, too? "

" Tweet! tweet! tweet! I've been here for ages,"
le little fellow said, saucily, and he perched on
le tip of my outstretched finger. " Don't you
Remember when you were a small boy the wind blew
ly cage over and killed me, and you cried — I've
jever forgotten you. It is just sweet to see you
lere," and he twittered, and gently rubbed his beak
wer my fingers, and fluttered his tiny wings, till
caught him up and hid him against my face.
It made me feel queer and like a girl; actually
lere were tears in my eyes. Here I was, set down
a strange island, and there were creatures that
lew me, and were glad to see me. It seemed
very homey, and my heart got lighter than ever.
, if mother were only here! She had loved these
features.
" Rag, old fellow," I said, in an undertone, " isn't
lis great ? "
He was grinning from ear to ear. " I never felt
kind of satisfied before," he said. " Seems as
I'd never have a care again. I say. Master Sam,
's step down and speak to those other animals.
ley're all dying to get close to you. My venerable
friend here says they don't see humans once in a
log's age."
His venerable friend was the old monkey, who lad been standing behind us. I felt quite
flattered, was a kind of show for them.
 " Come on then, Rag," I said; then I gaped at him. "Why — why, Rag," I stammered.
 " What's the matter, master? " he said, in alarm.
 " Your ears — they've grown on again."
He shook his head. " Why, so they have. Now where did those chewed bits come from ?
"

 " No animal remains mutilated on the Island," said the old monkey, gravely. " Could you
see the condition of some creatures who leave earth, you would realise how impossible it would
be for us to remain happy while contemplating them. No, soon after they enter the healing
atmosphere of this World of Islands they are made whole."
 I gave a kind of whistle. It seemed to me that I'd have to let off steam somehow or other,
while taking in all these wonders.
 " Tweet! tweet! " whispered the little canary on my shoulder. " Don't you remember,
dear Master Sam, how my wings and legs were broken ? — they are quite well now."
 " So they are, you little yellow morsel," I said, and I took him in my hands, and
examined him closely.
 " Tum, tum, tum," trum.peted one of the elephants, who was getting impatient, " can you
tell me the latest news from Central Park ? "
 I immediately stepped down toward him. He was the largest of the elephants present, and
he ran his trunk caressingly up and down my back.

I want to know about my keeper," he said, in lis huge voice, " I want to know about my keeper, ng Mike McGarvie. I loved that keeper. I want to see him. Hum, hum," and he trumpeted, loudly, ind raised his head to look over the ocean as if le would bring the missing man to him. " I was in Central Park last winter," I began. " Last winter! " he repeated; '* why, I hear every jw days from him. Has any one heard anything ibout Mike McGarvie on this trip to the earth?"

" No, no," said the old monkey, soothingly, " per-laps the next air-ship will contain some one who has ieen him."

I'll go to the bird telegraphy station," said le elephant, who was a splendid specimen of an Lfrican beast, and he tramped away, swaying dis-)ntentedly, and only half listening to the comforting fcmarks of a fawn Jersey cow that ran by his side. I tried not to laugh, but I couldn't help it. The old monkey didn't laugh. " I'll tell you that lephant's story," he said. " He was born in captivity, and loved his keeper passionately. When he ras full grown, he became ill with some hopeless lisease. It was decided to poison him. His keeper >rotested, but it was done. Done badly, for they)uld not regulate the dose of poison for such a big mimal. Then they tried to shoot him — anyway, he ras three days dying, and his sufferings were such

a shock to his keeper, that he lost his mind. Now he is in an asylum. Some day he will die, and some day the elephant knows he will be transported to another world. There they will be together."

I was silent, and didn't want to laugh any more.

" Don't you know me ? " said some one, softly, " don't you remember me ? "

I started and looked up. Without thinking, I had made a few steps toward the circle of animals, and now a pretty spotted deer was thrusting his damp nose in my hand.

" I'm the Indian chital from the Park in San Francisco," the creature went on. " Don't you remember you were there that autumn day when the other deer set upon me, and killed me? You were only a little boy, and you couldn't get over the paling, but you raged and stamped, and the last thing my dying glance rested on was your distorted little face. I've never forgotten you."

I threw my arm round his neck. I couldn't speak. Then I turned to the old monkey, and after a time got my voice. " I feel queer," I said. " What makes all these animals look at me so ? "

He smiled a kind of grave smile. " The animals on this part of the Island have nearly all been used to the companionship of man. He is a divinity to them, and they will never be perfectly happy till they meet their former masters."

I

"And when will that be?" I asked, eagerly.

He gave a strange far-away look out over the sea. " No one knows. Away off there is the World of the Blessed. Every little while a beautiful white air-ship comes gliding along, and takes away some of our best animals. That world is also full of islands, and they are said to be a thousand times more beautiful than this little paradise."

" Then every animal finds his owner there? "

" Yes, if the owner has already arrived. There are some very happy meetings there."

" But how is there room for everybody ? " I said. " People have been dying for thousands of years."

" Don't you remember I told you that there are other worlds besides this one and yours?" he said, calmly.

I kept quiet a minute, trying to take it in, then I said, " Worlds upon worlds ? "

" Yes, systems of worlds."

" And all with people on them ? "

" No, not every one," said my new friend. " Not all are habitable."

" Why, it is enormous to think of," I said; " it gives a fellow a kind of back-handed blow on his imagination."

The old monkey looked at me pityingly. " So you have been supposing that the great Maker of the universe had only your little sphere to command.

You are — oh, what are you, and we?" he said, choking all up, and looking at the sea and land.

" Our worlds," he went on, when he got his breath, " are only two drops of water in an ocean, two little stars in the field of the sky. We go on after death. People and animals, too, are transferred from one world to another. This satisfies the love of travel implanted in every breast."

" But when I die, I wish to be with my mother, my friends," I said, sharply.

" Your wish will be gratified, boy. Do you suppose your Creator would be cruel enough to set you down in the midst of a savage African tribe where my forefathers lived? No, families, communities, races, will be kept together if they wish, and yet there will be freedom for all; but we will talk of these m.atters again. You must be introduced to the President of the Island."

CHAPTER IV.

THE HOME OF THE SWANS

I SUPPOSE the President is one of your largest mimals," I said, as we walked along a firm white)ath running through the grass by the seashore.

The old monkey laughed. " Wait and see. He is full of dignity, I assure you of that — but let us

ove on."

I had stopped a minute to look behind. The throng >f animals that had gathered to welcome our arrival ^as all moving slowly after us, with their eyes fixed m me, and I felt foolish when it came into my head lat I represented boys and girls, men and women,)robably all of them much more important than lyself — persons that they had loved on earth.

However, I couldn't do anything but just be my-jelf, so I turned round and walked on.

This was a glorious walk. Above us were the)alms, beyond us a forest, and on the left hand was the magnificent sea.

" Look there," said the monkey.

I did look. Up and down the beach a common old ^oat was running, excitedly shaking his head, wag-

ging his beard, and occasionally stopping to kick desperately.

" Just see him/* said the monkey, in a queer voice.

We went nearer, and now I saw there were tears running down the old goat's beard, and that as he mournfully wagged this beard, he kept muttering something to himself.

" What is he saying? " I asked.

" Come nearer and ask him," said the old monkey. Then he spoke to the goat. " Come, Jerry, hold up a minute; here is an earth boy just arrived."

" Oh, if I only hadn't! " muttered the goat; " oh, if I only hadn't! " and he kept on shaking his head, as if he didn't hear the monkey.

" Don't be foolish, Jerry," said the monkey. " Look at this boy; perhaps he can tell you something of your mistress."

At this the goat stopped running and jumping, and turned his bleared eyes on me.

" Do you know old Widow McDoodle, of Bangor, Maine — lovely Maine ? "

" I was born near there," I said, " but I never heard of the Widow."

He gave a kick, and began to run up and down again, crying harder than ever, and wagging his old beard, till I thought it would drop off.

"What did he do? — what is the matter with him ? " I asked my friend, the monkey.

Walk on and I'll tell you," he said, in a low

roice. " It is a very sad tale. He was a lonely ridow's only pet goat. She loved him, and even it him sleep in her cottage on cold winter nights. Ine day she went to the well to draw a bucket of rater. She had just put on a new red wrapper, and le goat says the instant he saw her leaning over, le awful thought came into his mind, ' What a good lance to bowl her over into the well.' He says it lust have been the red colour exciting him. Anyway, he couldn't resist the evil thought. He ran to the old woman, he butted her, and she fell into le well. He was nearly crazy. He bleated and irried on, till neighbours ran and got her out; len he went down on his knees and begged her irdon, but she wouldn't listen to him. She gave im an awful beating, and sold him the next day. " He died of grief, and was brought here, and for le solid year he has run up and down that strip

|f sand, crying and muttering, * Oh, if I only Ldn't!'" The old monkey's face was a sight as he finished

us story. He was so sorry, so kind, but he did for le. I tried to hold in, but I couldn't, and the next istant I was in a roar of laughter. I shouted and

stamped, and finally rolled down on the clean, white md. I hadn't laughed as much since I played Hillington

the brick trick, — that is, my hat on the ground over a brick, — he kicking, I watching.

Well, I nearly frightened the old monkey to death. He thought I had been taken with some inward convulsion, and all the other animals came trotting up, and stared at him, kind of ugly, as if to say, " What have you been doing to this dear little boy? "

I had a lovely time. I rolled and rolled, and every time I looked up and saw that circle of animals' heads round me, I just yelled, and rolled some more.

Rag was the only one that understood me. I saw him standing grinning from ear to ear. He always had a keen sense of humour, and then he had been so much with me that he understood me.

He passed round the word. " Don't mind him. He always laughs when any one gets hurt."

I heard a low murmur, " Very like a boy," and then began to feel ashamed of myself in comparison with all those sympathetic animals, and tried to sit up.

" The goat amuses him," explained Rag, and upon my word the old sinner was laughing himself. I followed his glance over his shoulder. All the animals were looking at the goat now, and like an idiot I took another peep at his watery old eyes and wagging beard.

It set me off again. I suppose I was half-hysteri-

I

cal from my adventures, and the hot, clean sand was like a bath to my tired limbs. Anyway, I had another s^ood time, till Rag whispered to me that the monkey was making off, whereupon I jumped up, and ran after him.

Excuse me, sir,*' I said, wiping my eyes, " but ly grandfather was a great laugher."

The poor goat is much to be pitied," he said, sverely.

" I'll tell you what'll cure him," I said. " He's lock full of nonsense now. Bring the Widow to 5e him. He's idolising — what do you call it — lealising her."

We don't call it nonsense," said the monkey, :ill more severely; " we call it sentiment." " The name doesn't cut any figure," I said, impatiently. " You bring the Widow — I'll guarantee he'll shut off those water-works."

The old monkey looked thoughtful, then he said: " Your suggestion m.ay be a good one. I'll mention it to the President. By the way," and he hailed one of the flock of birds that I forgot to say was hovering over us, " where is the President ? "

The little sparrow-hawk he nodded to, flew close
beside us. His fierce little eyes took me in, his
mottled v/ings, as beautiful inside as out, waved
ge^tU^ like two of my mother's choice fans.

" The President is over beyond the Swan Lake,"
he said, " near the corral," then he flew back, and took his place in the procession.

" By the way, Mr. Monkey," I said, " how do birds of prey get things to eat ? You don't let them kill anything, I suppose? "

" There isn't a particle of flesh food eaten on this Island, or in this whole animal world," said the monkey, " but there are trees and shrubs here that bear wonderfully sustaining fruits and berries."

" What about killing the trees ? " I said, jokingly; " you're such particular people here, that I should not think you would want to kill anything."

The old monkey's face lighted up. "I have heard that in advanced stages of life or death, as you would call it, a tree when it is struck will cry out, and a flower will bend its head and weep if you hurt it."

I gathered myself up as if I didn't want to touch any growing thing about me.

The monkey smiled. " Do not be afraid. Our vegetation has not progressed so far. If a tree dies here, we cut it down, but I must say that we don't pull flowers as earthly people do, and cruelly throw them on the ground to die. We regard that as demoralising, — but come this way," and wavinsr his hand to the animals behind as a sign that they were not to follow us further, he abruptly .turned into a path leading from the ocean to the forest.

gUf %oiiie of tfie Stoatig ss

" Never mind, I'll see you later," I said, waving my own hand to the disappointed faces in our rear. " I'll see you later. He'll bring me back." Then I ran after the monkey, and said, politely, " By the way, what is your name ? "

" Soko."

" You are a good-sized monkey."

" I am not a monkey. I am a man-like ape — a :chimpanzee. Have you ever looked into the history lof apes and monkeys? "

" Never."

It would repay you. The chimpanzees are very proud of their bodily structure. We are more like man than any other apes."

When I go home," I said, " I'll look into this monkey business. I suppose you have no books on the Island?"

' Oh, yes, we have a number. They have been [brought from earth on the air-ships."

" And are all the animals as clever as you ? "

" They are like human beings. Some like study, some don't care for it, — but just look there."

Oh, what a sight! I am only a boy, but I felt like an angel. Very beautiful old trees stood over us. It seem.ed to me that their hanging arms were trying to smooth my shoulders, and birds, birds, birds, were everywhere, peeping at me, and talking to each other in their own language that I did not understand.

I haven't the gift to describe it prop'erly, but everything felt so kind, and the wood was just beautiful. Lots of the trees and shrubs I recognised, lots I didn't, and I couldn't make out which were earthly, and which were heavenly.

" Look here! " I said to Soko, " when I left the East, and we went to California, the first thing I wanted to do was to get into the woods. The fellows took me up a canyon, they showed me a creek, and upon my word, every single flower and shrub there was new to me. Now I can't make out whether these are magic things here, or whether they may be growths I'm not acquainted with."

" Every growing thing on this Island resembles some other growing thing in your world," said Soko. " There is nothing magic about our trees and flowers. I don't know why it is that mortals always imagine that in any kind of a future state, things must be reversed. A new world is only the old world made over — good things left, bad ones taken out."

He made me feel comfortable. " I am at home in this heaven," I said. " I would be all upset if I found m.yself in a place where trees were growing with their roots in the air, and people were walking en their heads — oh, what a glorious lake! What do you call it ? "

' The home of the swans," said the monkey, or the ape, as I suppose I must call him, " our whistling swans, and white swans, and black swans."

I just gasped — I wish I had some new adjectives
to describe the place before me. I don't seem to
lack words when I'm running straight ahead with
ilk, but when I come to a description I miss them.
lere's a dictionary beside me just chock full of
rords, but I can't seem to make them fit in, and
ist have to use the same old ones — " beautiful,"
specially.
Well, here goes — I'll do the best I can with plain
iguage. Imagine a lake in the woods, very quiet,
jry still — a beautiful lake — just heaps of flowers,
and blue, and green — no, the leaves were
•een. Well, all colours of flowers bending, and
liling, and nodding at themselves in the lake, and
irk shrubs behind them, and trees behind the
irubs, and everything calm and lovely, and dozens
white swans gliding through the water and trail-
!g after them such sooty little dolls of swans.
Oh, you daisy things," I cried, stretching out ^y hands to them like a girl.

I didn't expect them to come up to me, but they [id. They let me fuss with their feathers, and examine their bills. Some had red bills with a black knob, that Soko said was called a "berry," some had bills black at the tip and lemon yellow about the nostrils.

I felt as if I could live and die in this swans paradise, but the old ape urged me on.

" Where is the President, Dulce ? " he asked one of the swans that had come with our air-ship.

I winked something damp out of my eyes. She looked Hke my mother, as she queened it round that lake with one sooty dab of brown beside her.

" Over there," she said, and she bowed her beautiful neck toward a winding path.

" May I call again ? " I whispered, as she pressed her breast against the moss to reach my hand.

" As often as you like, dear boy," she said, like a lady, and with a final squeeze of her soft throat, I ran on after the ape.

He was journeying through the underbrush, picking big white raspberries as he went.

I imitated him. " Nothing magic about these," I said.

He gave me a half-moon grin from his enormous old face. " The only magic thing about our vegetation is, that products of temperate and tropic zones all grow together for the good of our mixed assembly of animals."

" But if there are only animals from the United States of America, why do I see so many African and Asiatic creatures here ? "

" There are not many in proportion, but creatures from warm climates have a way of spreading themselves. I should have said that all the animals that die in the Union come here, that is, unless they

Stoang 59

prefer to go to their own people in other islands. I was happier to come here after death, than to go to some island where I would be with my ancestors whom I had never known. I lived my life among American animals. I prefer them." " Where were you born ? " " In a monkey-house in a southern city." " Were you always kept in captivity? " " Always." "How did you die?"

" I went mad from the smallness of my cage." I guess animals suffer a lot that way." He shuddered. " They suffer unspeakably — but here is the President."

CHAPTER V.

A FIGHT WITH AN ANARCHIST

We had come to a small green clearing in the forest. An African elephant with huge ears was thrashing about on the grass, trumpeting, waving his trunk, and cutting up generally.

" Is that your President ? " I asked.

" That crazy thing! " and the ape gave me a pitying glance.

"He is so large; I thought he must be."

" More muscle than brain," said the ape, sharply. " No, there is the President," and he pointed to a group on a little green knoll to one side of the clearing.

I looked for myself. A sturdy, medium-sized dog sat under the trees. He had a following of a smaller dog something like himself, six pups, a liver and white field-spaniel, an Irish setter, a fox terrier, and a wolf, a white rat, a cur dog, a snake on the cur's back, and several horses.

" Yes, that is our President," said the monkey, proudly.

I

"That small-sized brown dog?" " Dignity isn't bounded by inches nor feet." " I guess not, if you have that small animal to rule over you. I thought you'd have a hippopotamus iat least."

' Is not the dog the nearest friend and companion [of man? "

I looked down at Rag. " I believe you're right." " And hasn't he by constant association with man [learned to be more like him than any other animal ? " You're right again. But that dog isn't even a thoroughbred." " A good mongrel is the best thoroughbred."Seems to me I've seen him before," I said, in a mzzled way. " Perhaps you've heard of him." "What's his name?" " Joe — Beautiful Joe."

" Joe, old Joe," I gasped. " Of course I've read if him, but he's a story-book dog. I thought this)aradise was only for real animals."

' Can't an animal be a real animal and a story-[book animal, too ? "

" The book said he was real, still I didn't believe it."

" Well, he truly was a real dog — people used to iread his story, then go to see his living self. He died a year or two ago, and we brought him here

in an air-ship. His false body is buried near his home, and if you choose, you can see it when you go back to America."

" Well, well," I said, in astonishment; then I stared at Joe. There he sat, well-preserved, firm-looking, a wise old dog, with his missing bits of ears and tail grown on again. However, I couldn't see any Presidential dignity about him.

" A queen died some time ago in Europe," said Soko, " a queen who was not a very large woman, yet every one who went near her said she was full of dignity and majesty. Wait till you get near old Joe. You will see that he is a ruler."

" It was a fine thing for you to make him your President after the hard time he had on earth," I said, " but I vow I can't see anything wonderful about him."

"Watch him then," said Soko.

I did watch. Joe never looked at me, and the animals about him were too much taken up with the elephant's antics to turn round.

"What's the matter with the beast?" I asked, when we had for some time stared at him thrashing round, throwing up earth and digging his tusks into the roots of trees.

" He's an Anarchist," said Soko, " only came here yesterday."

" An Anarchist — among wild animals? "

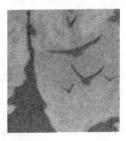

"THE ELEPHAINT WAS AN AWFUL LOOKING BEAST

I

" He is doubly wild. He was put out of the [world because he wouldn't submit to law and order. [It makes him crazy to find a model government lere. Look out — he's coming this way." We fell back a little, but the President and his Ifriends did not move.

The elephant was an awful looking beast. His tiny eyes shone like spots of flame. He was muddy ind earthy, as if he had thrown water over himself, md then rolled on the ground, and the air about lim was fairly hot with rage. I was concerned for the brave old dog. I had lade friends with him through the story of his life, and without thinking, I called out, " Take care, Joe."

The old fellow turned. His brown face fairly)eamed; then he looked squarely at the advancing >east.

For some reason or other the lunatic stopped tramping and waving his trunk in the air. "Brother!" said Joe, kindly. The elephant raved up and down before him. I ain't your brother. You're a boss and a liar." " Brother, what do you want ? " said Joe again, iand a kind of shiver ran down my back as he said it. There was power in the old dog's voice.

The elephant tossed his trunk in the air and waved his tusks. " I want equal rights, equal divi-

sion of labour, equal division of property, government by the animals as a whole, not by one dirty, low-down cur."

" Stupid brute! " said the ape, angrily, in my ear. " We have hardly any machinery of government — and what we have is rabidly democratic."

The elephant was worse again, and now the most of Joe's following had taken refuge behind trees. The old dog still sat on the knoll as if he disdained to move. He was very quiet, very sorrowful, and the elephant acted as if he were dying to kill him, but didn't quite dare.

At last Joe turned round. " It is of no use, he is utterly unreasonable. Send for the good elephants."

A whole flock of different kinds of birds, that had been perched on the trees overhead to watch the sorry spectacle, flew away like the wind at Joe's word.

" What does that mean? " I asked my guide.

" The good elephants will surround the bad one. If he resists, they will force him into a big corral that we built yonder, under those oaks, for refractory animals."

" Will you send him back to earth ? "

The ape shivered. " No, that would be toe great punishment. He will be sent to the Isle of Probation."

*'The Isle of Probation? Where is that?"

" It is another island, much smaller than this — an international spot where bad animals from all this world are sent. They are all raging anarchists, murderers, thieves, and other misguided ones. Nothing cures them like a dose of themselves. In a short time they invariably beg to be sent back to the island they came from, where they behave themselves ever afterwards. There is an Isle of Probation dog," and he pointed to the cur near Joe, " that Bruno."

" Bruno," I said; " not the Bruno in * Beautiful Joe,' who was so bad that Mr. Wood had to shoot him?"

" The same — he is a good dog now and devoted to Joe."

" I should like to speak to him."

The ape smiled. " Wait till this elephant business is over. Bruno is deep in that bunch of rhododendrons just now. Here come our warriors — aren't they fine ? "

A brace of Asiatic elephants were loping down toward the green clearing. Their small ears were wagging, their loose skin was wriggling, till their rounded old backs looked as if they had been ploughed.

" Good boys, Sumatra and Borneo," said the ape, "and look at Bengal coming^ to help them."

When the elephants ran, their posts of feet came

plump, plump down on the earth. The beautiful creature beside them leaped through the air like a cat. His eyes were two spots of light, and as he leaped, we could see, on the under part of his dark striped body, fur that was as white as milk.

" Now the Anarchist is dished," said Soko, coolly. " He might as well give in."

He didn't give in, though, for a few minutes. He steamed up to his three foes. He snorted and screamed, he bellowed and thumped the ground, and I got all of a perspiration. Imagine a fight between three elephants and a tiger!

But it wasn't as lively as I hoped it would be. It was more like a game played by rule. And there was too much mercy in it for fun — that is, speaking as a boy on earth, not in paradise.

The tiger sprang on and off the Anarchist's back as if he were doing duty work in a gymnasium. I could have watched him for ever, he was so supple, and while he did the graceful act, Sumatra and Borneo seesawed and crowded and pushed, till they got the Anarchist away from the greensward and rammed against the trees.

It was funny to see them — the three big creatures fighting with their three trunks in the air.

" Why don't they bang each other with them? " I asked the ape.

" They might hurt them. The trunk is exceed-

ingly sensitive, and exceedingly useful. See, the Anarchist tries to pin the tiger to the ground with his tusks. He could give him a tremendous toss with them, too, if he could catch him."

'* He'll never catch that tiger," I said.

" Never — see, they have corralled him."

I ran forward. The good elephants had driven the bad one into the strong enclosure, which was so covered with green climbing things that one scarcely knew it was an enclosure.

'* Shut the gate," said Joe, sadly.

The good old dog had come forward, and was looking in at the raving Anarchist.

" Now what happens?" I whispered to the ape.

" He will be left to think over his sins till hunger has made him manageable. Then he will be shipped ,to the Isle of Probation."

" Suppose he repents. Will he be allowed to ftay?"

Certainly, but Anarchists don't usually repent ithout a taste of Probation. We don't want any foolish sentiment, even in Paradise."

CHAPTER VI.

AN AUDIENCE WITH THE PRESIDENT

All the animals and birds round about were staring through the wattles at the captured elephant — all but Joe. He came up to me — the good old dog.

I looked down at him; then I dropped on my knees to be on a level with him.

Something shone out of that old dog's face, some force that made me feel, " Well, here's an animal that's only an animal, and yet he knows more than I do."

*' You old boy! " I said, and forgetting about his Presidential dignity, and treating him just as if he were a common dog, I threw my arm over his shoulder, and drew him toward me. " You good old dog, I never expected to stroke your back."

Joe's eyes were full of tears, upon my word they were, and there was something in his glance, some peculiar light, telling me that, hearty and jolly and glad to see me as the other animals had been, there

wasn't one of them to whom my visit meant as much as it did to Joe.

" You always were half-human, old fellow," I said. " You have lots of friends, do you know it? "

Still that same strange, steady glow in his eyes. " If I could have some human beings here! " he said. " I'm happy, quite happy, and yet it seems to me sometimes that I cannot wait for my dear Miss Laura md Mr. Harry, and the rest of the Morris family." ' They will come to you sometime, Joe," I said, rubbing his head. ** You don't want them to die." ' No, no," he said, chokingly. " The earthly life Is very sad at times, yet there are bright spots. 'Let them accomplish their journey, but how glad I shall be when I hear that they have gone to the World of the Blessed. When birds send word from earth of Miss Laura crying, it seems to me I shall go crazy. Think of tears in her gentle eyes. She that never hurt any one! "

" Never mind, Joe," I said. " There's an end to everything. Some day you will get what you want."

He licked my hand. " You are a dear boy. I've
leard how you stand up for persecuted animals,
ind when your heart was nearly broken over your
[dog's death, we all wanted to have you come here,
loko especially."

" Joe," I said, " you spoke just now about birds [sending messages from earth. How do they do it ? "

" You have heard of wireless telegraphy ? "

" Yes, Joe."

" Well, we have bird telegraphy. Birds fly to given points, and sing news all over the worlds from their beautiful throats. Thus we are kept posted."

" Goodness! " I said. " I've seen birds sitting on tree-tops nearly breaking their little windpipes. Do you suppose they were telegraphing?"

" Very likely — but I am forgetting myself. Seeing a dear human being has made me weak. Jess," he said, raising his voice, " don't you want to meet one of our earth friends?"

The comfortable looking little dog that resembled him waddled up.

" Why, Joe," I exclaimed, " this isn't your mother, is it? — poor Jess, who was abused by Jenkins ? "

He nodded, and the small, fat dog behind him smiled so widely that she showed every white tooth in her little head. " Yes, I am Jess, and here are my pups," she said, in a pretty voice.

" Hello, boys," I said, as the six of them came scrambling over each other to me. " There's no Jenkins here, is there? "

They wagged their little heads; then, too full of fun to keep still for a minute, they went rolling and tumbling over each other about the grass.

' It is a good while since they were pups," I said, " if the story of your life is true. Isn't it time they grew up? "

He curled his dear old lip in a dog laugh. " Oh, yes, but remember, my boy, you are still in time, and we have entered upon eternity. Think of the duration, or the want of duration of our lives. Puppyhood is immensely prolonged."

" But you are in Paradise, and you are not a puppy."

" No, Master Sam; I could not go back to puppy-hood just now and be happy. I like to be an old dog without the infirmities of age. But," and he grew thoughtful, and looked away out over the sparkling sea, in the peculiar way that the animals all looked, " I have heard that in a future state, after ages and ages, there is a re-birth and a re-growing, but I do not know. We have so much to learn, so much that is improving and delightful, and that keeps our minds occupied. I often think that if, to us, these unfoldings are so wonderful, what will they be to you beings of a higher order. I often, often think about it," and he wagged his old head wisely.

Then his eye fell upon Soko, who with every long hair in the dunnish fuzz around his dark face sticking out with pleasure, was watching us, eagerly.

" Ah, Soko, my trusty lieutenant," he said, " you are there."

" Why, Joe/' I said, " you were a President a minute ago, and now you sound like an admiral or a general."

" States and dignities don't count much with us," said the old fellow, smiling at me, " and I fear we get them mixed. We are a republic, pure and simple. I am nominal head, but all the others are with me. You see there are no jealousies here, no strivings for office. We are all on an equality."

" You have sorrow, though, Joe; witness the goat."

He became very grave.

" Send for the woman that owned him, Joe," I said; " do send for her."

" Would it please you ?" and his brown eyes shone at me.

" Down to the ground."

" Very well, Soko, you see to it."

" All right, sir," said the ape.

" And get the boy a comfortable place to sleep to-night."

" Yes, sir."

" Here's my dog, Joe," I said, pulling Rag forward, " he hasn't been introduced to you."

I put my hand over my mouth to keep from laughing. It was just " too sweet for anything," as the girls say, to see those two dogs run up to each other. I was impatient for them to get on their

hind legs. They seemed just Hke a pair of boys to me, now that they could speak. But they didn't. They touched muzzles, and grinned at each other, and then they were friends.

" This is a boss place, old man," said Rag, easily.

" Say ' Mr. President,' you dog," I muttered tinder my breath, and I gave him a push with my foot.

" Boss place, President," repeated Rag, still more jeasily.

" Very boss," replied Joe, gravely. He never msed slang himself, but I believe Joe would lie idown and die before he would hurt anybody's feelings.

Never saw such goings on," said Rag, " that ' elephant fight was scrumptious. Couldn't you give us something in the line of magic ? My master loves funny and puzzly things."

Joe's face clouded.

" Shut up," whispered Soko, " Joe doesn't like anything of that sort."

" I'm keen on magic myself," Rag went on, unabashed.

I felt ashamed, but I couldn't rebuke him, for he spoke my thoughts.

Old Joe looked at me lovingly. " You are a real boy, and boys like magic shows. Come with me, and we'll interview Her Necromancy."

" You go with Soko, Rag," I said, nudging him. " You're always putting your foot in it."

" Here's gratitude," he said, grumblingly, " and I sha'n't go with Soko. I'm not going to fall one step behind you, till we finish sizing up this place."

I wa:s afraid Joe heard him, and tried to make an excuse for him. " He's a spoiled dog, Joe. Bull terriers are always saucy, I think."

" He reminds me of Dandy," said Joe, with an indulgent smile.

" Dandy, Dandy, the tramp," I said, " one of the dogs in your book ? Where is he ? "

" He died in the book, don't you remember ? "

" Oh, yes, he snatched bread from a child, and her dog fought him — I'd like to see him."

" Well, we'll summon him," said Joe, and he nodded to a sparrow who had been perched near us, with its head on one side, listening to every word we said.

" Doesn't he keep to one place here ? " I said.

" Oh, no," and Joe laughed, " a tramp on earth will be a tramp in Paradise. The great Ruler of the universe does not change the proclivities of his creatures."

" Joe, what are proclivities ? " I asked.

" You know there was a race long ago on the earth called the Latin race?"

" Yes, Joe." '

I

" Well, this word is formed from two of theirs, * pro ' forward and * clivis ' a hill."

" Then proclivities are down-the-hillnesses."

" Exactly."

" Something like backslidings ? "

" No — backsliding is going down the wrong side of the hill. Proclivity is going forward."

" Do you get time to study Latin ? " I asked, admiringly.

" Oh, yes, we have eternity before us, you know," said Joe. " Come, let us go see the Cat."

" See the Cat, the Cat, the Cat," croaked some one. " Take Bella to see the Cat," and a stunning, gray parrot with red tail feathers flopped to my shoulder.

" Upon my word of honour," I said, staggering back, " if here isn't that wonderful bird, Beelzebub, or Bella, from Joe's story of his life. How do you do, old girl ? "

" Very well, very well," she said, giving me a claw to shake. " How's yourself? "

" Fine, Bella, all the better for seeing you. Well, you're a gay old resurrectionist."

"I'm the belle of the Island, the belle of the Island," she said, glibly. " Pretty Bella, lovely Bella, sweet Bella. Give Bella a walk."

I laughed, I roared; there was something so ^mpudent and funny about this saucy gray parrot.

She didn't care a bit, but as serene as possible sat
on my shoulder, only gripping slightly when I staggered from laughing.

" Toby," she called, " come forward; come see the earth-boy."

" Toby, Toby," I said to myself. " Who is Toby ? I seem to remember him."

" Toby," she screamed, " he doesn't know you. You've grown so handsome, Toby, so be-au-ti-ful, Toby — such a dude, Toby."

" Joe," I whispered, " who was Toby? I forget."

" Don't you remember," he whispered back, " Toby, Jenkins's horse, the miserable,
broken-down creature, weak in the knees, weak in the back, and weak all over, that the milkman
used to beat all the time to make him go ? "

" Well, Toby," I said, turning to the plump old horse, approaching, " I beg your pardon.
You're such a gentleman that I didn't know you."

He rubbed his nose on my shoulder. " Good boy, I'm glad to see you here."

" No need to ask whether you are happy," I said.

" Happy," he replied, with a thick, contented laugh, " I never even dreamed of such rich
grass on earth, such peace and quietness to eat it in. Do you remember Fleetfoot? He's my
greatest chum now."

" Fleetfoot — oh, yes, he was the chestnut-coloured colt in Joe's story, the pet of Mr.
Harry who
married Miss Laura. He could do tricks, couldn't he?"

" He does them yet," said Toby, with an admiring smile, and immediately the brown-eyed beauty stepped forward. He, of course, was a smarter looking horse than Toby, and he was
as graceful as a deer. The way he came up, pawing and bowing,
tmade us all laugh. Bella screamed with delight. *' Oh, my, oh, my, hat a face, what a
form, the King of Dudes. vVhere's my gentleman, where's Davy the rat? Find Davy, some one.
Davy, Da-vy, Da-vy, Da-a-a-a-vy! "

The pink-eyed white rat came scurrying from under some fig-trees, where he had been
stuffing himself.

" Come, Davy," shrieked Bella, in a gale of merriment. " Come show your paces. Jump
for Bella, dear Bella, and the pretty boy who has come to see you."

" That rat is a simpleton," grumbled old Toby in my ear. " He believes every word that
Bella says."

Davy was as fat as a pig, but he was as much Bella's slave in death as he had been in life,
old Joe whispered, and round and round the ground he went, leaping and flying through the air as
if he had wings.

I thought the parrot would suffocate herself laugh-
ing. She clutched my shoulder with her claws, and between her shrieks she would call
out, " Faster, Davy, faster, faster! "

By and by the rat gave out, and fell in a heap.

" Fan him, some one," said Bella, coolly, recovering herself. " Throw water on him."

No one did, and she screamed: " Sumatra, Borneo, have you got any water in your
reservoirs ? "

I didn't know what she meant, but I kept a still tongue in my head, thinking I would find
out.

Dear old Joe saw my fix, though, and he murmured in my ear: " An elephant has a stomach something like a camel's. He has a chamber in it that can be cut off from the digestive cavity. In this chamber he can store several gallons of water. Our elephants are very fond of giving themselves shower baths through their trunks in this way."

I looked across the green clearing. The two elephants, Sumatra and Borneo, were keeping guard over their prisoner, who was thrashing about inside his green barriers. Close to them, the tiger was lying on the ground, licking some slight wounds he had received.

Bella was a kind of tease among the animals, for when the elephants heard her shrill voice, they began some kind of grumbling talk in their own language that sounded like, " You go. No, I won't —you go — no, you."

However, at last, the smaller one of them got up — he had been lying with his hind legs extended backward, like a person kneeling, and he set his two or three tons of flesh in motion without any fuss. Then he waddled over to us, and, extending his trunk, gave poor Davy such a deluge of water that he was quite washed away.

"Where's my rat?" said Bella, skipping from my shoulder, and looking under every bush and tuft of grass near by. "Where's my rat? You great, big, hateful, ugly Borneo, I wish I could kill you," and she flew to his broad back and began digging her sharp beak into his hide.

The elephant made a big, rumbling noise inside him that sounded like laughter. Then he swung himself back to his comrade.

Bella was on the ground again. " Davy, Davy, dear, dear Davy, sweet Davy, precious Davy, where's Bella's rat, her angel rat?"

" Ba, ba, ba," said another distressed voice, " where's my tiger, my tiger brother ? I'm cold and lonely without him."

Ragtime snickered beside me. " 'Pon my word, there's the tiger's baby, looking for his keeper."

It was a fetching little lamb that careered over the grass and ambled right up to Joe. A stupid, little lamb, for it never saw the tiger lying right before it.

No, it went up to Joe, with the most beautiful, innocent look you ever saw, and bleated out a pitiful story about losing his friend.

It was all in ba's and ma's, but I understood. Lamb talk or any domestic creature's talk is easy compared with wild beast talk.

It was funny to see the tiger, in the minute that Joe took to tell the lamb about the combat with the Anarchist.

Mr. Bengal lay with his body on the ground, and his head raised slightly, and he looked for all the world like a huge, good-natured, happy cat.

His handsome tail just moved slightly, then he half got up, as if to say, " What are you keeping my lamb for?" fell back again, as if he thought, *' Oh, you're all right, anyway," and then the lamb went skipping to him.

The tiger didn't make any fuss. He just opened his paws a little, and it was as good as a play to see the lamb snuggle up to him. I noticed that Bengal stopped licking himself in the place where the lamb put its head, though there were several raw spots there.

" Look here! look at that! " yelled Bella, and drew all our attention to her.

She had Davy by the back of the neck, and was dragging him before Joe.

"He isn't dead, is he?" I asked.

THE LAMB WENT SKIPPING TO HIM "

" Oh, no," said Joe, " he can't die here. He's only overtired. It's Bella's own fault, for keeping

Iim running. Bella, let him lie in the shade. Don't rorry him. He will come to." Bella sat back on her tail and stared at him. " I'd ke to kill that Borneo." " Come," said Joe to me; "if we are to see the lat, we ought to be moving on." "Wait for me," screamed Bella. "I like that boy. I want to go, too. Some one carry Davy. Who'll carry Davy? Who'll carry my rat?"

" Give him to me," I said; " I'll put him in my pocket."

" Your pocket's not warm enough. Where's a Kangaroo? Where's Aunt Australia? Aus-tra-lia!"

A mild-faced Kangaroo came hopping out of the forest.

" She's got young ones in her pouch," said Toby.

" Chuck 'em out," shrieked Bella, " let 'em walk.

Here, Aunt Australia, put Davy in your bag.

Bella's going to see the Cat, and Davy must go,

too."

The Kangaroo obligingly put her young ones on the ground, and took Davy in. When Bella's tongue was still, our procession formed for the home of the Cat.

I was quite excited. Earthly magic was pretty good, but what must the magic of Paradise be ?

CHAPTER VII.

ON THE WAY TO THE CAT'S HOME

Our train swelled as we went along, and most of the animals that Soko had waved home came dropping in by twos and threes.

" You will be the real President of the Island while you are here," said old Joe, in a comfortable voice.

" I don't want to cut you out, Joe," I said.

" Human beings will always command where animals are concerned, and I am well pleased to have it so, dear boy," he replied.

" I believe you, Joe — you're a sensible old dog — no nonsense about you,"

We marched on, Joe and I in front. Now we were under fragrant bay-trees reminding me of my adopted home in California. There was a tangle of wild roses, lupins, and ferns under them, and not far away a little brook was singing softly to itself.

" This part of the wood is especially for Cali-

fornian animals," said Joe, as if reading my

thoughts, " soon you will see some bare, brown hills,

rhere squirrels and gophers live. There is also a lountain for lions, bears, and snakes." " I should like to see a real, good, resurrected rat-ler," I said, " and hear him rattle, without feeling 'd got to run." " There is a rattler on the mountain," said Joe, called Old G/ay Beard, but you'd likely run, for j's a snake with a keen sense of humour. He lives a cave, and has a numerous family, but even to le youngest great-great-great-grandchild, they all irry when they hear a stranger coming, to let him low."

What for? To bite them to death?" " Master Sam," said Joe, reproachfully, " you)rget we are in a land where death is unknown." " Beg pardon, Joe. Tell me what the snake does ?"

" He is a mischievous old fellow, as I told you. [e runs out, he rattles, then he springs. His vie-always runs, unless it is a creature that has been lere for years, because it is second nature with us to protect ourselves, and it takes an age to outlive it. After a time, when the rattler gets done laughing, he cries out to the runner to stop. Then he explains that it was all a joke; but it is a joke that is keeping him away from his second paradise, and sometimes I think we'll have to send him to the Isle of Probation."

" He likes his fun better than his prosperity."

" And he is so old," said Joe, in a disgusted voice, " a great-great-great-grandfather! "

" So no animals die here, Joe? " I said.

" Not one."

" Well, suppose that Anarchist elephant to-day had torn the tiger to pieces ? "

" He would not have been allowed, but even if he had, the vital spark would be left. The tiger would revive. There can be no death here."

" Only suffering."

" Very little suffering, unless the animals violate well-known laws. In future states there will not be suffering."

"And they fight here?"

" There is but little fighting. I wonder that there is not more. You see the animals come here direct from earth, many of them with evil passions. That there is not more quarrelling speaks loudly in favour of a good environment. Look, there is Squirrel Hill."

I did look, and like that old boy in Roman history, I could have stumbled and kissed the ground. This was a bit of California. There was a grain field, a grove of live-oaks, and a dandy hill for the squirrels and gophers, with never a rancher to fight them for the grain.

"Any poison oak, Joe?" I asked.

He smiled. " Plenty of it, but it doesn't poison."

We walked round the hill, the animals all coming put of their burrows to stare at us, and to chirrup to bne another that there was company. ' Behind the hill was a winding road, fronting a magnificent plain, and a twisting river.

There was no sign of house, or barn, or human creature anywhere, but the plains were alive with animals of different kinds, and the air was so clear hat I could even see them bathing in the smiling iver.

" Let us sit down here a little while," said Joe, * and admire the view. I dare say you are tired — nd hungry, too, perhaps," he added.

"I'm not tired, Joe," I said. "I feel as if I uld leap over this hill and back again, and vault e plain and river in three jumps, but I am most powerful hungry — I've a kind of feeling as if I'd been wound round a drum."

" 1 know that feeling," said Joe, gravely. " I had it all the time when I was a puppy. What would you like? "

" Roasted chicken and sweet potatoes, a slice of pork, and turnip, and cold tongue, and celery, and carrots, and beets, and squash pie, and ice-cream."

" Bring a chicken, some one," said Joe, turning his head.

He and I sat with our faces toward the noble view.

All the birds and beasts following us had politely grouped themselves behind.

I looked over my shoulder. A brown and white spaniel was hurrying toward the wood.

" You're going to get fooled, boy," chuckled Bella, in my ear.

"Shut up!" I said.

" Naughty boy! " she screamed, " naughty boy! " Then she went on in a wheedling voice, " Do you know that dog, nice boy, — that good spaniel dog that used to Hve with Bella?"

" No," I said, " I don't."

" Why, that's Jim," she said, " the sporting dog, Jim, that the cruel young man fired at and made him gun-shy. He can carry three eggs in his mouth at a time. He will bring a chicken for you, boy, a tender, sweet chicken."

I said nothing more, and we all looked at the view until old Jim came scurrying back. He had a plump, white chicken between his jaws, and his mouth was so soft that he had scarcely ruffled a feather.

He set it down before Joe, and then modestly ran behind all the other animals.

" Run, chicken," said Bella, slyly, but the plump little chicken stood there not a bit frightened, and keeping one bright eye on Joe, began to smooth down its feathers.

" Has any one a knife? " asked Joe.

A small monkey, who had a belt round his waist, came forward, and handed Joe a thing made of Kstone. im " Thank you, Howler," said Joe; " give it to the

K^ " It seems pretty sharp. What do you use it Hor ? " I asked, playing with it in a silly way. ^^ " For cutting roots and shrubs, young master," said the monkey, saluting me; then he dropped back.

Come put down your head, little white chicken," said Joe. " The boy will have to kill you himself, for no animal here would do it."

The little creature stopped making her toilet, and stepping up to a stone laid her head on it.

I was so mad with Joe that I could have stuck the knife into him; could I strike that bright-eyed thing looking up at me so trustingly ?

"Take your old knife," I said, and I threw it among some bushes.

" Naughty boy!" said Bella, from my shoulder, " naughty boy! "

I dragged her from her place, and threw her up into the air.

Such a shrieking and a chattering as she made. "Bad boy! Cruel boy! — you hurt Bella's claw. Poor Bella — where's Davy ? He's a good rat. I'm coming, brother," and she made her way to the animals behind us.

But Joe hadn't finished my lesson yet. " Here, pig, pig," he said.

A pink and white thing ran out from the crowd behind, the cleanest thing in pigdom that I ever saw, but before I could lay a hand on him, a glorious, flaming macaw flew before me, and held suspended in his beak a bunch of superb Tokay grapes. Another macaw brought muscats, an eagle had half a dozen bananas in his talons. Word had soon got about that I was hungry.

" Bring also breadfruit, and pineapples," Joe commanded ; then good-natured at the sight of so much food, I caught piggy by the hind leg. " This little pig goes to market, this little pig stays home," and I tickled him so hard under his clean little joints, that he ran off squealing for mercy.

" Don't you like my lunch better than yours ? " said old Joe, softly, when I had eaten.

" I'm not used to butchering my own dinner," I said, roughly.

" Some one has to do it," said Joe.

" If I had to slaughter all the animals I eat," I said, " I'd live on vegetables."

Joe laughed, softly. " I often think of the wolf slinking to the hut door of the^shepherd, who was partaking of roast lamb. * What a fine fuss there would be, if I were to do that!' said the wolf."

" Yes," I said, " we pity animals, then we eat them. It's queer, isn't it ? "

.

©It tftt Wius to ti^e €uVH ^omt 89

" I have heard," said Joe, " that on account of the progress made with regard to laws of health, and protection of animals, human beings will soon refuse to eat the more or less tainted flesh food."

" But, good gracious, Joe, what could we do? "

" You who are really not carniverous could get on better without flesh food than we do — and we are perfectly comfortable without it."

" But animals would overrun the earth ? "

Joe laughed. " Therefore you must eat up superfluities. My boy, if everybody gave up eating flesh, there would not be so many animals bred."

" And where would we get our shoes ? " I said, sticking out my foot, " and our clothing? "

" Men are clever enough to invent anything. Look at the different uses to which paper is put — but you must be thirsty — some brook water, some one."

A monkey ran with a gourd, and soon I had another drink of the crystal water of the Island.

" Come on, Joe," I said, jumping up, " I can walk to San Francisco now."

Our train of followers started up, and we wound along down a road skirting the plain below.

All the time I could hear Bella scolding and chattering behind. " Come here, old girl," I called out.

" Here I am," she cried, brushing my ear with her soft, gray wings. " Here's Bella, glad to see you, boy. Is your little temper over, boy ? "

" You hush up," I said, " or I'll box your ears."

" Davy," she called, shrilly, " Davy, he sends his love to you, and are you pretty well ? "

The old Kangaroo, taking this for an invitation, came hopping alongside with her young ones and Davy.

"Bella," I said, "how did you happen to die? I thought parrots lived to be a hundred."

She lost her saucy manner, and her feathers drooped. " Oh, it was very sad. Bella was caught napping. She never was afraid of cats, but one day when she was out in the garden with Mr. Ned, he went to sleep, and Bella went to sleep, and then a naughty Miss Pussy came, and she took a mean advantage of Bella's being asleep, and she jumped on her, and squeezed her to death, and Mr. Ned beat the cat, and took Bella away, but she was dead, stone dead. Poor Bella! "

" And Davy, how did he die ? "

Bella shook her head. " Nobody knows. He thinks it was a cat, but he isn't sure. Sometimes he says it was another rat."

" I should think an event like that would have been impressed on his mind," said Aunt Australia, unexpectedly and mildly.

" And how did you die, Auntie? " I asked.

" Of thirst, I and my young ones. It was terrible. Everything was baked; it reminded me of a drought in Australia."

"Oh, you died in this country?" " In the United States of America," she corrected, gently. " I was taken young from my own country, was brought up with American animals. At the ist, our menagerie train was crossing a desert. It)roke down; there was a fire, and many animals rere killed. Strangers came around me, and I [opped away. I looked for water for my babies, ■'here was none. At last I found a can half-full of)me liquid. I gave it all to them; then I wandered, fandered over the desert. My feet got sore, my)ngue cracked. At last I lay down on the hot sand. [y strength was gone. * I do not know where we lare going,' I said, ' but we will go together,' and ^I very gently choked all my young ones. There was short time of agony. Then there was perfect)liss. I slept, and did not wake till some one held a water-bottle to my lips. I was away up in the air in a beautiful, white ship. I could feel my children moving in my pouch. The good old ape Soko was saying, * Where shall we take you ? Take me with you,' I said, for I had been with him for a short time in New Orleans. Then we came here." " Poor Auntie," I said, " you had a rough time." " But this makes up for it," she said. " This makes up for the suffering on earth."

" You are a good-natured doll. Aunt Australia," said Bella, shrilly, " a good-natured old doll. Everybody likes you."

' Bella," I said, " tell me something that has often puzzled me about parrots, earthly parrots, not heavenly ones. Do they always know what they are saying ? "

" Of course they do," said Bella, briskly.

" I mean do they know what the words mean ? For instance, when a parrot says, * Good morning,' does he know what that means ? "

" Not a bit of it," replied Bella, " that's abstract, but he knows what * cracker ' means, 'cause when he says, * cracker,' you give him food. I used to know lots of words. How could I help knowing that' Joe ' meant ' dog?' Every time I said it he would look at me. And I knew '

Davy ' meant ' rat' — but I was an uncommonly bright parrot," she said, modestly.

" I guess you were," I said.

" And look here, boy," she added, sharply, " when in doubt about animals, remember this, they know more, not less, than you think. Every look, and movement, and squeak, and gibber, means something. Every one — humans are only beginning to understand animal and bird talk. See that stupid-looking green parrot back there on that monkey's shoulder ? "

" Yes," I said, turning my head.

" I'll just give him a glance," said Bella. " See, just a half glance. I haven't even spoken to him."

" You winked," I said.

" No, I didn't," said Bella, and indeed she hadn't. " I just looked as if I had something to tell him, some piece of news. Now you'll see him come blundering up here."

Sure enough he did, craning his neck, and with eyes goggling, for all the world like a curious person's.

" Get away, you old gossip," screamed Bella, as he flew beside us, " I haven't a thing to tell you, except that you look greener than usual."

" You mean bird," I muttered; then my attention was called from Bella to the Kangaroo, who was trembling timidly, and whispering, "There is the Cat's home. I'm half-afraid to take my children there."

" Never mind your children; look after Davy," said Bella, sharply. " Is he coming, too? "

" I think he's all right now," said the gentle Kangaroo, " perhaps I could tumble some of my young ones in."

" Come up here, Davy," said Bella, " up on this nice boy's shoulder."

" I won't have him on my shoulder," I said, " it is bad enough to have you here."

" Put him in your pocket, then. You promised," she squawked, as I hesitated.

I let the subdued looking rat slip into my pocket; then I raised my eyes.

CHAPTER VIII.

THE ABODE OF HER NECROMANCY

We had turned our backs on the grassy meadows and the river, and were facing a desert. There seemed to be nothing on it, but sand and heaps of stones that looked Hke ruins.

The slippery sand was hard to walk on, compared with the firm, winding paths, and the smooth greensward that we had just left.

" I don't see any house," I said to myself, looking away off to the rim of the desert where it met the sky.

" Look again," said Joe, " do you see those broken pillars ? "

" Oh, yes, a little to the left."

" Well, behind them is a group of doom-palms. The Cat has her home there under the ground — now let us consider," and he looked anxiously about him. " Her Necromancy hates to be stared at. This whole crowd can't go."

A murmur from birds and beasts immediately arose.

" Well," said Joe, diplomatically, *' I will make an exception in favour of the birds. They may all go, remembering to keep high in the air, and not to spy— all, that is, except the sparrows. Her Necromancy doesn't like them."

" Why doesn't Pussy like sparrows ? " I whispered to Bella.

" Says they're gossips," said Bella, " and so they are, hateful little things. They've told lies about me."

The sparrows looked as mad as fire. However, there was nothing to be done. Joe was President, and they had to mind him. Making a subdued twittering noise like that you hear from earthly sparrows about bedtime, they flew off a little way, and, perching on some dried up, old cacti, watched us going on.

" Do tell me something about this Cat," I said to Joe.

His old face looked troubled. He hated queer or mysterious things. He was a very honest dog.

" Her name is Isis, or Moon Face, but the animals mostly call her ' Her Necromancy.' She has lived in this Island a long time. No one here knows how long. She is very fond of accompanying the airships to earth, and we encourage her to do it, especially if we are to have dealings with mortals, as in your case."

" Couldn't the apes have made me invisible ? "

" No, the animals have very little power over mortals, though they can do about anything they like with those of their own kind. Very often they have most puzzling cases. Suppose an animal has been almost utterly destroyed — our good, persevering apes search until they find something belonging to it, if it is only a hair or a handful of ashes. When Mrs. Montague's Barry was burned in that dreadful fire in Fairport, nothing could be found of him but one tiny leg bone."

" That's the fire in your story where the Italian's performing animals were destroyed ? "

" Yes, — well, Soko took that tiny bone, put it under the cloth of gold, and Barry was resurrected."

" And can't mortals see the apes when they are at work?"

" Oh, no, no. They are quite invisible. They pass in and out among human beings all the time."

" But the Cat, you say, is different."

" Yes," said Joe, and he again looked troubled. " She was the pet Cat of an Egyptian princess who was a sorceress, and made a study of unknown forces, and other peculiar mysteries that I do not understand. Anyway, she was a very bad lady. I don't know where she is, but I think it is on some kind of an Island of Probation in the World of the Blessed."

" Why was the Cat sent here among these American animals ? " I asked.

" I think she has been on nearly every island in this World of Islands," said Joe, and he added, lowering his voice, " I will tell to you what I would not tell to an animal here. Pussy has — I know — been on, not one Isle of Probation, but several."

" Why, what a bad Cat she must be!"

" Yes, she is pretty bad, but she has some good qualities."

" Why, I should think she would upset all your good animals."

*' She has not that kind of badness," said Joe, still in the same low voice. " Her badness is not violent like the Anarchist Elephant's. It is all inside her. I think she has been sent here because we have some specially good and gentle animals, and the great Ruler of all things hopes that she will get some love into her heart. Without love, she can never progress into a higher state."

" I believe you're the model, Joe," I said, clapping him on the back, " you old bundle of goodness."

Joe blushed or acted as if he were blushing. " Hush, boy, don't speak so loud. To continue about Pussy. I think she is improving, for occasionally she shows a little kindliness toward a good, little white mouse that I gave her for a servant."

" Will she mind giving an exhibition of magic for me ? " I asked.

" No, I don't think so. She may even be secretly pleased. She is very undemonstrative. It is hard to find out what she really thinks."

While Joe had been speaking, we had come close up to the pile of stones. Behind them, under the palms, was a tiny brick pyramid, with a hole in it large enough for a cat to go in. Beside it was another hole large enough for a mouse.

" Why don't they both go in the same door? " I asked.

" The dear only knows," said Joe. " It is some of the Cat's nonsense. Pussy, Pussy," he said, going to the larger hole in the pyramid, " Pussy, will you come out? "

There was no answer, and we all gathered round the pyramid. There were Joe, myself, Bella, the Kangaroo, Ragtime, half a dozen monkeys, three or four horses, calves, panthers, wolves, foxes, an ox, a camel, goats, sheep, more pigs than I could count, and a lot of poultry.

While we all stood gaping at the pyramid, there was the slightest noise behind us, and turning round, I saw the Cat behind the pile of stones.

She winked at me, and I almost fell over. She had been so stiff with me on the way to the Island, that I felt as if she didn't like me. Now she was

putting herself on an equality with me, as if to say, "Just look at those silly animals, goggling at nothing."

" Pussy, Miss Pussy," said Joe, beseechingly, *' the earthly boy wishes to see you."

" Suppose you turn round," said the Cat, sarcastically.

All the animals turned their heads, and it was fun to see their faces. The birds, of course, knew all the time, and were snickering up on the palms.

Joe looked grave as if he were thinking, " Now, igsn't this just like some of her tricks." W " Madame Moon Face, Your Necromancy, or Pussy," he said, " whichever you prefer to be called, I am here to ask you to give an entertainment for the amusement of our earthly visitor. Will you do so? "

" Don't I have to do so," she said, coolly, from her pile of stones, " if the President of the Island commands? "

" No, you don't," said Joe, firmly. " You know you don't. You will not submit to any one on this Island."

" But you know I want you to send a good report of me over yonder," said the Cat, quite simply, and with a longing glance across the desert toward the sea.

All the animals giggled. They were uneasy in

loo 3ot'u Ji^uvuxaut

her company, and had been so often fooled by her, that they didn't believe her when she spoke the truth.

She drew her black brows together, and Joe went on hastily, " Will you give the entertainment? "

" Yes."

"And when?"

" To-morrow night."

"And where?"

" In Fifteen Foxes Valley at eight o'clock."

" Very well," said Joe, " thank you," and he was about to leave, when the Cat spoke again, " Would the boy like to visit my palace ? "

"Your palace?" said Joe. "Why — why, certainly, if he wishes."

The good, old fellow told me afterward that he was confused, for she had never before offered to confer such a favour upon any one.

To tell the truth, I didn't want to go. I was afraid of her. Everything in the Island seemed so square and above board, but her Catship, that I mistrusted her.

"Cold feet!" said the Cat.

Her sneer reminded me of Hillington, and I called out, " I'm not afraid."

" Come, then," she said, and getting up, she coolly walked past all the animals present as if she did not see them, and crawled into the large door in the pyramid.

lOI

" Do you expect me to wriggle in there? " I asked.

" Wait a minute," she repUed. ^ There was a pounding down below, then the pyramid swung back, as if it were on hinges, and underneath was a pair of magnificent doors, laid slopingly in the ground like the old-fashioned outside cellar doors in the farmhouses in the East.

These doors were gorgeous and no mistake — dull brown metal with gold pictures on them, and they were set into a marble wall.

Now I had plenty of room to descend. The door swung back, and I saw before me a flight of white marble steps. 1 ran down them, to show off to the animals behind.

Rag ran after me.

" Oh, your dog is coming, too, is he? " remarked the Cat.

" He always goes where I do."

" But he wasn't invited."

" Hello, master," said Rag, " I'm stuck."

I turned round. There the old fellow was — grinning from ear to ear, but rigid.

" I've been turned to stone," he said, " never mind me. Go on, I'm not suffering. I suppose Blackface will unstone me when she comes back."

" You shouldn't try to enter a lady's house without permission," said the Cat.

I made a step backward. " You release that dog, madam, or I'll not go another step."

to2 3?o^'g ipatairtee

" Will you send him back ? "

" Yes."

Rag immediately found the use of his limbs.

" Skip," I said, pointing to the steps. " Stay with Joe, and if I'm not back in an hour, come after me."

Pussy curled her lip. Then she laughed. The faces of the animals peering down the doorway were too funny. They had enough to amuse them till I came back, for they were gaping at the gorgeous doors, and the long marble hall as if they never meant to stop.

" You have a very fine house," I said.

" Yet I'm not happy," said the Cat, with a sigh.

" I knew now she was speaking honestly, so I looked sympathetic.

" I want my old home and my dear mistress," she went on — " my dear Egyptian princess."

" But there are no Egyptian princesses now."

" My princess was a daughter of the Pharaohs," said the Cat, proudly.

" Je whillikens! " I said. " You must be old. These American animals must seem like mushrooms to you."

She hung her head. " I have had a sad story. My mistress did not do good things. She taught me to be bad. So closely do we animals follow our human leaders. She is working out her probation. So am I. But I cry every night to be reunited to her, and to be in my old haunts. I hate this Island."

grtie ^tioire of %er TSTfetotnantj? 103

" Poor Pussy," I said, softly, and I stooped down and stroked her fur.

' Don't tell the other animals this," she said, brokenly, ' they don't believe in me. All the cat was educated out of me by the princess — I was worshipped by human beings. I love to have you here, though a girl would have been more to my taste."

I told her I was sorry for her sake I was not a girl, and all the time we were speaking, we kept walking down the marble hall. Open doors were on either hand, and looking into them I could see magnificent rooms with pictures and vases and queer ornamental kinds of furniture. And all the paintings and decorations looked odd and square, like the pictures in my illustrated Bible.

I felt about a thousand years old, till the hall came to an end, and then what I saw took all thought of myself out of my head.

In front of us, the hall widened into a square courtyard, and this courtyard was about the most striking thing I ever saw. There was a fountain in the middle of it, and flowers — scarlet, and blue, and all kinds of colours. I'm a little colour blind, but they were bright and dazzling, anyway. Well, around the fountain and flowers, there were seats, and back of the seats were windows. The palace was built round this courtyard. All up

and down were windows, and balconies, and hanging flower-boxes, and baskets, and strips of gay carpets, and rugs thrown over raihngs.

" Why, this is splendid," I said — " never saw anything like it. Now, if you only had some people."

" People," said the Cat, " oh, yes, certainly, — don't you see them ? " and then I rubbed my eyes.

At nearly every window, there was a dark head, with long, black hair, and queer, stiff-looking gold combs and head-dresses, and their heads were nodding, and bowing, and smiling, and I even heard talk — soft, low talk, such as ought to be spoken in a king's house.

Near at hand, there were women and children, paddling in the fountain — such fat, chubby children, but all odd and foreign-looking. I didn't think they were real, so I went up to one fellow playing with some goldfish, and nipped his shoulder.

The flesh felt firm just like mine, and he screamed " Ouch!" and turned and gave me such a crack.

The Cat was showing every one of her shining white teeth at me. Those teeth didn't look many thousands of years old. Then she said, " We must hurry on, if you don't want to spend more than an hour here."

We went on, and she showed me all kinds of things. Big halls with gold and collections of precious stones, and for the life of me, I couldn't

help bawling out, " Oh, how I wish I had some."

" Fill your pockets," she said, and I assure you I didn't wait for another invitation. I chose diamonds mostly. There was a big bracelet I took for mother, and the middle stone in it was as large as my bantam ■len's eggs. How pleased I thought mother would be with that stone. Then I picked out a fancy kind of a head-dress for her — diamonds again, but with a few pearls thrown in. Oh, I was sharp, I assure you. I just looked round and thought, " Now a diamond is the most valuable of stones. When I get back to earth, that will command the highest price." However, I did sandwich in a few topazes, rubies, and emeralds.

When my pockets were stuffed, I tightened my waistband, and poked the jewels down my shirt. *' If I had a basket, I could carry more," I said to the Cat.

Her lip was curled. " You are a real, human boy. What can those pretty things do for you on this Island?"

" May I not take them back to earth ? " I asked, anxiously.

" Oh, by all means," she said, dryly, " but the hour is up. We would better get back."

On the way down the marble hall, we met a beautiful creature coming toward us — a haughty young woman with a touch-me-not air.

I

"Is that your princess?" I asked, eagerly.

The Cat looked mad, then she began to cry. " My princess! — No, did I not tell you that I am separated from her for thousands and thousands of years ? "

Then she said, snappingly, to this beautiful creature: " Follow us! "

I gaped, when the scornful young person fell meekly in behind that common looking black Cat.

Soon we reached the marble cellar doors. There was old Joe looking down anxiously. Rag and the other animals peering over his shoulders.

I looked behind me. Where was the princess? I wanted Joe to see her. She was gone.

I

CHAPTER IX.

A LODGE BY THE SEA

Where also was the marble hall, likewise the flight of steps, and the gorgeous doors?

Upon my word, they were gone too. There I sat blinking like an idiot, and looking down at the holes in that dusty pyramid, which was like the den of an animal, and at the Cat, now rather cross, with a faded-looking white mouse beside her.

" Till to-morrow, then," said Joe, gravely, " Fifteen Foxes Valley — eight o'clock."

" All right," snapped the Cat; then she wheeled round and disappeared in her pyramid.

Joe turned eagerly to me, " Did you enjoy yourself, dear boy ? "

" Yes, Joe, but I'm glad you're not a magician. Such tricks stagger me."

"But you like them?"

" Oh, yes, I love to be fooled and fooled over again. Just look here," I said in disgust, and I began heaving out the lumps of coal from my pockets and shirt front. " I thought these were diamonds."

Joe laughed heartily. " That Cat would deceive any one. All the time you were gone, she kept us amused with a little magic creature with sixteen legs and ten heads, that came leaping and dancing up and down the marble steps, making faces at us, and never getting twice in the same position."

" I suppose she just lives in a hole in the ground," I said.

" Yes, an underground place. She hypnotised you, dear boy, and made you see anything she wanted you to. People on earth do such tricks."

" Yes, I know. I've seen lots of magicians. But still, Joe, there's something we don't understand about some tricks, isn't there ? "

" There is, dear boy. There is the spirit world. Since coming here, I have learned that mortals puzzle themselves over some phenomena that they cannot explain, namely, the connection between the earthly and the unearthly. Some day all these mysteries will be cleared up for them. I may not speak too freely to you, since you are to go back to earth — see, here is Dandy."

We had all left Castle Egypt, as some of the animals called the Cat's home under the doom-palms, and we were travelling back over the desert.

A handsome brindled bull terrier was trotting easily over the sand, preceded by the sparrow that Joe had sent to find him.

" Well," he said, as he drew up and saluted Joe, "you sent for me. What do you want?"

" To introduce you to a boy from America who has read your story."

" I am charmed to meet him," said Dandy, elegantly. " Is he a dead boy, or a live boy? "

"A live one," said Joe; "he is going back to earth in a few days."

" I am glad to see you. Dandy," I said, " for as I remember you in Joe's story, you belonged to the race of tramp dogs."

" I belong still," said Dandy, " I hate to be tied to one place."

" Let me introduce my bull terrier Ragtime," I said. '* I would like you to be friends."
Ragtime stepped forward and made his best bow.

" Well, I can give him some pointers on Paradise," said Dandy. '* I get over this Island oftener than any other creature."

" Are you happy here. Dandy ? "

' Yes, almost. I want a master. I wouldn't stick to one on earth, but I'd even stop tramping if I could have one here. With your permission, I will attach myself to you, while you are with us." His manners were really fine, and as I remembered the story of his life, I recalled the fact that he had been used to good society.

" I should like to introduce you to my mother,"

he said. " She's a dear old lady. I used to hate her on earth, because she wouldn't stay home and lick my ears when they were sore, but she's given up tramping now, and we get on very well together. I love to roam, but I always want to find her in our httle home w^hen I return."

" I know men like that on earth," I said. " They tramp, but their womenkind have to sit by the fire."

" See, there she is," said Dandy, " just heaving in sight against the horizon."

A fat old bull terrier was indeed wagging along toward us. She and Dandy and Ragtime were the only bull terriers I had seen on the Island. They're pretty lively dogs, and I daresay a good many of them had to go to the Isle of Probation.

" What is her name ? " I asked, when Dandy's old mother came travelling up to us.

"Mella," said Dandy. "She doesn't look as if she'd been run over by a cart and killed, does she?"

" Is that what happened to her on earth ?" I asked.

"Yes. Don't you remember Joe tells about it? Well, we might as well jog along with you.

We seem to be interrupting the procession. Where are you going to sleep to-night, Mr. Sam? "

^ aotrge ftg tlie Sea m

Joe overheard him. " Soke is getting a place ready for the boy."

" I ask, because I'm going to sleep outside your V door," said Dandy, '* mind that." mt "You shall be first dog of the bedchamber," ^H said.

!^ " You're likely to have a crowd of courtiers," said Dandy; " but remember I spoke first."

" A crowd! Why, who will want to sleep near me?"

" Every domestic creature on the Island," said Dandy, promptly, " and a few wild beasts. You see, when night-time comes, animals get lonely. They remember their masters, and you'll have to play sub. But Fm keeping you from the President — excuse me. I wouldn't stand in Joe's light for an island," and he politely fell back.

I remembered how kind Joe had been to Dandy on earth. " Joe," I said, looking down at him, " it seems queer to have you so small. If I had my way, I'd swell you to the size of an elephant."

"Would you think any more of me then?" he asked, with a kind of a shake in his old voice.

" No, Joe, I guess after all it's easier to like the little things than the big ones, but I'm surprised not to find you larger. You used to look larger in your pictures."

" Oh, I was afraid of the photographer's camera,"

he said. ** I used to sit in front of one to please Miss Laura, but it frightened me terribly. It was so mysterious — now shall we turn a little aside to see how your lodge is getting on ? "

With our long tail of animals, we turned toward the seashore. Looking away ahead, past the big trunks of the trees, I could see animals hurrying about, and when we got near, I just stood and stared.

Under the trees, close to the belt of white sand, that ran round the Island, a large force of monkeys was working. Upon my word, they seemed like a swarm of smart, black carpenters. They had put up a lodge, or wigwam, or camp — I don't know what to call it. Anyway, it had sweet green walls of some flowering shrubs that just smelt fine, a roof of thick woven branches, and a big door and two windows that opened on to the sea.

" Oh, Christmas! " I said, stopping short. " That isn't for me, is it? "

" You don't like it ? " said old Joe, anxiously.

" It's scrumptious, but, Joe, what a lot of bother to make it."

" Bother, oh, no, it is a pleasure to any of us, to work for you."

" But you're not used to work in Paradise."

" To work," repeated Joe; "my dear boy, we are never idle, unless we are resting."

I was too excited to pursue the subject just then. 1 was so excited that I broke into a run, and all the animals trailed after me, to the lodge.

My mother's Angora cat and the canary Taffy sat on a tree outside, purring and chirping directions to the monkeys, and pretending that they knew all about the way that I liked to have things done.

The monkeys were listening good-naturedly. I was on them before they heard me. They were working very busily.

" Soko, old chap," I said, slapping him on the shoulder, ** you're a boss carpenter."

He grinned, and waved his hand toward the swarm of younger monkeys. " I have good workmen."

" Well, if this isn't ' just the sweetest,' as the girls say," I shouted, as I ran inside. There were two rooms, and the lovely smell of them was enough to make a fellow want to go to sleep at once.

" I think we'll leave you here awhile," said old Joe, thoughtfully. " Lie down and rest. You are tired and overwrought. Is that couch comfortable?"

I threw myself on the bed. I don't know what it was made of, but it smelt like lemon verbena, and orange blossoms, and wild thyme, and roses, and lilies, and bayberry leaves, and pines, and lots of other nice smells that I couldn't remember.

" Throw his blanket over him," said Joe.

" Why, Joe, old man," I said, " you don't have stores here, do you ? "

The old dog smiled, and I saw that the blanket that a young monkey was throwing over me was of some vegetable fibre.

There I lay, happy as a senator, animals looking in the window at me, and through the door, crowding and peering over each others' shoulders, as if I were some kind of a show.

The tallest had the best of it, and soon I heard some one squeal, " I can't see. Get off my toes. Oh, what does he look like?"

Bella burst into laughter. " It's Tiny Tim the Berkshire, the tiniest of all. Let him in, someone."

" Come, piggy," I shouted. " Come, look at me. I'm a sight worth seeing."

The animals all made way, and didn't a mite of a pig come trotting into the room? He raised himself on his hind legs, ran his little snout along the edge of my couch, squealed, " Pleasant dreams! " then scampered out. He was very fat and jolly looking, and I heard him squeak all the way outside. The animals all seemed to like a joke, and I think each one gave him a sly push as he went by.

" Now go out, everybody, please," said Joe, beseechingly. " We've been crowding the boy ever since he came. Let him have a little time to himself."

"All but me," said Rag, and he lay down by my bed.

" And me," said Dandy, and he stretched himself out beside him.

" And I'm going to stay, for I was his mother's bird," said Taffy, getting up somewhere among the leaves on the roof.

" And I was Mrs. Emerson's cat, President Joe," mewed the Angora, and she sprang to my pillow, which was of poppy leaves, soft as velvet.

" And I'd like to see any one put me out," said Bella, fiercely, and perching herself close to my ear, she began to sing in a cracked voice:

"Go to sleep, my darling, Go to sleep, my pet, Close your little eyesies, All your cares forget."

I laughed — I roared — that cracked voice, that beak rising and falling, those goo-goo eyes, nearly killed me.

" Bella, come out," said Joe, decidedly.

"Can't I just get a little bit of myself in?" rumbled some one at the window, and I saw that the elephant that wanted Mike McGarvie was hanging his trunk in the room. " The boy reminds me of my keeper. I'm going to be his body-guard while he's here."

I tried not to laugh, for it didn't seem polite, but upon my word of honour, I thought I'd suffocate.

Joe was overborne. Every blessed animal on the Island seemed to be crowding into that room to see me go to sleep. He was pushed up close against ray bed.

•'* Jump up, old fellow," I said, " youVe the best right here, and if you stay down there, you'll be crushed."

Then I wiped the tears from my eyes, and tried to see my way through lions and tigers, sheep and poultry, dogs, cats, birds, panthers, horses, cows, etc. Then I up on my bed, and made a speech.

" Gentlemen and ladies," I said, standing up as straight as I could, but still not being able to look down on a gaping old giraffe, that had managed by hook or by crook, I guess by crook especially, to insinuate himself into my sleeping quarters. " I feel highly honoured by your very prompt and pleasing manner of calling on me at the exact moment when I entered my new home. I will return your calls as soon as possible, and looking forward to seeing you soon again, I must beg the privilege of* a little time to myself."

Well, I sat down, and everybody applauded my speech, but no one went out.

" Ba, ba," pleaded some one in the doorway, " let

I

^ aotrge tig tfjt Sm 117

me in, and my dear tiger. The bad elephant has gone to sleep, and we want to see the boy. I think some one might have kept a reserved seat for my Bengal — please don't step on my hoofs — where is the President ? I think we might have had the private entree. My Bengal has been as public-spirited as any animal here."

" Oh, law," growled Rag, under my bed, " can't that lamb talk! I wish he'd keep his tiger out. I'd love to worry one of those yaller ears."

I don't know why Rag was so suspicious at first of that tiger. For a good while, he vowed that Bengal would eat the lamb sometime when no one was looking. I found the royal animal just about as straightforward a beast as there was on the Island.

Well, the crowding went on, until it got to be awful. Then Joe waxed dictatorial.

" Brothers," he growled, " leave this place. I am shocked at your want of manners."

Still they wouldn't go, and he whispered to me, ** Didn't I tell you they wouldn't obey me when there was a human being about? You are the real President of the Island. Speak to them."

I stood on tiptoe on the bed. I waved my fists. I thundered: " Get out of here, every mother's son and daughter of you."

They all went, and I could have bent double to see them shuffling out — tigers, and wolves, and

lions, and foxes, that could have eaten me as an appetiser before dinner, and never felt me. I remained standing and ugly, till they had all disappeared.

" Except Ragtime," I roared, like a bull, as I saw that my wrath was sending even my own dog slinking from the room.

Rag came leaping back, and went under the bed.

" Have a good sleep," said Joe, kindly; then he, too, disappeared.

I dropped on my pillow. " Isn't that an eye up there? " I said to myself, "a tiny eye about as big as a pinhead ? "

" Yes, it is I," piped Taffy the canary — " I didn't go."

" You little beggar — weren't you frightened of me when I yelled so ? "

" Yes, but I hid behind the leaves and waited. You'll not send me out, seeing I was your mother's bird?"

" Come down here, you little imp," I said. " What are you hanging back for ? You haven't got any one else up there ? "

" Just my little kid brother," said Taffy, *' little Tweet-Tweet. He's very cunning."

" Well, stay, you little wheedler," I said, sleepily. " What is in this air, Taffy ? It is as delicious to go to sleep as it is to stay awake. Do you have night here, Taffy, — does it get dark ? "

" Oh, yes, Master Sam, as black as pitch. Then we go to sleep."

" Well, good night, or good day for the present," I said, drowsily. " All these wonders have made me sleepy."

" Do not speak of wonders till you see what the Cat can do," said Taffy. " I hear she is going to give you an exhibition."

" Is she very wonderful ? " I asked.

I had to prop up my eyelids to keep awake to hear the little fellow's answer, and even then I didn't.

I fell asleep, and slept like a log — Never a ghost of a dream.

CHAPTER X.

THE ARRIVAL OF MALTA

When I awoke, it was sunrise. Old Joe and Ragtime lay on the floor, or rather the earth, which was carpeted with moss and leaves.

Taffy and his little brother had disappeared.

I looked through the open door of my lodge. What a view! Near at hand, the grass and the trees, then the sand and the plunging breakers, and the great stretch of sea, and over all a grand pink veil of sky.

" Good-morning, Ragtime and Joe," I said, " I've had a glorious sleep."

" I have been waiting anxiously for you to awake," said Joe. " It is just about time for the air-ships to arrive from earth. I expect Malta this morning."

" Malta," I said, " the gray cat in the story of your life? "

" Yes, the Maine birds sang of her death to the birds of the Middle States; they sang to the Pacific coast birds, and the Pacific coast birds sang to us.

They all knew Malta, for she had learned not to harm birds. Will you please hurry, Master Sam?"

" Haven't I time for just one plunge in those breakers ? " I asked, going to the door.

" Perhaps — if you make haste."

I ran toward the water, throwing off my clothes as I went.

Rag gathered them all up with his strong, white teeth, and dragged them out of reach of the waves.

Oh, what water, what air! It seemed to me there was something in it different from ours on earth. Something that made me feel lively, and as if I would never have a pain nor an ache, and would live for ever.

There were five or six lines of breakers. I dived through every one of them. I swam about. I felt little gay fishes touching my legs with their damp noses as I went. I even thought I heard them laughing and chuckling softly to themselves, but I hadn't time to stop and investigate. However, when I came out, and was putting on my clothes, I said to Joe, " Is this a fish Paradise, too? "

He smiled. " Oh, yes, the great Ruler of All Things would not leave out some of his creatures."

" Well, well," I muttered; then I burst out with a wish, " Oh, if mother were only here."

" Wait a little while," said Joe. " Some, day she will be with you in the World of the Blessed."

" That is, when we die."

" Yes, as you call death."

" How much longer am I to stay in this world, Joe?" I asked.

"You are not tired of us, are you?" he asked, quickly.

" Oh, no, but I was wondering how long I would be allowed to stay."

" Only a short time longer, I fear," he said, with a sigh.

" I suppose you don't feel like running," I said, as we trudged along under the trees.

" Running, — why, my dear boy, I run over this Island all day long. I only walk when I come in sight of the animals."

" Why do you walk then, Joe? Are you ashamed to let them see their President running?"

" Oh, no," he said, simply, " I go slowly, because they often have something to ask me, and they are all so kind-hearted that if they saw me running, they would think I was in a hurry, and wouldn't stop me."

" Well, you have got a fine lot of animals," I said. " However, let's have a run now, we don't want to stop; " so he and Rag and I set out like three deer for the Hill of Arrival.

There was a great crowd of animals there. They were all watching far-away specks in the air, for this was a time of day when air-ships were

coming and going between different islands, but they crowded round me, and asked me how I had slept, just like a lot of polite ladies and gentlemen.

I scattered pats, and pinches, and rubs, until an old wolf came up with a sneaky, goody-goody air, and said, " Billy wants to see you, sir."

"Billy," I said, "who's Billy?"

" The Italian's dog," whispered old Joe, " in the story of my life."

I tried not to laugh. If old Joe had a fault, it [.was his being stuck on himself because he was an luthor.

" Well, Billy," I said, looking down, " I remember lyou perfectly, but is this you or a lamb? "

I never saw such a dog, — a fox-terrier, pure white, barring ears, face, and tail. He was so good, so gentle, as he stood with his big eyes, too big for perfect pointing, fixed on my face. He was a kind of sugar candy dog, a dog that would melt in your mouth. Looked as if he didn't know what badness was — a kind of dog to be coddled and protected.

" You dear little brute," I said, " if there's any brute in you. I am glad to see you."

He immediately sat up on his hind legs, and cast an appealing glance at the slinking wolf, who came forward.

" Billy is my chum, sir. He doesn't care to talk much — never did in life. He was a most discreet dog, sir. Every one liked him."

" Well, what does he want now ? " I asked.

" I guess he's glad to see you, sir, and " — added the old fellow, hesitatingly — " you haven't such a thing as a piece of sweet cake about you, sir, have you? Billy is a dog that always liked cake better than meat."

" More than you could say for yourself, I suppose," I replied, running my eye over his lean form.

** I used to be fond of meat, sir," he said, meekly. " I can't deny it — but you must have some cake in your pocket, sir."

" I tell you I haven't a crumb."

"Would you mind looking, sir?" he said, persistently. " Billy never sits that way long unless he smells cake. Just notice the look in his eye, sir. Isn't it moving? "

" Well, now, how should I get cake here in Paradise? " I said, jokingly. " Don't you live off berries and raw vegetables?"

" Oh, no, sir. There's a bakery over the other side of the Island worked by the monkeys. I'd be happy to assist, but I can't use my paws the way they use theirs. I wish I were in it, for they're a little short in supplying us with cake."

" Come now. Gray skull," said an orang-outang near us, in a good-natured voice, " don't prejudice

the boy against the bakers. It's a great deal of trouble to make those sweet cakes, and the President tells us not to give out too many."

Grayskull turned his back on him, and said to me, " I wish you'd feel your pockets, sir."

" Well, I declare, if there isn't a cake," I said, bringing out a scalloped one. " I thought I'd eaten them all. I'm hungry myself, I guess I'll eat it."

*' Perhaps you'll give us half, sir," said the wolf.

I was only teasing him, and threw him the whole of it — such a tiny cake for such a big animal.

He laid it humbly before Billy. " Here, angel dog."

Billy surveyed him with his melting eyes, that looked too soulful for a thought of food, then he bit off three-quarters, and gave him the rest.

I snickered — what a queer pair! Then I watched them going the rounds, — Billy sniffing the air, and then sitting up before this animal and that one, and always getting something, and always taking the larger share, and giving the wolf the lesser.

On account of this three-quarters business, and also because his little carcass was so much smaller than the wolf's, he soon got filled up, and then he held up in his begging. The wolf sat beside him for a time licking his lips hungrily, then he too tried the sitting-up business.

As he propped himself up on his hind legs with his big fore feet dangling in the air, the whole bunch of animals burst into a shout of laughter. He didn't make the pretty little beggar that Billy did.

Then the animals took to cuffing him — good-naturedly enough, but it took all the spirit out of him, and he went and sat on the edge of the circle.

" The air-ship, the air-ship! " called Joe. " Come here, dear Master Sam."

I ran beside the old fellow. His brown head was turned up, a ship was just overhead, and an ape that looked as if he might be Soko's brother was looking down out of the car.

A pair of swans — black Australian ones this time — were hovering over us, preparatory to sailing away to their beautiful lake.

We all fell back, for the car was touching the ground.

The Cat sprang out, stared carelessly at all the animals round about, gave me a knowing look, then ran off to her palace, or castle, or hole in the ground, or whatever she chose to call it.

"How did the Cat get on this air-ship?" I asked Joe. " I thought this one left here some time ago."

" So it did," said Joe. " She went out to meet it yesterday in another air-ship. Here she is," he went on, in a deep voice, " here she is."

the whole bunch of animals burst into a shout of laughter"

A little gray cat was looking timidly out of the car.

"Malta," he said, "Malta, dear Malta, don't you know me? "

She hesitated no longer, but sprang out. However, she was a pretty surprised looking cat, and seeing the wild animals, put up her back, and began to spit pluckily.

" Malta," said Joe, " this is the Island of Brotherly Love. Animals don't fight here."

She put her back down, but crowded up to him, and said, " Joe, I'm frightened."

" Poor pussy," he replied, kindly, " you will have a lovely time here. Do tell me how you died ? "

" Old age," she mewed, shyly peeping round at us.

" Then if our Creator let you die, you didn't suffer much? "

" No, Joe, and I was glad. I was always afraid a dog would tear me to pieces," and she shuddered.

"Did you mind the long journey?"

"No, Joe; where am I?"

" On an island in a world where the islands slowly float about in a beautiful sea. We often come in sight of other interesting islands, and they pass us slowly like great ships."

" My head is pretty small," murmured Malta. " I can't seem to take all this in."

" Well, you have come through a good deal since you left New Hampshire," said Joe, kindly. " Just look about you for a few minutes, and don't talk."

Malta stared at the animals, who were all staring at her, and at a cargo of guinea-pigs that the ape who looked like Soko, and who was really his brother, was vainly trying to get out.

They would not come, and Joe asked: " Where did you get them ? "

" In Boston," said the ape, " from a medical school — vivisected pigs."

Joe shuddered. " No wonder they are afraid. You go speak to them, Malta. They don't know us."

The gray cat went up to the air-ship. " Piggies," she said, gently, *' this seems a very nice place. No one is hurting me."

One or two little snouts were thrust out of the car.

" Offer them some juicy grass," said Joe to the ape.

" Do you think that will do, sir ? " said the old ape, with a wise shake of his head. "That is what human beings" do. They feed them, then kill them."

Joe sighed; then he said, kindly, and with a very good imitation of a guinea-pig voice, " Squeak-a, squeak-a, squeak-a."

His tone was so kind, so inviting, that the little
I
pigs came dropping out, one by one, following each other in a funny fashion. Pretty little fellows they were, too — white, and tan, and spotted.

" Not as intelligent as some animals," said Joe, " but too intelligent to torture. Are there any pigs here, this morning? "

" Nary a pig," said Dandy, who had just come running up. " Like me, they love to sleep late in the morning — how de do, Malta."

*' Take them, some one," said Joe, " over to Guinea-Pig Settlement. Introduce them to the other pigs, and make them feel at home."

" I'll take them," said the wolf, who seemed as if he wanted to get the animals' good opinion of him, by doing something dignified.

The animals were roaring with laughter again. At sight of him, every guinea-pig had scuttled back again into the car.

Joe smiled himself. " Thank you, Gray skull,

It you are too large. Here, weasel, you take lem."

And don't sample their brains on the way," ried some one, mischievously.

The weasel turned, and threw a forgiving look

her his shoulder.

"Who said that?" inquired Joe.

No one spoke.

" Let the animal who slandered weasel step)rward," said Joe.

A red fox, simpering and smiling, came sauntering inside the circle.

" Shame, Velvetfoot," said Joe, " shame. Now go with weasel every step of the way, and think hard all the time, that no matter how bad an animal has been, a time comes when he may truly repent of his evil ways, and lead a better life."

The weasel, the fox, and the train of guinea-pigs set out.

" They say guinea-pigs are stupid things," remarked Rag, under his breath. " Just look at the glances they are giving their escort. There are volumes in each one. They wouldn't be a bit surprised if they were eaten."

" They have a great deal to learn," said Joe. " Come, let us escort Malta to my house."

The animals all formed a procession behind us as we set out down the hill and along the beach.

On the way Joe talked to Malta, who was quickly getting used to her new surroundings. " How is Mrs. Morris, Malta?"

" Not very strong, Joe. I fear she will not last long, and — and — "

" And Miss Uaura, or Mrs. Wood, as I should say?"

" She — is — not — well," said Malta, hanging her head.

Joe stopped short, and his old face looked bad. "Is she ill, Malta? — is she going to die?"

"I —I think so."

" Oh! " and the old dog gasped. " Is she suffering, Malta? "

" I am afraid she is, Joe," said the cat, reluctantly.

" My dear Miss Laura! My dear Miss Laura! " muttered the old dog, " she who never hurt a living thing. Oh, it is strange, strange!"

" It makes every one feel terribly to have her ill," said the cat. " She is so young and lovely. Joe, when she dies, will she come to this beautiful place? "

" No, Malta, she will go to one so much more beautiful than this, that we haven't the slightest idea what it is like. But how my flesh creeps to hear that she suffers. I seem to suffer with her — Mr. Sam," and the dear old dog stopped suddenly, and turned to me, " will you excuse me if I leave you? This bad news has upset me, and I am too sad company for you. I did want to take you to my house, but I think we would better wait for another time. Dandy will feel honoured to amuse you."

" Certainly, Joe, I will excuse you," I said; " go home and talk to Malta."

" Take him to Gray Rock, and let him see the fishes. Dandy," said Joe, " He is interested in them."

CHAPTER XL

AN IMPROMPTU CIRCUS

I HAD been very much entertained as we walked along, by listening to the conversation of the animals trotting down by my knees.

Dandy now came forward, but I stood for some time watching poor old Joe going sorrowfully toward his house, with Malta talking beside him. His head hung down, his old face was furrowed. He was in Paradise, but still he could suffer.

" What part of the Island does he live in? " I asked Dandy.

" On a hill back by the beaver swamp. He has a good-sized house, for he has a large family. You'll see it some time. Now quick march, for the fishes."

We walked on and on, keeping to the dark ribbon of a path that wound along through the grass fringing the sand.

The sun had come up strongly, more animals had joined us, and I felt my lips drawing gently back to my teeth.

"What's amusing you, Master Sam?" asked Dandy.

»I nodded over my shoulder. " Looks like a cir-s coming to town." " Well, we'll have a circus," shouted Dandy, springing on a sandy knoll, and barking to attract attention. " Ladies and gentlemen, it will please the boy to see you gambol. You are all walking too soberly. Come, do something, all of you. We've lots of circus animals here. Hurry up now, and show your paces. Jumbo, come forward. Get some boards and barrels, somebody, and a ladder or two."

The monkeys, who seemed to be the busiest workers on the Island, ran about as if they were crazy. Some went among the trees, others scampered down the beach.

A magnificent great animal stepped out from among the others. I had not seen him before. "Is that Jumbo?" I asked, "the New York Jumbo?"

" He's the genuine, real, veritable, amiable darling old Jumbo, the pet and pride of the children of two earth worlds," said Dandy, glibly. " He loves boys. Go up to him."

I hurried up to the old fellow. He ran his trunk over my figure, he smoothed me as gently as my

own mother could have done; then, in a low voice, he said, " This is like old times."

" Oh, you old ark," I said, trying to get one arm half-way round his leg. " I've heard of you, and I'm mighty glad to see you."

" Would you mind whistling a bit," he said, in his deep, true old voice. " It is years since I have heard a boy whistle."

I puckered up my lips and began " Old Black Joe," as fine as a fiddle, but something stuck in my throat, and I couldn't get on with it.

" Try ' Home, Sweet Home,' " said Jumbo, in a voice that seemed a soft echo rumbling from some deep cavern.

That finished me. " I can't," I bawled, and I rolled over on the sand, and wriggled among his gray pillars of legs; "I want to see my mother. I am a baby, a baby! "

Jumbo rubbed me softly with his trunk, and a sparrow flew hastily beside me. " Your mother is well — the earth birds have just telegraphed."

I sat up. " You are sure ? "

" We never make a mistake," said the sparrow, prettily. " We always sing back the messages to make sure. Your mother is well, and is sitting by your bedside, not too anxious, because the doctor tells her that your false body will soon come out of its trance."

" That's good," I shouted, and I sprang up. " I'll soon see her — now for the circus."

Dandy was barking at the top of his voice: " Come, gentlemen, this way, gentlemen. The circus will now begin. Wonderful leaps of the spider monkey. Red-face, from the backs of the flying foxes of Fifteen Foxes' Hill."

" You will enjoy this," whispered Jumbo. " Boys on earth never saw anything like this."

Fifteen pretty little kit foxes, all brothers or cousins. Jumbo told me, came scurrying down the hard wet sand, which was as firm as a floor, now that the tide had gone out.

A long-tailed monkey sat cuddling himself in a heap, but as they came by, he sprang — sprang like a creature that was all springs. I never saw such leaping. The fifteen foxes ran, they rushed, they flew back and forth like the wind, and that monkey kept up his springing, on the back of one, now of another; then didn't fourteen other monkeys come on? and they sprang and leaped, till my eyes got dazzled, and there was a perfect mix-up of foxes and monkeys.

" Bravo! Splendid!" I cried, clapping my hands. " I never saw anything like that before. Good fellows," and I ran up to the foxes, who were going off with their tongues lolling out of their mouths. I rubbed their steaming sides, and

praised them, and then I turned to the monkeys, who were clapping their sides with their hands, and looking as cool and gleeful as if they hadn't done a thing.

In some way or other I felt as if all these animals were my brothers.

" Come on, gentlemen, come on," said Dandy, who was a great trick-master. " Get your hoops, and balls, and whirling sticks. Little Billy's turn next. Billy's last master was an Italian, you know," he said, turning to me, " a professional animal trainer."

Billy's tricks were all good, but they were earthly dogs' tricks. A row of wolves held hoops in their teeth, and he jumped through, and caught the flying sticks between his little jaws. But what I thought most wonderful was his finding a grain of sand.

" Blind Billy's eyes," said Dandy, and an ape clapped his hands round the little fox-terrier's head, but indeed the honest little fellow didn't try to look.

" Now you touch a grain of sand," said Dandy, " any grain — remember the one you touched."

I had pretty hard work to mark so tiny a thing, but at last I succeeded, and the ape loosed little Billy, and didn't he go straight to the grain I had touched ?

*' It's magic," I said.

" It's a keen sense of smell," said Dandy. " None of these are magic tricks. Only the Cat does those. Earthly dogs could do this, and earthly foxes could play with monkeys if they would — now, some more sports, brothers. The President approves of these exercises. Let's play Prisoner."

The animals immediately began running about, here, there, and everywhere. Presently there was placed a high seat with a judge on it — who was a red, uncomfortable looking calf, with a pair of spectacles on, made of willow twigs, which spectacles kept falling down, getting over his nose, and bothering him.

" Why didn't they put a smarter animal in as judge ? " I whispered to Jumbo.

" Stupidity on the bench makes more fun in the court-room," he said. " Just listen."

Below the judge were four tables, which were tree-trunks cut off near the roots, and behind each table sat a donkey on his hind legs, pretending to scribble something on the table with a stick held between his front hoofs.

" Those are the lawyers," said Jumbo. " Look, here comes the criminal."

"Thief! thief!" called some one, and presently two sheep came bundling in a wolf — old Grayskull, Billy's friend.

" Ba, ba-a/' said the judge, " what is he accused of?"

" Stealing cakes from the bakery," bleated the sheep.

Every one shouted. It seemed that old Gray-skull's fondness for cakes was a standing joke.

" Ba, ba," bawled the calf, " what am I to say next? I forget; and will some one pick up my glasses. They've fallen on the ground. I'm fixed so nicely, I don't want to move."

" Say ' Guilty or not guilty,' your worship,'* remarked one of the donkeys, scowling at the sheep, who were both trying to talk at once. One sheep was black, one white, and they looked pretty sharp for sheep.

" Guilty or not guilty, your worship," blundered the calf —" Dandy, no one has picked up my glasses."

" Oh, you're too stupid for anything," said Dandy, impatiently. " Drag him down from his seat, some one. Hyena, you be judge.'*

A laughing hyena, making the most awful faces, went to the bench, where a whole crowd of animals was jerking and pulling at the calf, and having a regular spree over turning him out.

" Now the case will proceed," said Dandy.

" You're guilty, prisoner," said the hyena.

" I'm not," said the wolf.

" You are."

" I'm not."

" We'll soon settle that," said the hyena, laughing horribly, and licking his lips.

He was preparing to leap off the bench and have a bout with the prisoner.

" I never saw such a set of idiots in my life," shrieked Dandy. " What will the boy think of you? Why, we played Prisoner only the other day. Hold your tongue, judge, and get back to your seat. Counsel, there, examine the prisoner."

One of the donkeys jumped up, ran to the wolf, and putting his hand, or rather his hoof, under the wolf's leg, pulled out a sweet cake, that one of the sheep had just placed there.

*' You true donkey," shrieked Dandy. " I meant you to ask questions, not to play policeman."

The wolf grinned. You're guilty, wolf," said the hyena, " I just

Lw that cake taken from between your joints."

" Which the sheep put there," said the wolf.

" What matter how it got there, if it was there,"

lid the hyena. " Somebody has to be punished." You're a pretty judge," said the wolf. " You've ["ot a twist in your morals, as well as in your temper."

Now, I'll give it to you for that," said the [hyena, and his laugh was something ghastly.

" Come on," said the wolf, and shaking off his sheep policemen, he laid his nose on his paws and looked at the hyena like a provoking dog.

The next instant, wolf and hyena were out of the court-room, flying into the woods.

" Will they hurt each other ? " I asked Jumbo.

" Not a bit of it. This is only rough play. They like to tease one another."

Dandy was roaring at the demoralised court. " Another judge, there. Here, meek-faced Billy, you step up. Condor, you be prisoner."

A big American condor flopped heavily up to the sheep and lighted on the ground between them.

"Now, Billy, sweet Billy," said Dandy, "the prisoner has stolen a sweet cake that has been found under his wing. What shall be the penalty?"

" Death," said Billy, gently.

" Now, Billy, darling Billy," remonstrated Dandy, " just open those lovely eyes a trifle wider. Would you sentence that fine bird to death for merely stealing a little cake — one of those tiny cakes you are so fond of ? "

" Yeth," lisped Billy, gently.

" Stop lisping," said Dandy. " You never lisped in life. You're putting on airs. Why would you sentence that fine bird to a cruel and ignominious end, Billy?"

" Cauth," said Billy, " he stealth my caketh."

I

" Now, Billy, be merciful; remember how you suffered when you died."

" I forget all about it," said Billy, " cauth I'm havin' such a good time now."

" But the poor condor won't forget. It will hurt him to die."

" It won't hurt me," lisped Billy, gently.

Dandy got mad. " Condor," he said, " you be judge."

The animals fell on Billy, jollied him 'most to death, pushed him in the prisoner's place, and put the condor on the bench.

" Now, condor," said Dandy, " here is a little dog who is very fond of cakes. He loves them better than anything else on this Island. He likes to steal over to the bakery, and see them coming fresh and sweet-smelling from the oven. Probably there was a panful cooling on a rock. Probably he stretched out his little paw and concealed one under his little white leg where wings ought to grow, for he is such a good little dog. What is your sentence on this little prisoner, this good, trembling little prisoner?" for Billy was shivering, and shaking, and rolling his big, beautiful eyes as if he expected to be killed the next instant.

" Life," said the condor, mildly.

" Life! " repeated Dandy. " That is, you would not punish him ? "

" I'd give him a pan full of cakes, then he wouldn't steal any."

" Hurrah for the condor," shouted Dandy, " hurrah, hurrah, the prisoner is discharged," and he sprang up and ran about. " The judge is a gentleman, the court is dissolved," and as if glad of an excuse for a frolic, the animals ran hither and thither like crazy creatures.

I pulled up Dandy, who was scurrying about the beach with the best of them. " What about the fishes, old man ? "

He stopped short. "Oh, yes, I forgot. Come on, we'll make for the ancient Gray Rock."

CHAPTER XII.

FISH PHILOSOPHY

" Good gracious! have they killed each other ? " I said.

We were tripping along over the sand, and saw upon our right the laughing hyena and the wolf, lying with their heads crossed and bodies extended.

" Yes, with fatigue," said Dandy. " They're dead tired. You don't understand these animals. They're always poking fun at each other."

"Weren't they really angry?"

" Oh, just a little bit, perhaps," said Dandy, airily,

:" but they'd soon get over it in the heat of a chase.

'here is Gray Rock," and he pointed ahead of us to

[a large gray surface that looked like an immense

twhale stretched out on the water.

Ah, what fine fun we have playing on that old [rock," he said. " We rub it with seaweed to make it slippery, then we play games on it, and fall in the water, and scramble out again. Come, let us go fto the end of it."

We had a gay time tiptoeing our way out to the 143

part of it that entered deep water. Only Dandy and I went. All the other animals stayed behind, and either went in bathing or lay down in the shadow of the rock.

"Look away out there," said Dandy, suddenly, " can you see the Triplets, and hear their children playing? "

I raised my head. Some distance beyond us were three other gray rocks, these half-covered by sea-lions, who were sunning themselves or plunging about in the water.

" Don't their grunts sound happy ? " said Dandy. " Now look down here, and see if it that isn't the prettiest fish garden you ever saw."

I got flat on my face on the rock, and peered down.

" Oh, glory," I said, " I wish I could take off my clothes and have a tail and fins."

"Oho there," said Dandy, putting his muzzle down to the water, " come up and talk, some of you."

I held my breath. There was a little paradise below in the water; then came a flop, flop, and a gray seal, so graceful in the water, so awkward out of it, came hitching up on the rock beside us.

" Oh, get out," said Dandy, " you're only half fish," and he looked again into that magnificent pool full of fishes in full dress, and the loveliest seaweed, and sponges, and bright-coloured anemones, and little sea animals, whose names I didn't know.

jaws out of the water, " we heard you had an Eastern boy on the Island — is it true? "

" Yes," said Dandy, " he's here, wants to interview you — says he'd like to be a fish."

" I'm a true blue Down-Easter," said the fish — " was caught, cut open, and my false body was dried and sent to the West Indies, where I hope the blackies enjoyed it. Excuse me, till I get a breath of water," and he popped below.

Presently he reappeared. " What else does the boy want to know ? "

" Speak to him," said Dandy.

" I want to know how you got here," I said. " The monkeys can't bring you in the air-ships.'*

" Yes, they do — part way. Then submarine boats meet us. I lok alive there, seals. Bring up a boat for the earth boy to see. What part of the East do you come from, boy?"

" I was born in Maine. I live in California now."

" I dare say you've eaten the false bodies of some of my family," he said, as if that made a tie between us.

" How is your paradise different from your earthly life?" I asked.

" Oh, we don't eat each other here. No worry, no care to get out of a bigger fish's way." "What do you live on?"

" Succulent grasses, and juicy seaweeds — we' vast tangles of them. They're sweeter than flesh" food when you get used to them, and cleaner, too."

" And do the weeds like to be eaten ? "

" They've made no complaint yet, but I hear in a greater ocean to which we shall one day go, there will be no eating at all. Seems to me, we'll miss lots of fun. I always enjoy a good meal, but I suppose it will be all right."

" And do you just swim round this Island? "

" We don't go far away. Fishes like their home as well as you do— Here's the submarine boat; what do you think of it? "

" Reminds me of a torpedo-boat," I said, looking at the queer cigar-shaped thing coming up out of the water. "And who manages this boat?"

" Seals," said Dandy. " They can do wonderful things with their flippers. Here, Snorter, tell the boy the story of your life."

The gray seal, whose, fur I found had become lighter with age, poured a long story into my ear, all about life in a " rookery," and fights between seals, and the clubbing of cruel men-hunters, and all the time he was speaking I seemed to be swimming in the good nature of his soft brown eyes.

It was so queer to sit there on that rock, listening to him, with Dandy and Rag beside me, the great blue ocean in front, the bright sun in the clear sky

" IT WAS A BIG ISLAND FROM THE NORTH
I
Overhead, the crowd of animals gambolling on the md behind.

Hist," said some one, suddenly, " there's an iland coming. Stop and let the boy observe it."

The cod, whose name I found was Yankee Tom,
ras speaking. He had been diving below in the
rater, and now with his mouth elevated, and his
yes sticking out with interest, he had cut in upon
the seal.

" How do you know ? " I asked. " I feel a lower temperature — it's an Arctic island."

T stared far out to sea. Something white and towering was coming — something that looked as if it were covered with glittering steeples of churches. It soon drew near, for it was going very fast. It was a big island from the north, Dandy told me. Up in the middle of it was a huge ice mountain, and on its drifted slopes we could see dimly the forms of white polar bears. Monsters they were. Dandy said.

' Look, look," he suddenly cried, " there is a mother bear with young ones."

Sure enough, there was a fat old bear, making her way down the mountain slopes with two little rolls of white trotting beside her.

" You are favoured," said Dandy; " strangers rarely see a mother bear with very young ones.

They conceal themselves in the ice and snow, until their cubs grow to quite a size." j

" And there are other animals," I said, pointing to the lower slopes. The island was not all ice and snow. The part near the water was open and brown. It appeared to be frozen ground, and on this ground seals, walruses, and many Arctic birds were disporting themselves. j

" They are looking for lichens," said Dandy." *' They do not eat each other, any more than we do."

" How is it this Arctic island comes into these warm waters ? " I asked.

" To give the critters on it a change," said Yankee Tom, smartly. " You don't want monotony, if you are dead."

" It won't stay long," said Dandy. " The animals are not very comfortable down here in their warm coats."

" And see how their mountain is weeping," remarked Tom.

Rivers of water w^ere indeed running down the face of the mountain.

" How our birds are telegraphing," said Dandy — " just listen."

I looked behind me. Larks, robins, nightingales, finches, and thrushes were flying away up, up into the air, and as they flew they sang.

I When they stopped, beautiful white birds sang rom the mountain of ice — such pure, clear, cold ongs. " Now we'll get the news," said Dandy, with atisfaction. " Lots of our animals will have friends in that island." " Can you understand what they say ? " I asked Dandy.

" Yes, when I can hear, but the birds fly so high
and sing so fast, that I can't always make them out."

" There's a crested seal," said Dandy, quickly,
*' look quick, boy — do you see the kind of helmet
on his head? "

I looked and wondered. The creature had a thing on his nose like a small bag, his colour was blue-black, and he was marked with irregular whitish spots.

I never knew there was such an animal," I id.

" Some boys and some girls, too, would be the

letter for a dip into natural history," said Yankee [Tom, dryly. '* If I were a fond parent, a human larent, I'd give my children books of information, ■ather than so many novels — however, I'm only a codfish, and I suppose my opinion isn't worth my salt," and he dived below.

Dandy smiled. " You're a pretty cute codfish, bm. I guess your opinions are worth something."

Tom came steaming up again. " Say a good word for the cod tribe, boy, when you go back to earth. We're pretty numerous."

"What shall I say?" I asked.

" Say * kill me quick, and I'll love you,' " replied the cod, with a shake of his tail.

" That message will apply to about every one you meet here," said Dandy, bitterly. " ' Kill, but don't torture,' might be written in flaming letters before every human eye — But, hello, the Arctics are signalling. Hello, brothers, how are you ? "

The beautiful white island had come nearer and nearer while we were speaking, and now we could have tossed a biscuit to it.

An ungainly old walrus, a regular sea-horse, was down on the Arctic beach waving one of his fore limbs wildly. Other walruses, seals, otters, and a number of birds were beside him.

"How do you stand this heat?" he bellowed. " I'm 'most roasted — am trying to fan myself."

" This isn't hot," roared Dandy, " it is just a nice, mild day."

" It's awful," groaned the walrus. " I'd give one of my tusks to be back home again. How's the boy? We'd heard you'd got one on your Island, and now we see him."

"He's all right," said Dandy, proudly. "Do you want to borrow him for awhile? "

" N-o-oo," said the walrus, doubtfully, " boys are cubs of men that hunted us in life."

" You great simpleton," called Dandy, " don't you know that no one could kill you now ? "

" He might beat me," said the walrus, cautiously.

" Suppose he did, you mountain of fat, it would do you good — increase your circulation."

' I don't hear very well," said the walrus, in a thick vpice. " I have a good deal of flesh — it takes talk a good while to get inside of me. I think I'll sit down awhile," and he subsided on the rocks. A wiry looking Arctic fox took his place.

" Have a good look at him," said Dandy to me, " for he is widely different from all other species."

I did take a good look at him, and not being up in ^ foxes, didn't see that he was different from his brothers, so I asked Dandy about it.

Dandy pointed out lots of things, — a less pointed muzzle, shorter and more rounded ears, a ruff of long hairs round his cheeks, and so on. His colour, I could see for myself, was a dull red and yellowish white.

" This is his summer dress," said Dandy. " In winter, he gets white, so that he won't be seen among the snow-fields."

" What does he live on ? " I asked.

" In life he lived on birds. Now he eats seaweed. Hello, brother," called Dandy, " did the hunters on earth ever find out what you did to get a living in winter when the birds had left the country ? "

The fox showed his white teeth. " No, brother — they never searched the crannies of the rocks, where we stored our nice, sweet lemmings."

" What are lemmings ? " I asked.

" Rodents," said Dandy, " first cousins to voles. They are heavily built, have an obtusely snouted head, very short tail, and tiny feet covered with hair. Length, about five inches."

" I should like to see one," I said.

" Did you ever hear of lemming fever ?" asked Dandy.

" No."

" Well, in Norway, where lemmings are the most abundant of any rodents, they have a curious custom. At certain intervals, thousands and thousands, and sometimes millions of them descend from their homes in the mountains, to the cultivated plains. They dash across fields, swim rivers and lakes, eat their way through fields of corn and grass, and plunge into the sea, where they are drowned."

" Why do they do such a crazy thing? " I asked.

" Nobody knows. On their way to the sea, they tumble into wells and brooks, and the water becomes so polluted that the people get * lemming' fever — but excuse me, I must talk some more to the fox," and he called out, " Can you give me news of Marco, the big sea-bear ? "

The fox could, and did, and they had a short gossip about various Arctic animals, the island meanwhile passing so speedily by, that the fox had to walk smartly along its side to keep near us, for our island, for some reason or other, was taking things much more quietly.

I found that the scenery varied on the Arctic island. Different kinds of trees appeared, and also a few swamps, and ponds and lakes. There were also rounded hills, some snowy, some brown and frozen, and also vast fields of ice stretching far inland.

The island was very thickly populated, and every animal and every bird looked happy.

" They don't mind the cold," I said.

" Not a bit," replied Dandy. " Alas, they are going — there is the end of the island. Good-bye, brothers."

" Good-bye, good-bye," came from the island, and we regretfully saw it disappear.

After its glittering white pinnacles and attendant icebergs had swept out of sight, Dandy turned to Yankee Tom.

" Tom, can't you bring up some of your queer fishes to show the boy? "

" Certainly," said Tom, and he dived below.

For a long time, I was pretty well amused. I had never dreamed of such queer fishes. There were

the gurnards, ugly, bright-coloured things, with enormous heads and fingerlike fins, which serve for walking on the sea bottom, and as organs of touch; tlie climbing perch, that Yankee Tom went up a small stream to get for me.

The creature actually climbed up on the rock, and hitched itself along some stiff grasses that grew on the further side of it. I could scarcely believe my eyes. I didn't know that there were such fishes in the world.

Dandy told me that a man called Daldorf wrote that he once saw a climbing perch ascending a palm. It suspended itself by its gill covers, and bending its tail to the left, it fixed its anal fin in the cavities in the bark, and by swelling out its body, managed to climb five feet from the ground.

" Come now. Dandy," I said, " that's a fish story."

" Look in your natural history when you go home," he said.

The ribbon-fish was an odd-looking thing. It had a body like a silver belt. The unicorn, too, was a queer coot, with his rosy fins and his businesslike horn running up on his back.

I think I laughed most at the odd little sea-horses. Yankee Tom made one stand on his tail, and showe(me where the good little father carries his younj in a pouch, he looking after them rather than th(mother.

No, I didn't laugh most at him, either — I am forgetting. I laughed most at the globefishes that Yankee Tom floated up for my inspection. They looked like the globes from our schoolroom table.

" Mostly wind," said Tom, when I clapped my hand to my mouth, " spit it out, boys."

Immediately there was a hissing sound, and the fishes became quite small.

*' Swallow air again," said Tom, and didn't they grow big and begin to float back downward ?

" In your world this used to make them safe from enemies," said Tom. " See how their bristling spines stand out."

I played with the globefishes a good while, then I had some fun with a spoon-beaked sturgeon, who went round holding out his nose as if he wanted you to put something in it.

However, he was eclipsed by the next comer — a hammer-headed shark from the Indian seas.

" What is he doing here? " I asked Yankee Tom.

" Formed a friendship for a baby American shark who was kept in the same tank with him. When they died, they both wanted to be brought here."

" I think we'd better be going," said Dandy. " We'll come back another day."

" Oh, just wait a minute," I said. " I want to see some salmon, and haddock, and herring, and other common fish such as I've been used to all

my life — and some barracuda, too, from California."

" All right," said Tom, and he went below for about the fortieth time.

I had a good talk with some old acquaintances, then after solemnly promising Yankee Tom to call on him again, Dandy took me round by the eel lagoon, and had an old electrician give me a shock.

It was a good one, I can tell you, and Dandy and Rag had a fine time laughing, till I made them step into the water. Dandy pretended he didn't care, but Rag made a fearful face.

"That's nothing," said Dandy, airily. "These eels are overrated. Some people used to say that electric eels were formerly caught by driving, horses into the water to receive shocks from them, but that's all nonsense. Let's get home now, so you can rest before the entertainment this evening."

CHAPTER XIII.

THE FOX ESCORT

Night was coming on. I had just made such a good meal of oranges, figs, dates, plums, a kind of bread they made on the Island, sweet cakes, and cocoanut milk. And other things, for I must not forget to say that an air-ship had been sent to San Francisco for some food for me.

To think of a special ship going all those miles made me feel queer and shy, as if I didn't know what to say, and upon my word when I saw what those animals had brought to this lovely island, where it was a forbidden thing, I didn't know where to look.

The food cargo was all pie and meat — meat of all things. " I'll eat the pie, Rag," I said, " but I'll be jiggered if I touch anything that has grown on an animal. Here, you take it."

He sniffed at it. " I can't, master, I've turned against it. It smells fleshy and nasty."

"What will I do with it?" and I held up the slices of under-done beef and well-cooked mutton.

" Throw it into the sea." 157

"And insult the fishes?"

" I'll dig a hole for you, master, and we'll bury it."

We buried it deeply at dead of night, or rather of dusk, for I gathered that it was about eight o'clock. I hadn't a watch with me, and there wasn't one on the Island, but the animals all seemed to know the time, and not only the time, but the days of the month and the year. Well, as I was saying, Rag and I had had our supper. He wOuld eat fruit as quick as I would now.

We finished our meal, and then there weren't any dishes to wash, for we had been sitting about on the grass and eating the fruit á la nature. So we just went on sitting by our lodge door, and looking of? at the last faint colouring of the sky before the blue blackness came on.

Presently Dandy came trotting up, head in air as usual, and licking his lips. " Have you dined, Master Sam? " he said.

" Yes, Dandy, like a king."

"Any news. Dandy?" asked Rag, with such an air of being at home that I could have roared at him. However, I didn't make a sound, and Dandy went on.

" Yes, the goat's Widow is on Her way here."

" Oh, Kafoozelum! " exclaimed Rag, " won't that be a daisy of an interview. How's the goat taking it?"

"He doesn't know — it's to be a surprise."

" Water-works still going, then? " said Rag.

" Oh, yes, cascades, rivers, Niagaras of tears. His eyes are a swamp, his head a marsh. But I prophesy the old Widow will knock some sense into him. It's a bad thing, Raggie, to have too much sentiment."

" I believe you, my boy," said Rag.

I kept as quiet as a mouse. It was such fun to hear the two scamps talking. It was like hearing two men over their cigars, or some of my mother's friends over tea.

" Have a chew. Rag? " said Dandy, and he took a piece of gum out of his mouth.

" Thank you," said my animal, so Dandy went shares.

Then they chewed and talked, and I listened.

" What do you think of this place, Rag? " asked Dandy.

" A number one," said my beauty.

" It's fine after the hustle of life," said Dandy, thoughtfully. " My! what frights I used to have. I'd be all of a quiver. Now here, I'm always happy, and yet I'm not dull."

" It's queer that they let Master Sam come," said Rag.

" Oh, once in a Hog's age they have a human being. I think Joe's idea in bringing people, is that

they may be able to understand animals better, and do more for them when they go back to earth."

" There's room for improvement on earth," said Rag, grimly.

" You bet your paws there is. Did you ever think how queer it is that there has to be so much suffering? "

" I have since I came here," said Rag. " I didn't on earth."

" Some people think we animals are smarter than we really are," said Dandy.

" Yes, they do."

" Now on earth I didn't think as I do here. I just knew. For instance, when I sat near any one I happened to be interested in, and that person formed purposes in his or her mind, I knew it like a flash. If my first master was going to tell the coachman to give me a bath, I knew it as soon as he thought it, or if old Mrs. Tibbetts was going to give me a dose of medicine, I felt it as soon as the idea entered her mind. Once there was a man robbed and nearly beaten to death in a house next hers. I felt there was something going on there, though I didn't make a fuss as I would have done if it had been in our own house."

" I know that feeling," said Rag, " and people who like animals think that because we are smarter in that way than they are, we must be smarter in

I

E^ttt jFor iSgCOtt i6i

everything. But we're not. We're not up to human beings, Dandy."

" No, never will be, but we're a help to them."

" Lots of people would get more fun out of life if they would cultivate animals more," said Dandy, after a long silence, during which he chewed gum for all he was worth. " I don't know any better cure for selfishness than a young dog. I'd give every old maid a fine, healthy, mischievous, young pup to bring up, to keep with her every minute of the time, to drag round her stockings in the morning, and worry her laces, and chew her ribbons, and give her something to think about during the day. And I'd let him have colic at night, so he'd wake her up to get medicine for him — 'cause she hasn't any children to worry her, see? "

" Good for you, Dandy," said Rag, with a laugh, " and what would you give an old bachelor ? "

" Oh, I'd give him a monkey and a parrot, and when one wasn't pestering him the other would be — Hello, boy, what do you want ? "

I roused myself. A brown and white spaniel was coming softly up to us.

" It's Jim," said Dandy. " Well, messenger of the gods, you look as if you had something to say."

Jim was shy looking, but he had one of the best faces I ever saw on a dog.

" And he's good all through," said Dandy, turning suddenly, " no make-believe about him."

" Do you know what Fm thinking of, Dandy ? " I asked.

" No, Master Sam, I can't tell that, but your thoughts were painted on your face just then."

" Good Jim," I said, fondling his long, silky ears.

He pressed his dear old head against me. " The President says, Master Sam, that he hopes you will excuse him this evening. He tried to come, but his heart failed him. He is afraid he would be a wet blanket on your fun."

" He is still grieving about Miss Laura," I said.

" Yes, Master Sam," said Jim, very gently, and very respectfully. " If you will release me, I will run back to him. He has asked the Fifteen Foxes to be your escort."

" Now I call that mean," said Dandy; " Fm going home."

" Come here, old fellow," I said. " You shall be second escort."

" You forget," said Jim, mildly, " that the entertainment is to be on the grounds of the Fifteen Foxes. It would be impolite not to honour them. Here they are now," he added, hastily.

" Where ? " I asked. " I don't see them."

" I smell them," said Jim. " You, dear earth boy, know nothing of the power of smell; that is, comparatively nothing. You tell him, Dandy. I must really be going," and with a hasty lick of my hand, he ran away.

" The glories of smell," said Dandy, enthusiasti-illy, "oh, I could write a book as long as Joe's on it. You poor mortals with your almost blunted sense of smell, don't know the ecstasy of running with your nose to the ground. That sweet and odoriferous earth tells us news of friends and foes, of tragedies, comedies — in short, of everything in heaven or earth that we are interested in."

" Prove it," I cried, " go off there," and I pointed to the now gathering darkness. " Do something, show something, to tell me that your nose is more wonderful than my ears and eyes."

Dandy sprang up, ran about the grass a little, then down to the beach, and disappeared. After awhile, he came back, and lay down.

" Did you a few minutes ago, but since it became dark, hear anything down there?" and he pointed toward the sea.

" Not a sound."

" I did," he said, " and you saw nothing? "

I reflected a few seconds. I had been lying on my back on the grass, but on an incline, so that I could look out at sea. Just as it was getting too dark to see things clearly, I fancied I saw a thin cloud come between me and the ocean, but I was not sure, not sure enough to speak, so I said nothing.

" Well," said Dandy, " I was interested in talking, but still I heard some animal come softly down

to the shore, and I saw that it was one of the elephants, but I didn't pay any attention to him. Now I have just been down to investigate. It was the Central Park elephant. He came up behind your lodge, tramping very softly, so as not to disturb you. From his footprints, and the smell, I should say he had something he wished to communicate to you. Probably he decided that he was too overcome for a conversation, for he went down to the beach, ploughed up and down there, threw up the sand, and held a quiet kind of a commotion. That elephant when he is deeply moved, doesn't make a sound. When he is only partly moved he is apt to be noisy. Now I should judge from his tracks, that he has heard the best sort of news that could be told to him, and that would be that Mike McGarvie is dead."

"Poor fellow!"

" Poor fellow! — the elephant is happy beyond words. Mike's troubles are over. He is in the World of the Blessed. Now you'll see self-restraint and goodness on the part of Central Park. He will be crazy to get with Mike. In just about a month, that elephant will be ready for transportation."

" Dandy," I said, " you're pretty clever, if that is true."

" There come the foxes," he said. " Look at their illumination." . I could not see as far as he could, but presently

there came bowing and smiling up to my lodge the

Iifteen pretty little x\merican kit foxes. ' They were fifteen of the most gentlemanly foxes : ever saw. All had dark gray backs, the tips of the ails black, and the under parts white. This I had observed when they were running races, for now I couldn't tell, as it was getting dark. However, I might have examined them if I had thought of it, for upon my word they were all covered with fireflies.

" Hail, highly esteemed young man," said the biggest fox, bowing before me.

" He thinks to flatter you by calling you young man, when you are only a boy," said Dandy in my ear.

The fox went on. " Owing to the clearness and perspicuity of our vision, we are able to circum-locute easily at night. You, young sir, we feared might come to mischance by the way, therefore, having no occult powers as has her feline majesty, we felt constrained to implore the assistance of our tiny but accommodating brethren of the lamp," and having finished, the young fox looked at me with rather a cunning air, as if he didn't know just how Fd take the mixed firefly and fox escort.

Dandy was bowing low before me, his bright eyes shining, his whole manner showing that he was dying to make fun of the fox.

" Your serene majesty, the boy," he said, " may I acquaint you with the fact that although this fox was born in the Northwestern States, he was brought up in a yard within smell of Boston, and that he thinks the universe is shaped like a bean."

"Oh, get out. Dandy," I said. "I'm a New Englander, and you New Yorkers are so buried in your own conceit, that you can't see over your own State line."

The fox was delighted. He waved his fine bushy tail, and immediately the other fourteen foxes came forward and bowed profoundly, each with his fur in a twinkle of light and distinction.

" Now the procession will form," said Velox, grandly, and he, as the leader, placed himself by my side. " Advance, guard," he said, " look well to the circumjacent woods. Let no careless quadruped interrupt the train."

Velox, Rag, Dandy, and I tramped on in state, in the middle of our illuminated guard.

" By the way, Velox," said Dandy, " is there any news?"

" Yes," said the fox, " news of the most favourable kind for the Central Park elephant — news of the demise of Mike McGarvie."

" When did he hear ? " asked Dandy, eagerly.

" Within the space of two hours. The news was communicated to the first flock of wireless telegraphers, by an earthly flight of carrier-pigeons."

" So this bird telegraphing goes on all the time," I remarked, half to myself.

Dandy thought I spoke to him, Velox was sure

rp[had addressed him, so they had a kind of a squabble. " Brother," said Velox at last, " we are arriving. Let us have no unseemly disputes."

Dandy made a face at him; then both stopped talking, for we had arrived.

CHAPTER XIV.

BLACK ART

We had come along through the darkness until now. There was a dark pit of a valley before us, Dandy said. I could see nothing, but he told me that this valley was full of animals.

I could hear a low growling and rumbling, but all the noises were subdued.

" Around the valley are pretty wooded hills," said Dandy, " and the trees of those hills are now covered with birds who have come to see the show. Here, follow the foxes. Your seat will be away up in front."

"So you have the entertainment out-of-doors," I whispered, " I should think that your magic Cat would want a building."

Dandy laughed, then he said, " Wait and see."

The foxes were pressing up ahead, going round the mass of animals rather than through them.

" Make way there," Velox kept calling, " make way for the boy, the American boy. Remove yourselves aside from his path, absquatulate, skedaddle,

I say," and then he would give a snap of his jaws, and make a leap in the dark.

The fireflies held on like good fellows, shedding quite a bit of light immediately around us. I don't believe a single one lost his foothold on the fox fur, and it was fun to see the illuminated little kits bounding through the throng of their fellow beasts.

I tried to keep from snickering. It was just like being late for a play, and stumbling down to the orchestra seats, with the usher tripping before you, and getting in everybody's way.

" Where is Miss Pussy ? " I asked Dandy.

" Up in front, on the slope of the hill, on a bare spot — a clearing. You'll see her soon enough," and he laughed again. " She always sits there till she's ready to have the lights on. I think she likes to hear us crowding and pushing in the dark."

Suddenly there was a tremendous voice heard. It filled the valley, it must have gone far out to sea — " Has the boy come? "

" The boy is present," called Velox, in a would-be mighty voice, that ended in a squeak.

*' That's Pussy speaking," whispered Dandy, " a pretty good pair of lungs for a lady, hasn't she — and all the time she knows you're here."

The tremendous voice roared out again. " Bring the boy this way."

My escort conveyed me in the direction of the voice.

" Put him in his seat," was the next order, " and don't any of you get in with him."

I don't know how they found the seat, but they did, and I felt Velox and Dandy gently pushing me against something that felt like a throne.

" Now look out for an illumination," whispered Dandy, " she's apt to do it quick."

" Turn on the lights," said the awful voice again.

*' Animals, bow your heads, and look humble before the boy."

I had been warned, yet my eyes had become so used to the darkness that, when the lights were turned on, I blinked helplessly.

After a long time, I winked myself into seeing. Turned on — there wasn't anything to turn on, no gas, no electricity. There were magic lights suspended in the air above our heads in soft coloured globes. It was pretty, anyway, and I lifted my eyes to the Cat.

There she sat — same old Cat, same old, plain, black animal, reposing on a green hillside, and looking down at us. I squirmed round on my seat. I must have a look at the audience.

Good gracious! Think of the farms of New England, of the Southern States, of the Middle West, the Pacific Coast. They were all represented, well represented, with a generous sprinkling of wild animals. And the birds — there seemed to be mil-

lions of them. Not a big animal, but had his back covered. They were roosting, even on the antlers of the stags. The giraffe had a whole row swarming up and down his slippery neck, and when he swallowed, or turned his head, they would fall down, and fight, and scramble up again. They were on the trees, too. I could see them dimly in the distance. Every branch was black with them.

" Her Necromancy won't let all the animals and birds come," said Dandy. '* Only a certain number to each show."

I turned round. He was sitting quietly at my feet. And I — where was I ? Upon my word, perched up on a big thing like a dentist's chair, and feeling just about as foolish as if I were going to have a tooth out.

There were folds upon folds of red cloth hanging about me. I pushed them aside, and said, '* Rag and Dandy, come up here, and stop grinning at me. You know I feel like an idiot."

*' Excuse me, master," said Dandy, and he slunk under my chair.

" Excuse me, too," said Rag, and he went under, too, but stuck his head out, so that the red stuff fell round his neck like a cloak.

" I'd go round ten corners to avoid Miss Pussy," he said. " I'll just stay where I am and keep out of her notice."

The Cat lay crouched beyond us, apparently engaged in trying to lick a speck off her paw, then presently she stopped, and the big voice went on.

" Animals, salute the boy."

They did salute, and for one minute the boy wished he were dead. And all the time I was suspicious of the Cat that she was making fun of me.

I think I was prejudiced by the animals. The Cat wasn't as black as they made her out to be.

Well, when the braying, and the rumbling, and the roaring, and the squeaking, were all over — and while it lasted, it was like fifty Fourths of July rolled into one — the Cat began her actions.

" So you don't have any theatre here," I whispered to Velox, who was cringing beside me, trying to make himself small, so the Cat would not find fault with him. " Somehow or other, I expected one."

He straightened himself up. " On earth," he began, grandly, " when entertainments are in progress, one anticipates a building, but here the building is a sequence of — "

" When all the foxes stop their prosing," began the awful voice again, " the entertainment will begin."

The Cat had got the speck off her paw, and was looking right at us. The fox crouched till he was almost as small as she was. He had been the only one in the crowd speaking.

" Theatre!" called the Cat in her own rather squeaky voice, " appear! "

The awful voice had stopped, but there was power even in her squeak.

Immediately a fine building surrounded us. I stared, you may be sure. There was the roof, there were the walls, where a minute before there had only been blue sky and trees. There was also a stage covered with red cloth, where the Cat sat by one of the wings on a big, yellow stool.

I turned round again. What a huge building, huger than the biggest cathedral I had ever seen! I could scarcely see the end of it. And there were some seats now, on which many of the smaller animals stood. The birds were on the network of rafters above us. I nodded and waved my hand to many of the animals that I recognised, and I just wish that some of the people who hate animals could have seen how their faces lighted up. Lots that I didn't speak to would grin, and bow, and pretend I was noticing them.

"Look at the stage, Master Sam," whispered Dandy, " look for your life."

I did look. There were about fifty black cats whirling through the air in circles of flame. Then the number increased till the stage was alive with them, and then they disappeared.

For a minute there was silence, then the applause

broke out. Fancy about a thousand barn-yards, and another thousand forests, and half a dozen menageries roaring, " That's good — go on."

The noise 'most finished me, and seeing it, a dear little crested grebe flew to me with a tuft of soft, downy feathers in her beak.

" Stuff that in your ears," she said, " and the noise will be deadened."

I was just thanking her, when the stage suddenly became black and still, and the awful voice thundered out: " Let the boy lead the applause."

That fixed them. Not a mouse squeaked now, unless I squeaked first. By the way, I forgot to say that the rat was on one of my shoulders, and Bella on the other. She had been quick to spy me out, and to come to me, but she was keeping pretty quiet, through fear of the Cat.

After awhile, the stage lighted up again, and we had a candy tree. The animals made about as much fuss over this as boys and girls do over a Christmas tree.

It was like this — a green tree sprang up in the middle of the stage, loaded with lemon drops, chocolates, caramels, Turkish delight, big lumps of sugar, and lots of other sweet things.

A beautiful princess came out from behind the scenes, and picking the candy and lumps of sugar, threw them to us.

There was no scrambling, no pulling, but all the animals got some, even the birds had their share.

" What did you get, boys ? " I asked, looking down at Dandy and Rag.

" Cocoanut cakes," they said.

" Well, look here," I replied, " I've got a fist full of crystallised violets, and they are real violets. My teeth go right into them, and I taste them. This isn't magic."

Dandy shook his head, but I noticed that he gobbled up all of his candy.

"If I feel sick afterward," he said, "it's real candy, if I don't, it isn't; for I've eaten enough to upset ten dogs. Wonder what we're going to have next."

" Would the boy like to see his home ? " squeaked „Pussy.

mLl nodded, and bless my heart if Market Street l^^sn't before me. I could see the people going up Pand down the wide pavements, the crowds coming from the ferries, the electric cars going straight, and the cable-cars whirling round on the turntables, the little one-horse Sutter Street car wagging along by itself. I could see the blue sky overhead, the tall buildings on either side, I could smell the flowers on the sidewalk by the Chronicle Building. I almost called out to a child running across the street, " Look out for that car." But the policeman at the fountain

corner gave him a clip with his hand and helped him along, then he took hold of two old women and helped them across.

" I'm homesick," I muttered to Rag, " I want to go home."

In an instant the picture flashed away, and we had some soldiers marching across the stage. I don't mean to say that these things were like moving pictures. Everything looked real and alive.

Well, that Cat went on and on, and thinking it over, I'm puzzled to know what she didn't show us. There's too much to tell. She seemed to get in everything in air, and earth, and sea. There were magic balloons flying through the air, full of fairies that laughed, and sang, and flung down roses at us. There were flying fishes, too, and dancing fishes, that flopped all over the stage on their tails, and held fans in their fins, and languished at us, and made eyes and especially mouths, till we nearly died laughing.

Then there were queer animals, such as I had never seen before, with extra supplies of legs, and tails, and even heads. One eight-headed, eight-legged monkey nearly finished us. He danced a set of lancers with himself, he did tricks, and cut up didos till the building was in one solid roar of laughter.

Finally, when we were all sore from laughing, the whole thing was over just Hke a flash. The Hghts nearly all went out, just enough were left for us to see to get home by, and we were left staring at each .other.

I gave a blank look round. The building was gone, there was a " whish! whish! " in the air of tired bird wings setting out for home, and a tramp and rumble from animals doing the same thing.

Just one little glimmer of light shone over the hillside. There was nothing there but the black Cat, looking cross and tired, and a faded white mouse crawling round where the back of the stage had been.

" Bet your life she's been working that mouse to death to-night," said Dandy. " She does the show part, and the mouse the real."

"Why doesn't the mouse run away?" I asked.

" Hasn't spirit enough. She's nothing but a slave."

" Come, say good night to our hostess," I remarked, staring up at Pussy, whom I could just see.

" Thank you," said Dandy, " I haven't any manners just now. Good night," and he ran away.

"Come, Rag," I said.

He slunk after me, looking like a fool, while Bella called to the rat in a voice so husky from laughing that she sounded as if her throat were full of bread crumbs, " Come, Davy, it's time for bed."

She flew off, and he ran after her, while I made my way to Miss Pussy.

"That was a fine show/' I said; "I'm much obUged."

She got up and stretched herself. " I didn't care a fig about those animals. I only wanted to please you."

I tried to think what to say to her. " Don't you think it would be better for you to try to like those animals more? You would probably be happier."

" No," she said, " I want my princess and my Egyptian home."

" How much longer do you have to stay here? "

" I don't know," she said, and she dropped her head down on the damp grass, and looked miserable.

" Will you let your mouse come and make me a little visit?" I said.

" Oh, yes, if she likes. Minerva, come here."

The little dragged-out mouse came running to her.

" Go with this young gentleman," said the Cat. " He kindly wishes to give you a holiday. Don't gabble and tell secrets."

" Very well, mistress," said the mouse, submissively. Then she turned her pink eyes on me. I don't suppose a mouse was ever so glad before to get a little outing.

" Come up, mousie, you look tired," I said, and I slipped her into my shirt pocket, where she cuddled down and went to sleep like a shot.

" Well, I must be going," I said, looking off to

the spot where my fifteen illuminated foxes were patiently waiting for me. " Good night, Pussy."

" Good night," she said, " but I'll see you again, as I did last night."

" When did you see me last night ? " I asked.

" I crawled up on your roof, and made a hole to look down at you. When you are asleep, you look omething like my princess."

I felt bad. "Are you all like this?" I asked. "All longing for us human beings?"

" For some of you," she said, " the kind ones. Yes, we are like that. Once let an animal associate with a human being, and it is spoiled for animal society alone. It wants to see something of its old master or mistress."

" And human beings are often so hateful to animals," I said. " It's enough to make one mad. Well, I'm off, Pussy."

" Pleasant dreams, boy," she said, and I think I heard her add under her breath, " dear boy."

Rag and I plodded along beside the foxes, all of us yawning and sleepy.

We had got nearly home when I felt a breath on my forehead stronger than the breath of the wind. I knew it was the bird that you feel, but do not hear, and, looking up, I saw a small screech-owl hovering over my head.

" Mr. Boy," it said, " Her Necromancy told me

to tell you that the Widow will arrive to-morrow morning at eleven."

"All right," I said; '^ thank you."

He just flicked my forehead with his velvety wings, and flew away.

When I got into my lodge, the foxes politely thanked the fireflies, who flew home, while the young kits turned tail in an opposite direction.

You may be sure I thanked the foxes before they disappeared, and then I made for my bed. On the way I stumbled over a chimpanzee, a lamb, ten dogs, but the cats, among whom was the Angora, were too clever to be caught napping, and crept out of my way.

Dandy was under the bed, and snoring enough to lift it into the air.

" Stop that, old fellow," I said, pushing him, " or you'll go out of this."

" Oh, excuse me," he said, rousing himself; then he went on worse than before, but I hadn't the heart to turn him out.

There were some birds up aloft, for I could hear them rustling, and some old scientist's pet snakes had playfully festooned themselves round my pillow. I gave them a cuff to make them scuttle away, then tumbled on to my poppy leaves.

Rag showed his teeth at the snakes, and jumped

up beside me. " There's a lot more animals outside," he said, " I smell them."

"All right," I said, drowsily, "let them stay. The door and windows are open, so we shall have plenty of air."

Then we slept.

\

CHAPTER XV.

THE TIGER IN THE MARSH

When we got up in the morning, I just doubled up laughing.

The sight reminded me of stories of those old kings and queens who used to dress and undress, and have their meals, with a crowd round them.

I decided to wait and have my plunge in the breakers when there weren't so many spectators, so called for breakfast.

I forgot to say, that the mouse had slept in one of my fists. I never saw such a chummy, affectionate little mite. It wanted to be petted all the time.

" Rag," I said, " isn't there some cheese left from that Joe had brought for me in the air-ship from San Francisco? "

Rag said there was, and I wish you could have seen the mouse eat the crumbs he unearthed.

" I like you," she said, in her little, thin voice, " I would like to live with you."

" Perhaps we will meet again some day, mousie."

" Yes," she said, and didn't her little, pink eyes 182

gfie gfgrt in t^t JWargfi 183

run out over the ocean just as the big-ger animals* eyes went. " In the better Paradise," she said, " I will be your little mouse."

" You don't like the Cat," I observed.

" Oh, yes," she said, cautiously, " but when she has an industrious fit, I have to work very hard."

"What kind of work do you do, mousie?"

i" I was told not to gabble," she said, timidly. " All right, just clean your whiskers, and that will Jceep you out of trouble— Hello, Dandy, what have we got for breakfast?" " Cocoanut milk, fruit, and bread." " Good — let us have it."

Rag called a monkey. The monkey tribe was the working tribe, on account of their being so handy with their paws, and having so many of them about, I began to feel quite lordly, like a person with an army of servants.

The first monkey called other monkeys, and soon my breakfast was spread on the grass outside, where I ate and drank the glorious view at the same time with my food.

" The most of the animals have gone," said Dandy.

" The most," I replied, looking round upon the few hundreds left. " How many were there? " " How many. Dandy ? " said Rag, turning to him. " About ten thousand, I should say," replied

Dandy, " not counting birds, slept within sight of your roof last night."

I would have been flattered, but I was too surprised to have room for anything else. " Why, I should think the place would be laid low after an army like that," I said, " there isn't even a shrub broken."

" The animals on this Island have to learn to be tidy," said Dandy, " that is part of our training. If one breaks a branch, or upturns a stone, it must be carried away."

" Then that is why the whole place is so parklike," I said. '* Do you put your rubbish in the sea? "

" Oh, no, that would spoil the fish gardens. There is a deep pit in the middle of the Island, where we cast what we do not bury. Then a large band of dogs goes round the Island to remove unsightly objects. It keeps them occupied, and the Island neat."

" Do all the animals work ? "

" Every one. Not a bird nor a beast, but what has something to do."

" Well, now, what could an eagle do ? "

" An eagle can break off dead twigs from the tops of high trees," replied Dandy, " and carry them to the pit. The eagles are our park commissioners."

" Well, what can rabbits do ? "

" They can keep clean the little runs through the

underbrush. You must remember that all these animals have to spend much of their time in looking for food, and in keeping their homes in order."

" It seems queer for you to eat, and drink, and build homes in Paradise."

" It is very homelike. It is just what we have been used to on earth, and many of us are very fresh from it. You must remember that we are being drafted away all the time to the next world — the World of the Blessed, which is a less material place than this."

" But you are happy on this Island ? "

" Happy as the day is long, so happy that I often wonder how I could be happier; but come, if you have finished your breakfast, let us walk along toward the Hill of Arrival. I wouldn't miss the Widow for a barrel of sweet cakes."

The animals fell in behind us, and we went mostly like Noah's procession — two by two.

Well, on the way, a melancholy thing for me happened, and I feel half ashamed to tell it, but this is a faithful chronicle, so here it is.

In going to the Hill, we had to pass a marsh. It was a lovely marsh — a regular Paradise marsh, not stagnant and slimy, but soft, and velvety, and smooth-looking, with bright green water-plants, and shrubs with glossy leaves.

As we were going by, I admired it, and Dandy smiled, and then sighed and said, "Poor tiger!"

" Is there an animal there? " I asked.

" Yes, a tiger — we call him the sensitive one. Really, he's absurd. You have only to point your finger at him, and he slinks."

"What's the matter with him?"

" He was a very fierce tiger in life, and was badly used — hot irons and that sort of thing, to make him tame. It took all the spirit out of him, and then he has an unfortunate name."

"What is it?"

" Tammany — Tam, for short. Now I don't call that an ugly name, do you? "

" W^hy, no, it's a pretty sounding name."

"Just what I say, but there's some ugly story attached to it on earth, and the bird telegraphers sang to our birds that it was a disgrace to be called by such a name. That finished the tiger. Some of the mischievous monkeys teased him, and he ran away from every one. No one teases him any more, now that we know how seriously he takes the business of his name, but he has got so thin-skinned, that you have only to think a mischievous thought, or imagine a wink, and he rushes into the depths of this swamp. We've all tried to coax him out, but he won't come, and I'm afraid he's half starved, for none of the things he likes grow in that swamp. Why —" and Dandy stopped as if struck by a sudden thought. " I daresay you might wheedle him out."

I was greatly interested. Of course I had not known Dandy in life, but in reading about him, I had been impressed by the fact that he was a selfish dog. Now he was acting generously.

" Done," I said, " I'll help you if I can."

" Of course he's heard that you're here," went on Dandy; " the birds have sung it to him, and of course he's anxious to see you. Now I'll tell you what I'll do. You stand back a little, and I'll go to the edge of the swamp and call him. — Back, brothers."

The animals all fell behind with me, and Dandy trotted ahead.

" Hello, old man," he called out over the sluggish water, "how are you this morning?"

There was no response.

" We've got a stranger here," continued Dandy, " a boy from earth, and he wants to see you. Come on, don't be impolite."

Suddenly Dandy scratched the ground with his paw in a vexed way, and came to me. " There now, I've done it, asking him not to be impolite. I shouldn't have said that. You'd really think he was made up wrong side out, he's so sensitive. It hurts him to be breathed on."

" Suppose I go call him ? " I said.

"He hasn't a name," replied Dandy. "We daren't call him Tam.many, for that sends him into the depths of the swamp for days."

" Can you see him now ? "

** No, but I can just tell that the bulrushes away over in that corner are trembling. That's where he is."

" Give him a new name," I said.

" Good scheme — you choose one."

I think I mentioned a hundred names in the next five minutes. There were so many animals on the Island, that all the names were used up.

" ni tell you what," I said, " we'll give him a double treble Christian name like the old Pilgrim ones, such as Leave-Your-Sins Barebones. Suppose we call the tiger I'11-Be-Jiggered-If-I-Do-It-Again, and Jigger for short."

"Jiggered, if he does what?"

" Goes into the swamp."

" Just the thing," said Dandy, " and so original. Let me tell him. You're my last card, and I won't play you till the others are out."

He stepped forward again, " Hello, boy, listen to your new name that the earth-boy has given you — Jigger. Isn't that a fine one ? No other like it. Now, Jigger, boy, come out, and show yourself worthy your new name."

The bulrushes quivered a little more, but still Jigger never budged.

" I give up," said Dandy, in disgust, " you try."

" Rag," I said, " old fellow, go and bring him [out. He's shy, and you're the only one that doesn^t [know how shy he is, so maybe he'll come with you."

My plucky dog sprang forward, and leaping, wading, half swimming, and sometimes wholly swimming, reached the tuft of bulrushes.

Soon we all saw him turn toward us, accompanied by a large, striped animal with hanging head.

Dandy looked round on the other animals. " Now, look here, fellows," he said, " you pigs, dogs, goats, calves, sheep, you lion, and you young panther, keep your mouths shut, unless you can say something pleasant. If any one dares to lisp ' Tammany,' he'll get a thrashing."

" Would he scuttle just for his name ? " I asked.

" Like lightning. He thinks it's the most awful word in the language. Look, here he comes. That Rag is a beaut."

" Yes, isn't he; you and he must be friends when I am gone."

" So you've made up your mind to leave him," said Dandy, with a twinkle in his eye.

" Don't I know I've got to," I said, fiercely. " Don't bother me."

I wish you could have seen that picture. Rag's dear, old, honest, white face, and the tiger's cowed, sneaky one. Poor wretch, he looked thin.

" Well, Jigger, old fellow," said Dandy, heartily, when the tiger dragged his last leg ashore, and

stood wet and dripping and hang-doggy, " I'm glad to see you! Come up here. Come, brothers, stop staring, and help clean him."

The tiger looked overwhelmed. He had not go enough to clean himself, but every animal that could get a lick at him took off some of the mud, and at last he stood clean and decent before us.

A chimpanzee ran like the wind, and got a loaf of the bread they made on the Island. The tiger ate it ravenously, then, twice the beast he was before, ran his tongue over his chops, and looked about him in a way that in an earthly tiger would have suggested, " What next? "

" Let's move on," said Dandy, who didn't want too much attention paid to the tiger, lest he should become embarrassed.

We walked on slowly, for the tiger seemed tired, and as I watched him dragging his limbs over the grass, a low-down cur of a thought came sneaking into my mind.

Suppose any one said Tammany — would he really run? Dandy said he would. I thought how much I would like to see those velvety limbs spinning ever the ground. He was dragging them along so loosely now.

" Tam," I said, in a dead-and-alive sort of way.

" What did you remark ? " asked Dandy, sharply..

" I was going to say that tam-o'-shanters are very becoming caps to girls."

THEN I SAW HIM RUN

"Oh!" said Dandy.

I We walked along, and the thought crept back. Tamma," I said, with a twist of my lips. Dandy caught on to me. *' What are you ying ? " he asked, half angrily. The little imp inside of me slipped down to my uoots. This dog was better than I was.

" I merely remarked that Tammas was Scotch for Thomas," I said, shamefacedly; then I patted the tiger's head. " Good boy, Jigger."

He looked up, gratefully. He was pleased that I had given him a new name.

I began to throw bouquets to myself. What a lovely kind of a boy I was! What a guardian angel to animals! How they loved me — how I loved them!

Those bouquets were my finish. An evil spirit tossed them to me, and words beginning with T just waltzed into my mind.

I was most crazy, and at last, to keep my mouth occupied, I began whistling, " Tramp, tramp, tramp, the boys are marching."

It didn't do a bit of good. Something awful came over me. If I died for it, I must see the tiger run. I stopped short, I dug my heels in the grass, and just blazed out — " Tammany! "

The tiger stopped, too, gave me one dreadful look, and then — then I saw him run.

It was lovely while it lasted, but it didn't last long. I never before saw a big, wild beast skedaddle from fright. But when it was over, my quarter of an hour came.

Splash he went into the marsh. We could see him panting, rushing, swimming, and leaping to his haunt, and then — then, I felt mean.

And no one said a word to me, not a beast nor a bird. They just left me to myself.

And what did I do — big boy in baseball suit, big ninny that ought to have known better — I sat down on a green hillock, and hid my face in my hands.

I could have howled, and I was dead homesick. I always am, when I'm in trouble, and I wanted my mother as much as a baby would have done.

The animals gathered round me. Not one bore a grudge, not even Dandy, who was the smartest there, and who had tried to steer me clear of the mischief. They licked my hands, there was a whole procession of noses touching against my arms and back, and animals pushing each other to get near me.

" Never mind," said Dandy, " he's been out once, he'll come again. We'll coax him out, when you're gone."

" That's the worst of it," I blubbered. " I've done a. mean thing, and you've all been so square with me. you*ll remember it against me. I can't wipe it out."

artie gtget in titt jwatgift 193

" Never mind," said Dandy again, " you're only an earth-boy. By and by you'll be a heavenly boy, and then you won't want to do mean things. I used to love to be bad when I was on earth. I would just have revelled in a trick like that. Come on now, or you'll be late for the Widow."

I got up; there was no use crying over spilt milk, but I vowed it was the last mean trick I would play any one on the Island. I would keep my record clean after this.

" Animals," I said, " I'm ashamed of myself. I'm meaner than the meanest thing that lives. Do your best to get that tiger out after I'm gone, and tell him I'll never forgive myself for having hurt his feelings, and I hope I'll have a chance to tell him so some day when I have become more of a gentleman."

" Good boy," said Dandy, "now forward march, animals."

Soon we came up to the goat, running and bleating, and not having a single idea of what was in store for him.

I went up to him, but his eyes were so bleary that he could not see me, and he was making such a racket with his mourning, that he could not hear, so I went on.

" Run," said Dandy, " there's an air-ship."

CHAPTER XVI.

THE WIDOW COMES

We could see an air-ship away in the distance — the Hill of Arrival was also in the distance, but we ran about half as fast as the poor tiger had run, and managed to get there just as the monkeys were throwing out the anchor.

It was the air-ship that we were expecting, and Soko stuck his head out. He had been chosen to go to Maine on this special trip, and he only had one passenger — the Widow.

That was enough for him. He looked ten years older than when he had started — such a haggard face. The Widow McDoodle was no handful, I assure you.

Well, she looked out over Soko's shoulder. Then she gave him a slap that made him jump.

" Out of the way, ye dirty beast, and where in the land of light and liberty have ye brought me ? "

" Step forward," said Dandy, giving me a push,

" the President isn't here."

I did step forward, and having no cap to take 194

off, for the lovely climate made one unnecessary, I made the lady my best bow, and tried not to grin.

If it hadn't been for my late painful experience with the tiger, which had sobered me, I would have grinned, for the Widow was the funniest, dirtiest old woman I ever saw. Ugly-tempered, too, and yet with a queer streak in her that made you laugh. Fortunately she wasn't too old to laugh at.

" And is it a boy? " she said. " And what is he doin' among all these dirty beasts ? "

I looked round me. There wasn't an animal in sight that wasn't as clean as a whistle. The calves were as white as milk, and as red as clover. The dogs were spick and span from bathing and licking each other. The horses looked as if each had just had a groom at him, the sheep as if they had just taken their wool out of very clean curl-papers, but the lady — the old woman!

Well, she was a sight! She still had on the red wrapper that had been the cause of the goat's ruin. It might have been clean then. It was sloppy, and spotty, and wrinkled, and torn now. Her old carpet slippers were just falling off her feet, and her hair hung in tousled rings about her face.

" Mrs. McDoodle," I said, with another bow, " my mother tells me not to argue with ladies. I will just say briefly that these are very decent animals, and that you have been brought here by my request."

" By your request — I like your impidence, and what was I monkeyed from my quiet home for, to come to this heathenish place ? Where is it, anyway — such goin's on — flyin' over the tops of houses and trees, and me afraid of fallin' out."

" You will be taken back safely," I said, when she held up for a minute. " You are here for a purpose. You remember a goat you once had, called — "

" Remember him ? — and how could I forget him, pushin' me down the well. Oh, it's worlds I'd give for a sight of him."

There was something queer in her voice, but I thought it best to lose no time talking to her. If she was mad with the goat it would do him good.

" Oh, the sweet old lady," bleated a sheep near me, " she is going to forgive her dear pet, and make him happy."

We all moved down the hill and across the sands, the Widow and I leading. Her face was delicious. She would look behind at the animals, then ahead at the lovely scenery, then she'd stare at me, till I had hard work to keep from bursting out laughing in her face.

" There he is at last, the poor goat," I said, solemnly, " just look at him."

He was so used to the comings and goings of animals that he paid no attention to us. There

was nearly always a group staring sympathetically at him, and always a bird or two perched on the palms looking at him.

But there was a transformation scene when the old woman caught sight of him.

" Is that me goat ? " she asked, and her wrinkled old face went knobby and queer.

" Yes," I said, " there he is, and he's dying of grief to think he pushed you down the well."

"Could ye give me a club?" she said, eagerly,

a good, stout club ? "

The animals began to catch on.

" I don't like the way her mouth is working," said Dandy, behind me.

" Let her alone," I said; " ask a monkey to run up among the trees and get a good switch."

An orang-outang brought back a beautiful willow switch, limber and lively.

" Now let me at him," said the Widow, snatching it, " now just let me learn a lesson to a low-down, sneaky, snivellin', cowardly — "

She went on till the words flew so fast that we couldn't make them out.

She got there, though. She ran over the sands like a young girl. She crept up to the weeping goat, she fetched him one crack, she fetched him another, till ' he had to dry up and turn round.

" That feels like my dear old mistress," he said,

touchingly, " my dear old mistress. Surely she has ijot come here."

" Surely she has," said the Widow, and she danced, and flew, and circled round him, lighting again and again with her switch, but never on the same spot.

" Oh, mistress," howled the goat at last, " you hurt horribly. Do stop, till I tell you how sorry I am about that well affair."

" I'll well you," she cried, giving him another rap, " I'll well you, and sink you, and drown you — you dirty, murderin', unclean, heathen beast!"

" She's not a woman, she's a machine," observed Dandy. " What was her profession in life ? She gives beautiful clips."

" She is a washerwoman," said Soko, who was grinning behind us, " she had some very clean clothes hanging in a very dirty back yard. Her fists are like hammers. She pounded me all the way over New England and the Middle West. Don't you think it's time she let up. Master Sam ? "

" No, let her run a little longer," I said. " See, the goat is getting disgusted. Look at his old beard wagging. In ten shakes of a lamb's tail, he'll butt her again."

" Law me! " exclaimed Dandy, " you'll kill him. If he butts her once more, remorse will finish him."

" You let me alone about that goat," I said. " In

gjie gggttroto eomefii 199

some ways I'm not half as smart as you animals, but I have a feeling that I can run this goat affair successfully."

" But isn't it time to call her off ? " said Dandy, anxiously. " Look at the hair flying."

" I guess the goat's back must be pretty sore," said Soko, but so moderately, that I saw he wasn't as much incHned to interfere as Dandy was.

The old woman had given him an awful time m his voyage through the air, and he had an idea fl was planning some sort of discipline for her.

* Mrs. McDoodle," I said, running up to her, ^** will you not stop now, and forgive your goat ? He las been punished enough."

" Forgive him!" she yelled, and hit out like a prize-fighter.

I got a cut with the end of the switch, and retired to rub my cheek-bone.

The goat had crouched down in a heap. " Oh, you silly thing," I roared, "you've no spirit, run away! "

He raised his head, looked round as if he had caught sight of a new idea dangling in the air before him. The Widow closed his eyes with a crack.

" Unkind lady! " cried the goat, suddenly, " I give you up." Then he started to run.

The Widow got in his way. He planted his head before her, butted her aside very gently, and started again.

She took after him, beating and screaming, and every time she caught up, he would push her over on the sand. He was very polite, very gentlemanly, but very positive. Even a good goat will be mean when he makes up his mind to be so.

" Give him a cheer, animals," I said, " this is a turning-point in his career."

The roars, and shrieks, and calls made the Widow wild. She could not catch the goat any more. He was frisking along the beach, tossing up his head, kicking out his hoofs, and acting like a life sentence prisoner out on a holiday.

Now these actions made the Widow so mad at losing him, that she charged us with her switch.

Didn't we scatter! She caught a few slow-going animals, and the way they drew in their tails and ran was a circumstance. " Reminds me of earth again, and my old master," said a horse, galloping by me.

" Never saw a switch before in Paradise," grumbled a dog, limping after the horse. " She caught my fore paw sure enough. Nasty thing, I wish you would send her home."

Dandy, Soko, Rag, and I stopped in a little grove, and looked back at her.

The Widow McDoodle had the beach and the beautiful sea all to herself. She thrashed round for some time, then she sat down on the sand.

" Better get her into the air-ship, Soko," I said, " she's served her time."

" Oh,' me, the animals! " laughed Rag, " just look at them."

As far as we could see, they were peeping. Every rock, and tree, and shrub had its concealed noses, and tails, and legs, and bodies, but observing eyes; and the birds on the trees were snickering, and telling each other to keep quiet. The Widow was as good as a circus to them.

t" We can't do anything with these earthly people when they don't want to mind us," said Soko. " I'll go see Joe, and ask him if we can't get the Cat to hypnotise her into the air-ship, for I give you my word, I don't feel like being beaten all the way back to earth again." " Come on, boys," I said to the dogs, " I want to Interview ^;he goat. Bet you anything, his views of life have changed."

CHAPTER XVII.

A CHANGED GOAT

I WAS right. He was a changed goat. We found him in a little green spot where many of the smaller birds went to drink and bathe.

There was a tiny stream running down a hill, leaping from one pool to another, till it formed a big, beauty one, and by it were beds of ferns and soft, green mossy places.

The goat was lolling like a lord on one of these beds of moss. A crow had just brought him a sweet cake in his beak, and the goat was alternately eating it, and giggling and talking to the little birds who perched on the ground, and in the shrubs around him.

He was perfectly silly, but there was never a tear in his eye.

" Oh, I'm so happy," he was gurgling in his throat as we came up.

" Isn't your back sore? " piped a robin. " Mine would be after all that larruping."
" My back is sore, birdie," giggled the goat, " but

"A CROW HAD JUST BROUGHT HIM A SWEET CAKE "

my heart is light. Oh, what a sweet thing is peace of mind, I gaze into this lovely water mirror before me. I see a shattered ideal."

" Why, what beautiful talk," said a lark, sentimentally. *' I had no idea you could be so poetical, Mr. Goat."

" What is life? " the goat went on with a smile that met around the back of his neck. "

Life, sweet birdie, is a comedy."

" Well, I should think so," called Dandy.

The goat partly raised himself from his reclining position. "Ah, my friends, are you there?"

" Yes, and have been for several months," replied Dandy, " but you haven't thought it worth while to cultivate us."

"Ah," called the goat, **the scales have fallen from my eyes. I was blinded, deluded, and all for a faithless woman. I loved that Widow on earth. I idealised her in Paradise. When I saw that vulgar red whirlwind, I thought, ' Can this be my glorified mistress ?' My soul revolted, yet I submitted to her chastisement. Now, thank fortune, I am released. Now I shall be happy. Come, let us tread a measure," and getting up, he began to skip gaily about the moss.

" Jerry, you're an idiot," remarked Dandy.

" Then, if this be folly," cried the goat, treading his measure alone, since no one would tread it with

him, " who would be wise ? Oh, how sweet are the pleasures of tranquillity. I long for no one. Now I am perfectly happy. I even think I could sing," and as he ran up and down by the pool, he began in a tea-kettle voice,

" Once I was grieving, Now I am gay. Once I was sorry, All the long day."

" Now I am happy, By this sweet pool. Now I'll rejoice me — '*

" Now, I'm a fool," added Dandy, loudly. " I'll wait and talk to you when you have more sense," and he ran away.

I was very curious about the goat. " Sit down and tell me exactly how you feel," I said, going up to him.

He squatted on the turf. " Earth-boy, I feel as if I'd had a load of turnips on my brain, and some one had suddenly rolled them off."

" But what made you feel that way ? — come now, don't be idiotic."

He turned his bleary, bloodshot eyes on me, and now his expression was serious.

" I tell you, boy, I bowed down and worshipped that Widow, but I made sure she'd forgive me. I

I

thought she'd be as tender as a spongy carrot after my death."

"Oh, you thought that would touch her?"

" Yes, I thought that Death, the great softener, would touch even her flinty heart, and that she would say, ' Well, I was too hard on him. I ought to have forgiven him.' "

" But it was a serious offence to push an old woman down a well."

" It was awful, abominable, but look at the worse things human beings do to each other, and to animals on earth. She ought to have forgiven me, specially when I died of a broken heart and poor feed."

" Well, do you feel as if you could ever love her again? "

The goat shook his beard thoughtfully. " I feel exactly as if I had lost my old woman. I have been thinking of her all these months as a sweet old thing sitting by her fire, sorrowing because she would not forgive me. That old woman has been put to flight by this old woman. Perhaps if this one forgives me, and I meet her, in another and a better Paradise, we may be friends again, but I doubt it. I feel as if I'd like a change now, a new owner. I guess I'll be your goat."

" Thank you," I said, hastily, " but I'm going to have quite a following of animals." Then, for my curiosity wasn't satisfied, I went on, " Don't you

want to look at her again? She's going back to earth pretty soon."

" Has she got her switch ?" asked the goat, anxiously.

" Yes, clutched tight in her hand."

" Then I guess I'll just stay here with her souvenir," he said. " I'm glad she's going back to earth. I hope she'll have a lovely journey, and now I think I'll sing a little more. Wouldn't you like to hear me? " and he got up and began to gambol again.

" No, I wouldn't," I said, and I made off as fast

as I could, but the first part of his song floated after

me.

" It is a gay and pleasant thing, Late along the fruitful Spring, To roam the meadows fresh and gay, Eating grass and drinking hay."

" How can you drink hay ? " I bawled back at him.

" You can't," he said, stopping and laughing like an idiot, " but how in time can I make rhyme, if you don't let me use words? Words were made before boys, anyway," and the old simpleton went on plunging and yowling.

«If you meet a little kid Dancing o'er the bounteous grid, Ask him to come play with you, He'll delight to frisk in dew."

I

^ etiangetr ggoat 207

" Oh, let up," I called back, " let u-u-u-p." But he went on.

" If a boy should come along, Greet him with a dance and song. Greet him gaily, let him go, 'Specially if he's pretty slow."

" Well, I call that gratitude," I said to Rag, who was the only animal left with me, the others being all taken up with spying on the old woman.

" He doesn't know that you were the chief one in having the Widow brought here, and I guess tears have kind of washed away his underpinnings," said Rag, soberly.

" Rag, if ever you make doggerel, I'll kill you," I said.

The old dog winked. " I guess I couldn't, master. My brain goes slow, and my body goes faster."

" You old imp! " I said, and I began to chase him.

He ran, and I ran after him, and neither of us paid much attention to the way we were going, till we landed in one of the prettiest spots on the Island.

CHAPTER XVIII. joe's home

It was Joe's home, and it was a lovely place. We were at the foot of quite a smart hill, and up at the top of the hill was a green lodge something like mine, only larger.

Old Joe was sitting at the door of his lodge, looking out over the sea. The morning sun shone on his old face. He was simply fine — I can't describe him. The doggy part seemed noble and grand, and then there was the look of a human being about him.

I didn't feel like speaking, and just stood staring up at him.

At last he saw me, and the dreamy look went out of his eyes. " Aren't you coming up, boy? "

" Yes, Joe — I'm sorry you've been having trouble."

" It's over now," he said, and he turned his old face up, till it looked yellow and shining as the sun.

" Is Miss Laura dead ?" I asked, for I knew 208

3ot^^ Jkotnt 209

enough now to be sure that while suffering gave the thoughtful animals pain, death pleased them.

" Yes," he said, " she is dead. I have just heard," and following the glance he gave, I could see a dove as white as snow up in the yellow sunlight.

"Then she is happy," I said, in a low voice.

" Yes, boy." H " And you want to go to her ? " j^fe He didn't say anything for a long time; then he ^replied: "As soon as it pleases the Master of all things to let me go."

" This is a pleasant place to leave," I said, and I looked round me. Strawberry plants, blackberry and currant bushes, and all kinds of New England things grew right up the hill to Joe's door, and behind the lodge I caught glimpses of a real pine wood.

There would be lots of little white wild flowers in there, such as we used to find in the woods back East, and what a fine place for squirrels and rabbits 1

" A pleasant place," murmured Joe, " but nothing to the place we are going to."

I fell into a brown study. Sometimes, in talking to these dead animals, I felt dreadfully alive.

Joe was very absent-minded, but after a long time he went on, in a low voice, " I am thinking about her all the time. Think how blessed to have

all the pain over. She was so merciful. She suffered with the tiniest fly that broke its wing."

I couldn't speak for a minute. A week ago I would not have understood him. Now, Rag's death flashed upon me. I was beginning to take hold of these things.

" All right, Joe," I said, and I threw my arm round him, " I understand, old dog."

Just then, Joe's fat little mother came sniffing up to me. " Good morning," she said. " I am glad that at last you have called on us. Don't you want to look round and see where the family sleeps ? "

I smiled at her, and leaving old Joe sitting gazing out over the sea, she took me round the place.

First we went through the front door into a long, low room, where my head almost touched the roof. The lodge was built like mine, only more substantially— green branches twisted together for walls and roof, and little flowers growing on the walls in some places where earth had been put in nooks and crannies.

All round the floor were raised boxlike sleeping places.

I turned to Jess. She was looking over her shoulder at Joe.

"He's watching," she said, gravely, "watching for messengers from the World of the Blessed. He thinks Miss Laura will be sure to ask for him. He may be sent for at any time."

" Don't talk about it," I said. " I feel all broken up, when you speak about Joe's going. Tell me who sleeps in all these cunning little bedrooms."

" Bedrooms," laughed Jess, showing her little, white teeth at me. " That's a very grand name for these cubby-holes. But Joe will have a separate nest for every member of our large family. Miss Laura taught him that. Even I don't have my pups to sleep in my nest, because I am no longer young — and I'm pretty stout," she added, apologetically, " and like plenty of room. I never had enough to eat in life, and my besetting sin in Paradise is to stuff myself. This is where my pups sleep," and walking into another room, she pointed to a fresh bed of hay in a cunning, green bower.

" Where are the pups ? " I asked.

" Off on a bay-leaf chase."

" Like a paper chase ? "

" Yes. You know pups must have fun, so a monkey goes ahead and scatters bay leaves. The pup that gathers most leaves gets a prize. Sometimes they have a plain chase when they follow the track of some animal — the bloodhounds teach them that."

" But how can they tell the monkey's bay leaves from those dropped by the tree ? "

" Oh, by the smell," she said, with a surprised air. " Every one the monkey touches, smells of him."

I didn't say anything. I didn't feel up to a discussion on scent.

" This is where Malta sleeps," said Jess, showing another little compartment, " this one lined with feathers. Dropped feathers, of course," she said; " no bird is killed here — Davy and Bella sleep together. Where are you, Bella? Here is your dear boy."

" Coming, Mother, coming," cried Bella, and she appeared from somewhere, strutting on the ground. She reminded me of parrots on earth who so often prefer the floor, where they are so ungraceful, to flying on the backs of chairs and sofas, where they look so well. Perhaps being kept in captivity causes them to partly lose the use of their wings.

Well, Bella came and got on my shoulder, and played with my nose, and bit my ear, and pretended she was going to hurt me.

" Mind the Widow, boy," she said, " the Widow with the big, big switch. She'd clout Bella's back if she could, but Bella is smart. She keeps out of the way. Ha, ha, ha! " and she burst into a screech.

" I hope the Widow won't get at my pups with her switch," said Jess, anxiously.

Good Jess — I thought of the cruel way in which her pups were killed on earth by the miserable Jenkins, and how she took them to her nest in the straw, and tried to bring them back to life.

I

3loe»g IS^omt 213

" What a different life you lead here," I said. " I suppose you're as happy as the day is long."

" Oh, so happy, boy," she said, " so happy. I lie here on the top of this lovely hill, and look away toward earth, and think of the animals suffering as I did. Sometimes I call out to them — only of course they can't hear me — ' Oh, animals, be patient, the Island of Brotherly Love is a long way off, but sometime you will get to it.' "

I stooped down, and patted her little brown head.

She winked away the tears in her eyes; then she said, " Come see the sweet-smelling place old Toby has. He was Jenkins's horse, you know."

She trotted away through more rooms, all with their green nests of different sizes, and going through the house, led the way to a big, thatched bower outside.

On the way she stopped, and said, softly, " When you go back to earth you may know of some mother dog who is going to lose her pups. Please ask the men who are going to kill them, or give them away, to take them from her very gently, for it hurts a dog to lose her young ones. Not as much as a woman, of course, when they steal her children from her, but it IS the same kind of pain."

" I'll remember, Jess," I said, " and if ever I have a dog, and she has pups, I'll let her keep them if there are fifty thousand."

She laughed heartily. " Well, you see, that wouldn't do. Some animals have to be killed, but there's a kind way of killing, and an evil way."

" Jess," I said, " I see where Joe gets his goodness."

She shook her little head, " Not from me, not from me — now look at Toby's home," and she entered the bower. " He isn't at home. He has gone on a picnic. He is old, and he never had much fun in life — you know he used to be a cab-horse before Jenkins got him — so Joe encourages him to have just as good a time as he can here. He associates mostly with thoroughbred horses. That was his ambition in life, and whatever your ambition in life may be, it is gratified in Paradise, if it is a lawful one. He has all the company he likes, too. See the six stalls Joe had the monkeys make — and he keeps them full of his friends all the time. He'll come home to-night as tired as can be, and he'll probably have six friends with him, and they'll sleep like colts till morning."

"Does he do any work?" I asked.

" Oh, yes — he helps draw the bread and cakes from the bakeries. The monkeys rigged him a kind of rough sled."

I walked into the thatched stable or bower, for it was as dainty as a girl's summer-house. " Why this is sweet-scented grass, isn't it? " I said, sniffing at the woven partitions between the stalls.

I

^ot^n %oine ^

" Yes," said Jess, in her little, humble way. " Joe wants Toby to have everything of the best — Toby and the cows."

" I suppose you animals who were so badly treated by Jenkins have a peculiar feeling toward each other," I remarked.

" Oh, yes, trouble binds together," said Jess, gently.

" And why are you so meek about your good luck now? " I asked. " You speak as if you were almost .doing wrong to have such nice things."

" I've never got over my old earth habit," she replied, in her little mousie way. " Joe talks to me about it, but I always felt I had no right to live when I was alive, and now I'm dead, I feel as if I had no right to enjoy anything."

" You had all the spirit taken out of you," I said. " I'd like to kill everybody that abuses an animal."

There was a step behind us, and turning round I saw that old Joe was standing in the stable door. The light was behind him, and his face was bent on me so earnestly, so very earnestly.

" Boy," he said, " I want to have some talks with you before you go bade to earth. Every American boy is a King. When you reach manhood, you enter your inheritance. If the boy understands the principles of good government, he will rule wisely; if he does not, he will be deposed and another will reign in his stead."

" What is my kingdom, Joe? " I asked.

"Yourself."

"Myself!"

"Yes — and if you are your own ruler, your kingdom is a city with walls. If you have not firmness enough to control your own spirit, your city is broken down and without walls — another ruler enters."

I laughed. " That means self-government, Joe, so I'm not fit to be an American King yet. I'd like to be a Turk. I want to cut off the heads of people that don't please me."

Joe looked thoughtful. " There's something about boys I don't understand. Even in the best of them, there is a sanguinary streak."

"What does sanguinary mean, Joe?"

" Bloody," he said, reluctantly.

" I never faint when I see blood," I remarked, proudly. " Mother does."

" Keep it down," said Joe, energetically.

" Keep what down ? "

" Your savagery, your fierceness, your desire to rule. No good will come of it, boy. Cultivate a meek and quiet spirit."

Jess was following us, and just here she remarked, timidly, " I've heard America called * Sweet land of liberty.' "

" I'd give them liberty," I said, for I still felt

cranky. ** I'd give them liberty, especially liberty to hang the people that aren't good to animals."

Joe smiled. " Boy, I think you would do better on another line of argument. Let the question of kindness to animals alone. I'll fall back upon first principles — once upon a time a King stepped from his throne. He saw a beetle in his path. He put out his foot. He was just about to crush it, when the beetle cried with a loud voice, * Justice!'

" ' Justice!' said the King, drawing back his foot.

* You mean mercy.'

" ' I mean justice, brother,' said the beetle.

" ' Brother!' repeated the King, holding up his head, proudly. * You, the meanest of things created, dare to address me thus!'

" * Who created you, brother ? * asked the beetle.

" * The Master of All Things. I am his noblest work.*

" ' Did he tell you so ? ' inquired the beetle.

" The King said nothing.

"' I am his noblest work,' continued the beetle.

* Look at my wonderful jointed body, my beautiful sheath wings.'

" ' Impertinent animal,' said the King, angrily.

I tell you I am highest in the scale of being.'

" * And I can soar a mile above your head,' said the beetle.

" * Now I am going to kill you,' said the King.

" ' Very well, brother/ replied the beetle. ' There will be one more sin upon your head.'

" * One more sin/ repeated the King, in a rage.

My courtiers tell me that I am a divinity/

" * The King the murderer has liars for servants/ said the beetle.

" The King's rage ceased; his head fell on his breast. He pondered deeply for a long time. Then he looked intently at the beetle, who was cleaning his wings. * Tell me, beetle, by what right do you make these monstrous assertions ? '

" * Tell me, brother,' said the beetle, kindly, ' by what right you question them ? '

" ' By what right!' blustered the King. * By the divine right of Kings.'

" ' But, brother, we are all Kings,' said the beetle.

" * All Kings!' thundered the frightened monarch, * this is some secret sedition — kill him, some one.'

" But none of his courtiers would silence the talking beetle, who went on cleaning his wings.

" ' Beetle,' said the King, in a wheedling voice,

if you will furnish me with news of this conspiracy, I will give you a province.'

" ' Very well,' said the beetle, shaking the last remnant of dust from himself. ' I will confess. It is the conspiracy of brotherhood. Every created thing has a right to live, and to do as he likes, pro-

vided he does not interfere with the rights of any other created thing.'

" ' Why, that takes me in!' cried the King, in astonishment.

" ' Yes, sire,' replied the beetle, ' you ought to be head of the brotherhood.'

" ' I will be head,' burst out the King. * Pass on,

tbrother, you are nobler than I.' f " * Not so, brother King. You go first. I will tollow.' ' " The King went on his way. ' Severe punishment to him who interferes with the rights of my brother behind me,' he cried."

" What a fuss about a beetle," cackled Bella, when Joe finished. " Nasty things — I hate 'em. They tickle Bella's claws."

" I know a story," said Rag. I looked down at him. He was sitting at my feet, his eyes dancing with mischief.

" Go on, old boy," I said. " Let's have it." " Once there was a Queen," said Rag, in a queer, solemn voice, " and she was going out for a walk. Just as she left her palace, a gray parrot with red tail feathers brushed her with its wings. * Awkward creature,' cried the Queen, ' let all gray parrots with red tail feathers all over my dominions be put to I death.'"

" Oh, the nasty Queen! " screamed Bella; " oh,

the cruel, hateful Queen, to kill all her sisters, the little, teenty, weenty, sweet and lovely gray parrots. Where are your ears, Rag? Let Bella get at your soft, white ears. She'll nip them; she'll make them tingle," and she chased Rag round the hill.

I watched them for awhile, grinning from ear to ear at the way Rag was coming out. Soon he would be as sharp a dog as Dandy. Then I turned to Joe. " Look here, old fellow, do you think animals have souls ? "

His dear old face grew troubled. " I am puzzled about many things, boy, but I do not think animals have souls as you understand them, though there is something very beautiful and wonderful wrapped up in that loose word * instinct.' We are more material than you are. We have not your capacity for worship. We have only a blind and dumb idolatry for our owners — we shall. learn more in progressive stages, but though I do not know, I feel that we, the lower order of animals, will never keep pace with man. He has in him a divine spark that is wanting in our slower, duller fire." \

" But you are better than some of us, Joe. You are not so revengeful. You don't hate Jenkins, do you?"

"Oh, no, no — I often think of him. I wish earnestly he could be in a happy place like this. There was a soft spot in him, but he was poor and

dirty, and of bad parentage. Things were mostly against him."

" Rag," I said, calling to him, as he lay panting near us, " do you hate Hillington for having killed you?"

" I never thought about it," said Rag, good-humouredly. " I just took things as they came."

Bella had made friends with him, and was perched on his back. Now she leaned over and squawked kindly in his ear, " I'd have nipped him, I'd have made him squeal. Maybe Bella will get her claws in him yet."

" Here, Joe," I said, " is a creature that doesn't like anybody."

" She is like some human beings," said Joe. " She doesn't mean more than half she says."

Jess heard me, and called, anxiously, '* Bella, won't you try to be more gentle? I would like all our family to go together to the World of the Blessed."

" I'll never get there. Mother," said Bella, mournfully, " never get there. I'm too bad!" and screaming, " Too bad, too bad! " she flew away into a tree, and cried and chattered to herself.

" Master Sam," said Joe, earnestly, " have you forgiven Hillington ? "

" No, Joe," I said, " I haven't."

" Won't you do so ? "

" And take half the pleasure out of life? No,

Joe — I just dream of the sweet black eye I'll give him, first time I catch him alone."

Joe sighed. " Master Sam, there's no real pleasure in revenge."

" Isn't there, Joe — that's all you know about it. It's glorious — it makes you feel warm all over, and comfortable, as if you had eaten ten Christmas dinners — I just wish I had Hillington here."

" In theory, you believe in all the virtues, but in practice, you prefer to leave out a few," said Joe, kindly.

" Yes, sir, talk is all very fine, but who lives up to the tallness of his tongue?"

" Some boys do," said Joe.

" Oh, yes, the Morris boys in your book, but they were extra good. I'm just a common, medium, bad sort of a boy. I don't do things some fellows will do, but I'm no saint, my friend."

He licked my hand. " You've a kind heart toward animals. Master Sam, — wouldn't you Hke to see them at work ? You've only seen them playing since you came."

"Just down to the ground, Joe. When shall we go ? "

" Now, if you like. The bakeries are running busily. Ragtime, you will come?"

My old beauty got up, stretched himself, and came toward us.

CHAPTER XIX.

ON THE WAY TO THE BAKERIES

" We have some distance to travel," said Joe,

and I think you would better ride. Where is Jumbo? — Barry, will you ask him to come?
"

A beautiful, yellow canary, who had been sitting On a rose-bush, eyeing us with a very knowing look, flew away.

"That is Mrs. Montgomery's bird," said Jess. "You remember he was burned to death with her in the hotel fire. He always stays with us. The animals in my son's book keep together," she added, proudly.

Ragtime winked at me. " That was a great book," he said, mischievously.

Jess drew a long breath, and began to talk about Joe's story. She was for all the world like a woman running over the charms of her darling child.

I gave Rag a push. " See here, old fellow, you stop making fun."

" Tweet, tweet!" piped Barry, coming back, 223

" such good luck. Jumbo was just coming to call on President Joe."

I ran to the front of the hill — the part overlooking the sea. Away down below, there was the big elephant trundling along like a good-natured old mountain.

You wouldn't think an elephant could act pleased, but he can, and old Jumbo did make a fuss over me.

" How am I to get up? " I asked, after he had mounted the hill, and I stood looking at his tableland of a back. " I have often ridden on elephants' backs in parks, but there was always a ladder."

" I'll be your ladder," said Jumbo, with a rolling laugh, and stretching out his trunk, he swung me gently up.

" Joe, you come, too," I said, " and Rag."

Dear old Joe smiled, and didn't Jumbo swing him up, and Rag, too.

"Bella, Bella," I called, "I hate to leave you moping. Come along."

" I'm bad, too bad," she shrieked, wildly, " bad, too bad!"

" Come along, old girl," I said. " Joe will tell you how to be good."

" Can Davy come, too ? " she called.

" Yes, hurry up."

She flew joyfully from the tree, screaming, "Davy, Davy, where's Bella's good rat? Come, Davy, Davy, sweet Davy, precious Davy!"

" Her love for that rat ought to help her along the upward way," I said to Joe.

" It does," he replied, gravely. " Not one particle of love is lost. All counts up for us in the day of reckoning."

" Here comes Davy," said Rag, " a little behind time, as usual."

" Pick him up. Jumbo," squeaked Bella, " don't hurt him. Bella will fly up," and she lighted on my shoulder.

"Won't you come, too, madam?" said Rag, politely, to Jess.

" Oh, I couldn't," she said, anxiously. " My pups will be coming home, and will want their mother. Good-bye, have a pleasant time."

"Good-bye, Mother," called Bella. "Bye, bye, take good care of everything. Such a housekeeper! Maybe Bella will bring you some fresh cakes."

Bella was in great feather, and as we plodded along, she screamed a greeting to every bird and beast we met.

That was a great ride. First Jumbo took us down the hill, going very carefully, so we wouldn't fall off; then he marched along under the trees, keeping within sight of the shore, so we could enjoy the view of the sea and sky. Sometimes he took us close under the branches, so we could pick fruit from the trees. We pulled oranges and apples that were

clean, and not black and sooty as they so often are in California groves. Plums, too, and pears, and cherries, and many other American fruits. Sometimes he broke off for us limbs that were out of reach, and would politely hand them up to us.

"Jumbo," said Joe, presently, "we will shorten the distance, if we cross the desert by the Cat's house."

" Could we go by the swans' lake, too ?" I asked. " I want to see them again."

" Certainly," said Joe, and Jumbo rumbled below, " All right! " and immediately turned his back to the sea.

We had great fun going under some low-growing branches. Jumbo stepped carefully, and told us when to duck our heads, and lie flat on his back, but still we had adventures. Bella was brushed froi my shoulder, but, of course, having wings, didn' care. I was .brushed from the place of honour, anj not having wings, did care, but the way that bii unwieldy-looking elephant flung his trunk behind! and broke my fall, was a caution.

Davy fell out of my pocket, and Bella screamed, " Oh, la, la, if you hurt my darling rat, I'll nip you! " Then she had to mourn again about being bad.

Joe didn't fall off, and looked as sweet as a peach, when I joked him about being dignified.

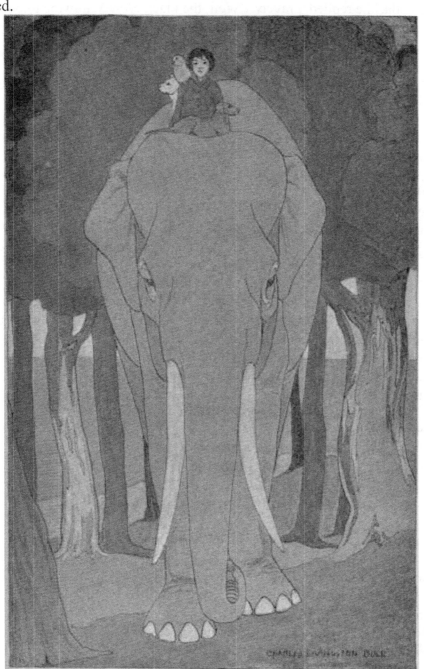

TURNED HIS BACK TO THE SLA

I" I don't believe you cx)uld act silly, Joe, to save ur life," I said. " I used to feel silly when I was a pup," he)lied. f Don't you ever feel silly now ? " " I'm afraid not," he said, in a voice almost as meek as his mother's, " but often I am very happy, and I just get by myself and laugh hard."

" And sometimes you laugh at the pups," said Bella, sticking her beak into our conversation. " You know you do. You can't help it. They're so funny. Such tricks. Oh, dear, dear — such a ' merry, merry bunch," and she went off into a cackling laugh.

Soon she stopped abruptly. " Sometimes I wish they'd grow up, but they've got six thousand years of puphood yet, haven't they, Joe?"

" I don't know, Bella," he replied, gravely. "Well, the black crow Wildwing told me, that Saucy Bill Sparrow told him, that Jenny Wren told her, that you said that — "

" I don't know anything about the divisions of eternity, Bella," said Joe, still more gravely. " Don't spread that gossip."

" Why, I never gossip," said Bella, in an injured voice, "but those sparrows — they gabble all the time." " Joe," I said, " how is it that your brothers are

pups, and you are an old dog? You were all born at the same time."

" But they were put immediately out of the world, boy, and I continued for some years in it. Earthly experience counts for much after death."

" Here we are at the Swan Lake," interrupted Bella. " Oh, ain't they sweet? "

" Aren't they, Bella," squeaked Davy, " ain't isn't proper."

I stared at the little fellow. He rarely opened his mouth, and just now Bella closed it by promptly boxing his ears. He pulled his head back into my pocket, and she raged at him. " Such impudence, correcting your betters. Ain't it impudence, boy? ain't it? Ain't he a saucy rat, oh, ain't he, ain't he? '*

" Aren't he," I heard Davy squeaking inside oi my pocket, " aren't he, aren't he."

Bella heard him, but could not get at him. " Oh, my, my!" she sneered, " what a rat, what a wonder-ful, won-der-ful rat! A fine grammar rat, an English composition rat, an American scholar rat! A torturing rat — just because a lady slipped on a word. A lady that rarely slips. Oh, she'll give it to you, Davy, you'll catch it, my lad. Put him out, Master Sam, dear Master Sam, put him on a tree branch. Leave him alone with Bella. Let her tickle him with her beak."

" Oh, shut up, Bella," I said, " look at those well-behaved swans."

the lake, a few were sunning themselves on the banks,

d a pair of black, Australian swans were making a

t — such an odd-looking affair, mostly of rushes.

I called out to the swans, and they came sailing

ward us, arching and bending their flower-stalk

s. " Oh, let me down," I said to Jumbo, " I must eak to them. I don't know why it is, but those

swans remind me of home more than anything else on the Island."

They really reminded me of mother, only I didn't like to say so.

While I was stroking Dulce's neck, she said in a sweet, whistling voice, " Do you know anything about loons, dear boy ? "

" No," I said, " except that they are some kind of little bears."

The animals all tried not to laugh, but they could not help it. Jumbo roared. Even old Joe smiled.

Rag was the only one that kept a straight face, for
he didn't know any better than I did.

" He is thinking of coons," said the gentle swan,
turning her eyes on the other animals. " Loons are
birds, dear boy — Great Northern Divers, they are
called — one of them is teaching her young one over
there. It is very interesting; perhaps you would
like to see her."

" Yes," I said, " I would."

She gave a shrill cry, and immediately a queer, solitary looking bird, like a big duck,
came swimming along with a little, dark gray creature beside her.

" Will you put your little one through some of his exercises here ? " asked the swan.

The loon didn't say anything. She was friendly, but offish.

" They are not used to associating with human beings on earth," whispered the swan, as
if to excuse her.

The loon, who seemed to be a very businesslike bird, had begun to show off. " If some
one would play hunter, I would do better," she said, suddenly turning round.

" I'll be hunter," said the swan, and she startec off — such a graceful beauty in the water,
such waddler when she struck the shore!

" Shoo bang go! " she cried, suddenly sticking her head out between some pussy-
willows.

The old loon had been parading round the lak(with her young one on her back. At the
noise the swan made, she dived like a flash.

"Where's the little one?" I asked.

Rag was chuckling. " Good play — the bit of down opened its bill, and held on to its
mother's tail."

" Did it really? " I asked Joe.

He nodded.

The swan was looking out from the willows. After a time, she drew her head in, and then
the loon came up in the lake ever so far from us.

" That was fine," I called to the swan. " Get her to do it again." .

The swan gave a cry — one thing I had learned on the Island was that every creature had
a language of its own. The animals could all talk to me, and I could understand them, but they
could also talk to each other, when I could mostly not understand them, but I knew that every
little squeak, and chatter, and twitter meant something.

Well, the loon came back, and the young one with her. This time he didn't ride on her
back. He went off by himself, pretending he was looking for food, but really keeping his beady
eyes on his parent.

" Piff, piff!" whistled the swan again from the willows.

The mother loon gave a deep, odd cry, the young chick scuttled to her, got on her back,
that was being quickly lowered in the water, and as she disappeared into the lake, wasn't chickie
downie holding on with all his might to one of her tail feathers.

" And that's how she drags him across the lake? " I said.

" Poor little loonie, she makes him practise every day," said Bella. " He gets quite tired out, and what is she practising for? There's no one here to hurt her baby."

" She's a good mother," observed Davy.

Bella made a bite at him. " Why, you're getting to be quite a talker! "

Jumbo had slipped me to the ground, and Bella and Davy had come with me.

" Dear Davy," said Bella, " come out with Bella."

He ran out of my pocket so suddenly that she never thought of nipping him. " Good boy," she said, after awhile, " Bella loves Davy, but he mustn't talk too much."

" I think we'd better go now," I said, patting Jumbo's trunk. " I know Joe is in a hurry. Joe, if I live to get home, I'm going to study about animals. Why, it's just like a story-book to see the differences between them."

" Many boys and girls will study natural history when they won't study anything else," said Joe.

" Numbers of children used to come to see me in Central Park," said Jumbo, " and then would go home and read about my family, and come back and tell me. I found out that I had some very distinguished relatives, who are no longer upon earth."

" Tell us about them. Jumbo," said Bella, " you talk so pretty."

Jumbo smiled, and began a short story about animals who used to live on the earth before man was created. As soon as he stopped, Bella began to tease for more.

When he put his foot down and wouldn't say another word, she turned to Joe, " You tell the boy about George Washington's mouse, and Abraham Lincoln's cat."

By this time we were jogging along toward the desert. There were no trees now, no shrubs nor pretty flowers, nothing but sand. We passed the little pyramid of the Cat's house, looking shut up and lonely under its clump of doom-palms. I forgot to say that the mouse had run home after having her breakfast with me. She never would stay long away from the Cat.

Well, Joe told us a fine story about Washington and a mouse.

" It happened at Valley Forge," he said. " American boys and girls learn all about that dreadful winter in their histories. You know what untold misery Washington and his soldiers suffered, and you will also remember that the general had two wretched houses, one to sleep in, the other to eat in. A little wood-mouse crept in from the snow and frost outside, and made himself a home in the dining-house. A soldier caught him stealing their miserable rations, and set a trap for him. The mouse went in,

and finding himself trapped, made a desperate attempt at liberty.

" Washington happened to come into the comfortless room, and heard him gnawing. He looked down at him, and said, * Poor prisoner, you are cold and hungry — so am I. You are panting for liberty — so am I. Go ' — and opening the trapdoor, he set the prisoner free.

" Some nights afterward, Washington was asleep. His wife spent the winter with him. Ah, she was a brave, good woman! The mouse says he often used to watch her from his hole, and admire her for making shirts with her tired fingers, and doing many other kind deeds for the soldiers. Well, as I was saying, Washington was asleep. His wife had shortly before been called out to receive a gift of fresh bread, and sweet, new cheese. Her husband had refused his meagre supper, and with a beaming face she placed these new articles of diet by his pillow, then hurried away to pay a last visit to a dying soldier.

" The mouse was as hungry as Washington, and here was no trap. As soon as the devoted Martha Washington left the room, he crept up to the bread and cheese. He smelt them, he was just about to eat them, when the thought flashed into his mind, * Here is the man who was kind to me — I cannot rob him.' Then he scampered away as fast as bis feet would carry him."

" Bravo, mousie," I cried, but Bella said, shrilly, " Don't believe a word of that story, not the mouse part. I believe the Washington part. Fancy a mouse loving anything better than his stomach! "

*' I believe it," and the little white animal in my pocket rose up on his hind feet, *' mice are first cousins to rats."

" You believe it," shrieked Bella, " you believe it! Oh, my, my! oh, my, my! "

" Mice are first cousins to rats," repeated Davy.

Bella suddenly became calm, and said, in a wheedling voice, '* Not to white rats, Davy, not to pretty, glossy, white rats with pink eyes like my Davy. This was just a common gray mouse, Davy, just a common mouse."

Bella was smart. Davy, after a lifetime and part of a death-time bondage to her, was beginning to assert himself, and if she didn't look out, she'd lose her hold on him.

Now she began petting him, and stroking him with her beak, till soon Davy looked as meek as ever-

" Now for your story about Lincoln," I said to Joe, when Bella had quieted down, " but first, Joe, tell me where is this Washington mouse ? I should like to see him."

Joe smiled. " Oh, he has gone long ago to the World of the Blessed. These stories are handed down."

" I'll warrant you that mouse is somewhere near Washington," said Jumbo, in his deep voice.

" I am sure he is," said Joe. " He loved Washington. I expect that good man is surrounded by the animals whom he cared for on earth in his beautiful country home. I know the mouse said when he was here that there was only one man for him in the World of the Blessed, and that man was George Washington. I am sure that neither Washington nor Lincoln would be surprised to hear of the Island of Brotherly Love, for they were both good to all created things. Lincoln said that he believed in a future life for animals."

" Do tell me about his cat," I said.

" Well, she was a black cat, another type from our friend under the doom-palms, a very gentle affectionate cat, and she lived for a long time in Lincoln's family when he was in Springfield, Illinois. She says that he was a wonderful man, for he never forgot to be kind at home, even in the midst of his stormy political campaigns, when he was battling for the life of the nation — no matter how tired he was when he came into the house, he would always stroke her when she sprang to his knee, and sometimes he would whisper strong and stirring words in her ear, such as * Union' or * Disunion,' ' Half-Slavery,' ' Half-Freedom.'

" On earth she did not know what such words

meant, but after she came here, she said that if she had had more intelligence, she would have known that war was coming before any one else knew it. Because she was black and homely, she used to remind Lincoln of the coloured people, and he would look at her and groan, with such sentences as, ' The black children suffer in bondage, the light ones live in sin. There is a sore in the side of the nation. She is bowed down — but the nation shall not die.' "

" He always wound up with that, she said, ' The nation shall not die.' Then he would push her aside, and walk the floor, and his face was gnarled and twisted, and he looked like some big tree in a storm."

Joe stopped, but I begged for more stories.

" I could tell you a book of stories about these two good men," he said, " stories from the animal's point of view that have never been published, but I have not time now. We are going to be interrupted. Later on, we will talk some more."

Joe was looking ahead at a queer-looking, brownish-gray, horned animal all alone out on the desert.

He was gamboling toward us in a peculiar way, and Rag, who was straining his eyes, said, " 'Pon my word, that creature's legs are in the air about as often as they are on the ground."

CHAPTER XX.

BREAD AND SWEET CAKES

" I BELIEVE it's the goat," said Rag.

It was the goat, alone, and as happy as a lark.

" Old tearfulness," said Joe, and his face was a picture of astonishment.

" Hasn't any one told you about the Widow ? " I asked.

" No, Soko called to see me, but I was busy talking to the dove, and Jess sent him away."

I told him of the Widow McDoodle's actions, and he laughed heartily. " We must send her back to earth. Soko is probably watching her — Good morning, Jerry, you look happy."

By this time we had come up to the goat, or he had skipped up to us. He was acting like an idiot, now on his head, now on his hoofs, now on his back.

" Jerry," said Joe, " stand still, and talk to me."

" Hold your tongue, dear President," said the goat. " I must listen to myself awhile yet. I haven't heard myself do anything but cry for the last twelve months — oh, I'm making such lovely

poetry, such sweet poetry. It just melts in your mouth."

Jumbo had stopped short, and Joe just sat still on his back, and stared down at the goat, as indeed we all did.

*' Here beginneth," said the goat, and diddling round us, and occasionally touching up Jumbo with his stumps of horns, he began:

" Oh, the great load of turnips has rolled from my brain, I can think, I can laugh, I can move without pain. I'm the happiest goat that ever was bom, I've come to the harbour, I've weathered the storm."

" Now, what do you think of that. President Joe?" he asked, when a few seconds of silence followed his recitation.

Joe gave him a kind smile. " Jerry, if that style of poetry — "

" Poetry," muttered Rag, " it's goatry."

" If it pleases you, it pleases me," finished Joe. " I love to see my friends happy. Now you won't cry any more, will you, and make us all miserable? "

The goat shook his beard and kicked out behind.

** Tears, silly tears,

They don't do any good, You might weep for a thousand years, No one would care a rood."

"What's a rood?" interrupted Rag, but Jerry was rattling on.

" Then let us all rejoice,

And go our ways with glee. Let's give the go-by to earth's prose, And take its poetry.

" Now I shall do some work, And never stop to cry. I'm going to be a better goat, If you'll all help me try."

" Isn't that lovely ? " he ejaculated himself, before any one else had time to say a word. " These rhymes just fly out of me. I don't know what I'm made of. I'm so taken up with the beauty and wonder of my literary ability, that I don't know what to do. Oh, how I pity animals that can't compose!" and he threw a melting glance at us all, including the President.

" Jumbo," said Joe, dryly, " I think we'd better be moving on."

" And leave him alone to his wonder and glory," said Rag.

Jumbo started off en his dignified walk, and the goat for a time ran below, serenading us.

" I think I'll go find me a nice little cave, One having a view of both forest and wave. I'll eat there, and sleep there, and work other times, And if nothing is doing, I'll make me some rhymes."

" Oh, what a goat," cackled Bella, " what a persevering, poetical, polydoodle goat. We've got a laureate now, President Joe. When this ride is over, Bella will weave some leaves for a garland."

The goat, with a waggish glance at her pert head, took her up.

" I'll wear a green wreath on my precious, gray head, Not being a beauty, I'll have honour instead; The ladies will pet me, the gents will be mad, And I shaU for ever be more and more glad."

** Ha, ha, ha," laughed Bella, ** the poet clown, the poet clown!"

" Jerry," I said, looking over Jumbo's head, " if you don't get out, I'll throw something at you."

He immediately struck into a side path in the forest, where he executed a kind of clog dance. We could hear his hoofs rattling on a big, flat rock as he marked time.

" Oh, he's got a little temper has our Master Sam, The cunning little temper of a gentle little lamb. But we like him all the better for his pettish little tricks. And I guess that when he leaves us, we'll be in a fix."

" Well, I never saw such a change as that," I said, with a groan. " Who would dream that that was the melancholy goat of yesterday! "

" Look, Master Sam," said Joe, " we're coming to the grain fields."

I did look. Away ahead, down the forest path, was something shining and waving in the sun.

" Heads of wheat," said Bella, " aren't they graceful? "

I nodded and kept my eyes fixed ahead. As we drew near the great field of wheat, I saw that there were dozens and hundreds of gray and brown spots moving along the ground by the roots of the wheat.

" Those are animals," I said, " aren't they, Joe ? What are they doing? They seem to be busy about something."

" They are our cutters," he said. " Wait till you get nearer, and you will see them biting the stalks in two. You were wondering what the animals found to do on the Island. Many of the rodents work hard at this grain cutting."

"Well, well," I said, "what a task!"

" The monkeys sow the seed," said Joe, " the rodents cut the grain, and the bears gather it."

"Bears!" I said.

" Jumbo, pause for a minute," said Joe.

The old elephant stopped, and I stood up on his back. The field before us was covered with a fine crop of wheat. I say field, but there was no fence round it. There was not one on the Island, except that in the corral where the elephant was confined.

I just opened my eyes, to see the industrious little animals at work^ and working so steadily that they

I

never stopped to look at us. There was a long row of them — rabbits, beavers, jerboas, rats, mice, squirrels, marmots, gophers, etc., and their little, sharp, chisel-like teeth were cutting down the wheat in fine style.

I slipped off Jumbo's back. Then just for a minute, I was frightened, and wished I was back again.

Two enormous bears had reared up from under some trees at the edge of the forest, and stood near us, towering away up in the air with their paws stretched out like arms. '^

"California grizzlies," said Joe; "they assist the rodents."

" Joe," I gasped, " for goodness' sake, how much do they weigh ? "

The old dog measured them with his eye. " About sixteen hundred pounds apiece, I should say — come, Silvertip and Kern, show the boy how you gather up the grain."

The two big fellows had evidently been having a nap, for they yawned and stretched their hairy limbs before they set to work. They gathered up the wheat in huge armfuls, then stalked away with it.

" Let us follow them," said Joe. " We'd better go on foot, we can see better, but you follow us, Jumbo, we may want you again."

I was delighted. We trod along in single file

through a path made by the animals in the middle of the field. As we passed the rodents, I stopped and patted a rabbit. He tossed his head, and gave the snorting noise rabbits make when impatient. He didn't want to be disturbed.

The bears led us through the field to a large, hard, flat piece of ground, where they flung their loads down.

At sight of the bears, a number of horses and oxen came running down a hill near by, and didn't they begin dancing and jumping, and running over the wheat.

" Thrashing," said Joe.

" Why, you ought to have machinery," I said.

" We are not clever enough to manage it; then this gives the animals something to do. Machinery would run them out of employment* Look at that old truck-horse, how gaily he thrashes beside his friend Fleetfoot!"

The truck-horse, whose name was Bonus, stopped work when he saw me, and came over to rub hisi nose up and down my flannel shirt front.

"Isn't this great?" he said. "I —an old broken-down horse — am able to thrash like a colt. I just love to work. I'd like to introduce you to a friend of mine, Palo Alto, a magnificent racer from California. He was worth no end of money, but he never puts on airs."

" Why, I've heard of him, Bonus," I said. " I've seen his grave."

" With his false body in it. Well, he's not too proud to thrash grain on the Island of Brotherly Love. He enjoys it. Then we have races sometimes on holidays, and when work is over we have a fine feed and a sleep, and then a good run to call on the horses on the other side of the Island. They have another big bakery over there."

" Well, well, well," I said. " I never expected to see anything like this."

" I must go back to my work," said Bonus. " We make good bread, and the animals all have such splendid appetites, that it keeps us busy. Goodbye."

" Good-bye, old fellow."

For a long time we stood watching the oxen and horses trample out the grain, and laughing at Bella's antics. She had perched on old Bonus's back, and cackling, " Faster, faster, faster," and spreading her wings, almost made the old horse crazy.

At last I took pity on him, and made her leave the poor old fellow, who stood with drooping head and downcast manner.

Joe gave some kind of a signal as we drew off, and suddenly all the thrashers stopped short, and stood aside, while an army of monkeys ran in, cleared away the straw, and with baskets threw the unwin-
nowed wheat into the air. When the chaff blew away, they filled their baskets with the winnowed wheat, and ran off.

" Let us follow them," said Joe, " and see the bears grinding."

Away in the distance, I had been hearing a noise like giants playing ninepins. Now we saw them.

The army of monkeys ran ahead. I saw them flinging down their baskets of wheat, jabbering and shouting at more bears, who were the giants. These bears held in their paws rocks like millstones, and as soon as the monkeys danced out of the way, they began to spin their stones over an enormous rock floor where the grain lay.

When we got near, the bears didn't seem so huge. They reminded me of big, clumsy boys playing at marbles.

I was fascinated. Their strength was immense, and they acted as if throwing a millstone was a nice little bit of amusement.

There was a ring of monkeys round them all the time, and whenever the bears stopped for a rest, the monkeys would run in with their baskets, fill them with the ground wheat, and dart off again.

" They are going to the bakery," said Joe, and he moved off after them.

I kept looking over my shoulder, as we left. The bears were grinding again, and the big stones were
rolling and smashing together. Beyond them, I could see the horses and cattle going on with their steady tramp, tramp, and away off, at the edge of the forest, was the waving wheat-field, where I knew the rows of little gnawers were at work. It was a busy scene, and the blood just tingled in the tips of my fingers. I felt that I, too, would like to get to work.

" Don't you think that my brothers make pretty good baskets ? " asked Joe, pointing to one near us.

I examined it. " Well, Joe, you animals beat everything."

" Do you smell the cakes and the nice fresh bread? " asked Bella, from my shoulder, as she elevated her beak, and sniffed the air.

" Davy would like a cake," said a voice from my pocket.

" Davy shall have a cake," said Bella, firmly, " even if his dear parrot has to fight for it."

When Joe said bakery, I expected to see a building. Then I thought how foolish I was. In this lovely climate, that was neither too hot nor too cold, they did not need the protection of a building. All that they did need, was a shelter to keep off the rain, and that they had in a great, wide canopy of •woven leaves.

Under this big green roof, scores of monkeys were running about.

" What are they doing? " I asked Joe.

" Mixing bread and cakes. They don't use yeast as bakers on earth do. They just take water."

" Hello, Soko," I said, as the old ape strolled to meet us. " I thought you were with the

Widow."

He grinned at me. " I am taking a rest, and watching my relatives work. I got Her Necromancy to go and hypnotise the Widow, and sent a lion with her to watch the fierce woman while she slept. He was dreadfully afraid of her switch, but I told him to roar gently if she ran at him, and of course Her Necromancy would settle her, before she could give him a cut."

" Ha, ha," laughed Bella, " I'd giggle if Miss Pussy wasn't a match for the Widow."

For an instant Soko looked startled; then he grew calm again, and shrugging his big shoulders, said, " She is a terrible woman. She gave one of my nephews such a cut that he can't use his hand for picking spices to-day."

"A terrible woman," repeated Bella. "She'd have caught this poor parrot, if Bella hadn't had wings."

" Do you spice your bread, Joe ? " I inquired.

" No, only the cakes," and he went on giving me ,. more information about bread-making, but my eyes | got ahead of my ears, and I could not listen.

There was a regular monkey parliament going on

under the trees. They were just chewing the air for all they were worth. Such jabbering and chattering, such rushing and hurrying, such a wagging of floury heads and floury paws.

" This is all whole wheat," said Joe. " We animals are more sensible than human beings, who mostly discard the best part of the flour."

" Where did you get the pots and pans, or whatever they are ? " I asked, looking at the big things in which the monkeys were mixing their dough.

" They are all wooden. We fell trees, and make them."

" Have you axes and hatchets? "

" We have very little that we cannot make ourselves. The beavers from the swamp near my house cut down the trees, and partly hollow these big, wooden bowls. The monkeys then take them, and use shell and stone knives. It is slow work, but they get done in time."

Joe and I walked on past the workers. They were all glad to see us, and every one would stop his work to thrust out a floury paw. They mostly worked in threes. One monkey would bring a bowl of the ground wheat, and would empty it into another bowl. A second monkey would begin to pour water on it from a gourd, while a third monkey would mix it.

They worked gaily and easily. They were not as intense as the gnawers out in the field.

" And how do you bake, Joe? " I asked.

" Come and see," he said, and passing by all the monkeys with their bowls of doug'h, we came to a place where there was an abrupt drop in the plain.

"Oh, my!" I said.

" Down below us was a kind of rocky basin, with pools of water and jets of steam.

" Geysers ? " I asked.

" Yes," replied Joe, " we have plenty of hot water there all the time, and fiery hot caves from the heat. Just come down. There is a safe path, but don't step to one side."

Rag, Bella, Davy, and I followed him. Rag and I on our own feet, Bella and Davy on my shoulders. This was very interesting. A few big monkeys were tiptoeing along the path ahead of us. Some carried big, round lumps of dough on slabs of wood, some had trays of small cakes, such as Billy loved.

" Wait a minute, boys," Joe called to the monkeys, " till we come up to you. I want Master Sam to see where you put the bread to cook."

A big ape stopped at the mouth of a cave.

"You don't let the little monkeys come down here? " I said, as we came up to him.

" No," he replied, gravely, " one day a hoolock fell in, and was terribly scalded."

"But he didn't die?"

" Oh, no, but we had a hard time to pull him out, and he had to suffer."

"AN ARMY OF PIGS AND BOARS

Then one can suffer in Paradise?" PB"Yes, in this Paradise, when one is foolish — see," and he rolled aside a rock from the mouth of a small-sized cave. " Put your hand in."

I put it in, but I didn't keep it there long.

" Come, Kula and Ranja," he said, and the other apes slipped their loaves and cakes into the hot cave.

The old ape put back the rock. " They will be baked in twenty minutes. Will you wait and have some?"

" Thank you, yes," I said. " What are you smiling at, Joe? "

" I want to show you our plough-boys," the dear old fellow said; "just step round the corner."

We edged our way round among the rocks, and went up a few steps cut in the side of the hill. Up above us was another field, this one, however, without grain in it, but newly ploughed.

" Come a little further," said Joe; then he began to smile again.

I stepped up beside him; then I held my breath. Out there in the sunshine, working up and down the hill, grubbing, snorting, pushing, and rooting, was an army of pigs and boars. One big fellow seemed to be boss, and kept moving around, prodding this one with his snout, grunting something in the ear of another one, and keeping things moving generally.

" Do you mean to say that your ploughing is all done this way ? " I asked Joe.

" Yes, boy, by pigs, and moles, and earthworms. The latter work as hard here as they do on earth at turning the soil over and over."

" Well, I never," I said, " you beat the Chinese for steady work."

" Now you will not think again of us as idle," said Joe.

" Never, old fellow," I replied, slapping him on the shoulder. " Here, pig, pig — "

I wanted to speak to one or two, but didn't the whole crowd turn? I saw their quivering snouts uplifted, the black earth clinging to them, their anxious, piggy, little eyes fastened on me. They wanted to pass the time of day with the earth-boy, but upon my word there were too many of them, and I turned and ran.

" Fm afraid you've offended them," said Joe, coming after me. " They're very clean pigs when they're dressed up. Of course they are in working garb now."

" Let them come call on me," I said, " when they are in dress suits, and we'll have a chat."

Joe's old muzzle was working. " Your cakes are coming out of the oven," he said, " I smell them."

CHAPTER XXI.

THE WIDOW AGAIN

The cakes were too hot to touch, but we all gathered round them and sniffed. Then we formed a procession back to the mixing-place.

" Please give me some of the nice, fresh cakes for Jess, the President's mother," called Bella, anxiously. " Here, you young crested sapajou, bring some fresh leaves and wrap a dozen in them," and she nipped the black tail of a young fellow, who was sitting watching us, with his eyes twinkling in the funny monkey way.

He ran and got the leaves, then Bella coolly asked ^me to put the package in my shirt front.

We all ate just as many cakes as we could manage, md I also took a piece of nice hot bread.

" No butter, Joe, I suppose."

" We never miss it," he said, " the flour is so sweet."

" Do you ever milk your cows, Joe? "

" No, the calves get the milk. They ought to have it. It makes them strong and well."

I thought of the Httle calves on earth crying for their mothers. " Joe," I said, " I wish every animal in North America could drop down dead and come here."

" It would be a great embarrassment to human ; beings if they should," said Joe. " Better let them | live, and have them kindly treated."

" But will people ever treat them kindly ? "

" You mustn't think of that, dear boy. Just go on trying to do all you can to make the world better. Every little helps, even though there is a great deal to be done. And animals are much better off than they used to be. Think of the state of affairs not a hundred years ago, when a kind-hearted nobleman, speaking on the rights of animals, in the House of Lords in England, was saluted with cries of insult and derision."

" England, oh, yes, I know that country," said a young ape near us, grinning over a cake that he was munching. " That is the country where ladies and gentlemen dress themselves up, and riding on big horses, chase a tiny hare or a fox to death. That is a lovely country, a beautiful country. I'd like to be a fox there, or a hare," and he took another bite, and grinned horribly.

" England is a fine country," said Joe, severely, " and much is done for animals there."

" And birdth," lisped a blue pigeon, perched on a heap of baskets near us. " I know an Englith-American pheathant. She tellth vewy thanguinary thtorieth."

" Good gracious! What's that? " I asked Joe.

" She means bloody tales," said Soko, abruptly. " Go on, pigeon."

" The Englith pheathant thays that birdth are raithed in parkth till they are vewy tame. Then they are thooed up in the air."

" Thooed," I repeated, " do talk straight, pidgie."

" Shooed, she means," said Soko.

" Thooed up in the air," continued the pigeon, "and gentlemen thoot them — bang, bang, bang! That ith fine thport, cauth the birdth are the tame, they don't want to fly away."

" The English are very fond of sport," said Joe, apologetically. " They are very brave."

" The pheathant thays," went on the pigeon, " that thome Americanth do thethe naughty thingth, too, and they chathe wabbits with dogth in courthing parkth. The wabbits are vewy much fwightened, and they wun, and the dogth pull them to piethes."

Joe sighed. " Well, Americans are mostly descended from English people. They have their bad ways, as well as their good ones."

" I wish I were king of the whole world," I said, angrily.

" It is a sad thing for us, and a good thing for yourself, that you are not, dear boy," said Joe. " Well, I was going to tell you some of the other erroneous ideas prevailing with regard to animals. It has been said that the life of a brute has no moral purpose."

"Moral purpose! I like that," muttered Soko.

The young monkeys were all laughing. I didn't see the joke, but when they went on choking, and spluttering, and thumping each other on the back, and winking, and cutting up generally, I asked Joe what it was all about.

" Jocko," he said, to one little fellow, who looked as if he had been led through life at the end of an organ-grinder's rope, as indeed he had, " tell the boy what amuses you."

The little monkey became grave, and stepping up to the President, bowed politely, and touched his head, as if he had a cap there.

" Please, Mr. President," he said, " we're brought up on morals. The old monkeys are always watching us, and tweaking us, and saying, ' Attend to your morals,' and 'Don't steal the cakes,' and 'Don't loaf,' and ' Don't run away,' and ' Don't tease the other animals.' We're jam full of morals, and it sounds funny to say we haven't got any."

Joe smiled. " Were you an honest little monkey in life. Jocko? Did you ever steal any of your master's pennies ? "

'* Never, Mr. President, and I knew, too, that they would buy juicy fruit. I liked my master, and I wouldn't steal from him."

" That will do," said Joe. " Mr. Sam — "

"Call me brother," I interrupted. "You all call each other that."

Joe's face beamed. " Well, then, brother Sam, I was going to tell you of a kind-hearted cardinal, who used to let busy little fleas bite him, because he said that he would have heaven to reward him for his sufferings, while the poor flea had nothing but the enjoyment of his present life."

"What a shabby flea, what a hateful flea!" squawked Bella. " Why didn't he tell the good cardinal about the Island of Brotherly Love?"

" He was a European flea," said Soko, " an aristocratic flea, and more reserved in his ways than we animals who are brought up in America."

" Some of us might imitate European animals in that respect," observed Joe. " A good many of us have very little repose of manner."

Bella giggled, and turning to Joe, I asked, " What do fleas eat here? You don't let them bite you, I suppose ? "

" They don't want to," replied Joe. " I offered a bite of myself to a homesick one just arrived from earth the other day, but he said I didn't taste nice. He'd lost his relish for his former diet. But

it cured his homesickness, and he took to a vegetable diet at once. Brother Sam, here is a doctrine once propounded on earth by a man called Descartes. He said that the lower animals were devoid of consciousness and feeling — "

A groan rose from the animals around us.

" Why, he was worse than the cardinal," said one sharp-faced monkey. " He didn't give us any life at all — neither in the world nor out of it."

" Another Frenchman called Voltaire made fun of him," continued Joe. " He suggested that the animals' exquisite organs of feeling had been given to them, just in order that they might not feel."

" Joe," said Soko, " that mischievous theory of want of sensation is at the root of much of the ill-treatment of animals."

" Exactly," said Joe. " Animals are animated machines to many good-natured persons. A child bumps his head against a chair. ' Naughty chair, strike it,' says the mother. The same child squeezes the cat half to death. The cat scratches. * Naughty cat,' says the mother, * strike it.' "

Soko replied to him. I heard long words — " experimental torture, analytical methods, scientists and naturalists, humanitarianism, emancipation, freedom of choice," and not understanding half of what the two clever old fellows were saying, I turned away. I was very ignorant, and my creed was short —

" There's an animal, treat him well. If a boy kicks him, lick the boy."

"Turn a few handsprings, will you?" I said to a brace of squirrel monkeys.

Off they went, in among the cakes and the dough bowls and the heaps of baskets. It was great fun. We all gathered round, and cheered, and laughed, till a sad event took place. My brace of imps rolled into a bowl of dough. Such a sight as they were! They skedaddled, and two old apes caught up sticks and went after them.

" Don't wallop them," I screamed, " it was my

fault."

He"s my adopted child, that golden brown
fellow," called back one of the apes. " I have to
cuff him a bit, for I want to make a good monkey
of him."

In the twinkling of an eye, they were all out of sight over the hill, and looking round for
some new thing, I discovered the big American condor that had taken part in the game of
Prisoner the day before.

He was away up in the air over us, but when I called, " Hello, old fellow, come down,"
he brought his huge old body down to the ground, and ate a sweet cake.

" You are big," I said, lolling up against his dark side, " I should like to have a ride on
your back."

" Come up in the air with me," he said, with a good-natured, hissing laugh. " I believe I
could carry you."

" Joe," I called out, " may I go for a ride on the condor's back ? "

" Well, he's pretty big," said the dear old fellow, leaving Soko, and coming toward me,
"but I scarcely think he could carry you, nor would I allow you to go with him."

" I want to make a tour of the Island," I said. " I am sure there are many wonderful things
I have not seen."

" You shall, boy, you shall," said Joe, " but I am afraid you might slip from the back of
the condor. We must have something more safe for you. How would you like an ostrich? "

" Finely; I once rode in a little ostrich cart."

" I tell you what you'd better do," said Soko, strolling up. " Let us have some races. The
animal that beats shall have the honour of carrying the boy round the Island. Birds not in it. We
mustn't trust him up in the air, except in an air-ship."

" Good," cried Joe. " You are fertile in plans, Soko. Will you kindly arrange details of
the race."

" Certainly, Mr. President," said Soko, with a smile, and he at once moved off in a
dignified way.

Joe looked affectionately after him. " There goes the animal that will be made President
when I am gone."

" How do you know, Joe ? "

" I feel it. No one has said a word, but he is best fitted for the position."

" It will be great, to have some races," I said.

" We have some swift runners here," replied Joe. *' We must send word round the Island,
and gather them all in."

" Joe, you must not leave before I do," I said, sharply.

" I must go when I am sent for, dear boy, but although I wish it to be soon, yet, for your
sake, I am willing to wait."

" Good Joe — and I am keeping you from home all this time. Let us go now."

" I am glad to be here, brother. I like to go round the Island every little while."

" How nice and respectful the animals are with you, Joe. Friendly, but not familiar."

" They are like human beings. They like to choose one of their own number to put over
themselves, and in doing him honour, they honour themselves — Bella, will you fly away and
see where Jumbo is? "

Bella flew off, but soon came back. " He is behind the bakery stuffing himself with cakes. Dear me, I'd be quite worn out if I had a trunk, and a chest of drawers, and a wardrobe, and a few extra rooms to fill with food. It keeps me busy to supply my own little stomach."

" Don't be vulgar, Bella," said Davy, properly.

" Vulgar! " she screamed. " You horrid little rat, I vulgar ? — I, the queen of the Island, the belle, the beauty, the dainty, delicate Bella? Oh, just come off that boy's shoulder for one minute, for a second, Davy, for half a second. Come now for one quarter — "

" Bella, hush up," I said, " you are vulgar when you scream."

" I sha'n't go home with you," she said, in a passion. " I'll not travel with such a low-down, correcting, uncomfortable rat, such a mock-modest rat, and with such a conceited, confusing boy. Goodbye, animals, Bella's going."

" Good riddance!" I said, wickedly, and she steamed aw^ay.

Our ride back was quiet. We heard the goat singing somewhere in the forest.

" A hunk of bread, a brook of drink, and me Running, and prancing, and singing diddle-dee, Oh, this is glorious ! Oh, this is bliss! How could a goat poetic find this Island aught amiss? "

However, he did not come near us, and we wei thankful. Jumbo put Joe down near his home, the carried me on to my own quarters.

" I will let you know about the races as soon we can arrange for them," were Joe's last words.

" It's a great mark of kindness in Joe to let yc

have races," remarked Jumbo, as we jogged along home.

"Why? He doesn't think that there is any harm in them, does he? "

*' Not the way we run them on this Island. But he is descended from the Puritan dogs, and you know that they growl at some things that other animals swallow whole."

" Jumbo," I said, when I reached my cabin, " don't go home. I like you. Can't you stay right here while I'm on the Island?"

His huge old frame just shook with pleasure. " I'd love to, dear boy. I come every night when you're asleep, but there's a good deal of me. Won't I be in your way? "

" No, Jumbo, lie right down under the trees. Be my elephant till I go."

" I'll be your elephant in the World of the Blessed, Master Sam," he said.

" Ah, now. Jumbo, you'll be looking for the young New Yorkers. You'll have no eyes for me."

" I knew some fine children there," he said, gravely.

. *' Tell me about them, Jumbo," and as he folded his legs and lay down, I sat astride his head, rubbing his old ears and listening to tales of the boys and girls of the Empire State.

While he talked and I listened, I at the same time

kept one eye on Rag and two or three monkeys, who were bustling about straightening my rooms out, and looking up something for dinner.

By and by Rag came and told me the meal was ready.

" I don't want anything," I said, " I'm chock full of cakes. Go on, Jumbo."

The old fellow prosed on, till my fiddling with his ears put him to sleep. Then I fell asleep, too, and only waked up when something went, ** Squawk! Squawk! " in my ear.

My eyes flew open with a jerk, and for an instant all was blue before me. Then my surroundings took on their natural colour, and the blue narrowed down to a jay, who hopped to my knee and looked fearlessly up into my face.

" I am from the President," he said. " I am directed to tell you, first of all, that the latest report from the wireless telegraphers is that your mother is well and not anxious."

" Good," I cried out.

" She is still watching by your false body," continued the jay, " and she believes what the doctor tells her, that you will soon wake out of your sleep. Therefore, the President says, you can stay on without fear of causing her undue anxiety."

" Good again," I said, " and I wish you'd just get a * Thank you' to those bird telegraphers for being so attentive with messages from home."

i

" Very well," squawked the jay in his funny voice; then he went on, " And I was also going to have a little talk with you about the races."

" Splendid," I was just saying, when I stopped and listened.

All the animals and birds about me were pricking up their ears. I didn't hear anything for a few seconds, then I caught on to a murmur in the forest, louder than its usual murmur, and presently a sound of animals running, and birds flying.

" What's up? " I said, and the jay, lifting up his nutmeg-grater voice, screamed suddenly to a cardinal-bird, coming like a streak of flame out of the forest, " Brother, what's up? "

" It's the Widow," wailed the cardinal-bird, in his rich, rolling note.

Just then the magnificent racer Palo Alto trotted up to my cabin.

" Master Sam," he said, " the Widow has broken loose again, and her face is turned this way. Don't you think you'd better get on my back? I'm the best runner on the Island, and I'd die before I'd let her catch me."

" Thank you, I believe I will," I said, and I sprang up from the ground.

CHAPTER XXII.

THE RESCUE OF THE CAT

"Can you ride?" asked Palo Alto, anxiously. " I was brought up in a stable where a whip was never used, and if the Widow shakes that switch at me, I'll be apt to get nervous and run pretty fast."

" Well, rather," I said, swinging myself up on his bare back. " I've got one of the finest ponies in San Francisco."

" You're all right," said Palo Alto, looking over his shoulder. " Now shall we start ? "

" Beg pardon, Bluejay," I said to the bird. " You were going to talk to me some more. Just keep me in sight, and after this excitement, we'll finish talking."

" Yes, sir," said the jay, harshly, and off we started, Palo Alto packing me on his back, and Rag and Jumbo running beside us.

" Jumbo," I said, " you're not afraid of the Widow?"

" No, Master Sam. I'll curl up my trunk, and 266

gjie Mtutut of tt|t eat 267

if it amuses her she can beat me all she likes. I won't feel it."

" She stuck a pin into Soko this morning," chattered the jay, " a long- pin that she took out of that grimy old bonnet of hers."

Jumbo looked anxious. " I'll have to trunk her, then, if she comes near me."

" How would you do it, old fellow ? " I asked.

" Oh, just take her gently round the waist, and wave her up and down in the air. That always has a quieting effect. No creature likes to be lifted off its legs. It makes a bird crazy to clasp it by the wings. I won't hurt the Widow, Master Sam."

" I'm not afraid of you, Jumbo," I said. " Blue-jay, who is to take her back to earth? "

" Soko," said the jay, glibly, " great, strong Soko. He's been getting his wife to massage his arms. Joe won't trust the Widow with any one but Soko. You see she is a mortal and precious, though she is so bad — there she is, boys."

Palo Alto stopped so suddenly that I almost lost my seat.

It was a funny sight. The Widow, worn out by her labours early in the morning, had had a beautiful nap, but it was over now, and she was on deck with her switch.

Her deck was a kind of cubby-hole between two sand-hills, with green shrubs growing up behind it.

making it lcx>k something like a nice, little flowery cave.

She kept sticking her head in and out this cubbyhole every other minute, staring up and down the beach, and shaking her switch at a little black thing lying on the sand before her.

Away as far as we could see, was a half-circle of animals, all frightened to go near, yet all so interested that they could not keep away. They acted just like people on earth who hang about a place where anything horrible or funny has happened.

The trees were black with birds, and presently a white gull swooped down to us.

" Hello, Master Sam. I'm a San Francisco bird. Don't you remember you used to feed me going over to Oakland in the ferry-boats ? "

" Did I, old fellow? Weil, I'm glad to see you," I said.

He perched on Palo Alto's back for a minute. "Isn't this dreadful?"

"Isn't what dreadful?" I asked.

" The Widow — hush, speak low, or she will hear you. Palo Alto, really I think you ought to skirt those palms, and take the boy round to the other animals. If the Widow made a rush, she might close round him here."

I began to laugh. " You are all mighty afraid of her. W^hy don't you circle round her, and take her switch away ? "

gfie iSitutnt of ti^e eat 269

" You see she is a human being," said the gull, hoarsely, " and we're all afraid of hurting her."

" Then why don't you get the Cat to hypnotise her ? You were speaking of it — some of you."

" The Cat," exclaimed the gull, " we did get her, but the Widow has hypnotised the Cat."

I was struck all of a heap. Hypnotised the Cat — that clever Cat — " Why, that isn't Pussy lying in that lump on the sand? " I cried.

" That is Pussy," said the gull, mournfully. " We are all talking of a rescue, but what can we do when the Widow is mounting guard like a soldier?"

" How did she do it? " I gasped.

Pi " Well," said the gull, sadly, " when we sent for Her Necromancy, she came. She looked fixedly at the Widow. She waved her paw once — no good — twice — no good; then up to twenty times. The Widow just stared at her, then she began to move her switch. Poor Pussy fixed her eyes on it, and was lost. She fell in a heap, and has been lying there ever since."

I was dumfounded, and before I could get my breath, we heard a pitiful, little voice at our feet. " Oh, please, some one rescue my mistress, my dear mistress."

I looked down, and there was the mouse. " Lift her up here, gull," I said, then I tried to comfort her.

" Brace up, mousie/' I said, but she only shook her head. Her pink eyes were full of tears. "I — I'm so unhappy," she said. " I'm afraid my dear mistress is suffering. She liked you. Master

Sam. Oh, please drive the Widow away, so I can get to the body of my dear mistress."

" I'll get Pussy, or I'll die in the attempt," I said. *^ Come, mousie, I'll be a knight like those of old, and you shall be my token," and I slipped her in my shirt front. Then I said, " Palo Alto, have you got the nerve to rush by the Widow and attract her attention, while Gull here seizes the Cat in his talons?"

All the animals and birds within reach of my voice began to snicker.

" Oh, botheration, I forgot," I said, " gulls are web-footed. Here, you golden eagle, come out of that tree, you have talons fast enough. Can you seize Pussy without hurting her ? "

" Yes," he whimpered, " if I go easy, but I've got seven little ones all depending on me, and if that dreadful woman gives me a crack across the eyes with her switch, I won't be able to find food for my nestlings."

" Oh, you .old coward," I said, " I'll feed your young ones. Come on — California to the rescue! Here, jay, you fly away and flap your wings in the Widow's face, and yell murder in her ear as we go by. Courage, Palo Alto! "

The dandy racer was trembling all over, and I must say I was kind of frightened myself. There was something so whirlwindy and earthquaky about the Widow, and her arm was like a steam-hammer.

" One to make ready," I whispered. " Jumbo, trumpet for all you are worth, and rattle her when we get near, and just break off a limb of that gum-tree. I'll shake it in her face as we dash by — Palo Alto, your goal is the semicircle of animals yonder. Now — two to prepare, three and we dare — "

We were off — I soon dropped my gum-tree branch, and held both hands tangled up in Palo Alto's mane. His feet just seemed to gently scratch the earth, his back was alive. His old chest heaved when we got near the Widow, and his eyes stared.

She was the only cool thing about. The sun was beaming, the breakers thundering, the animals roaring. They all appreciated what we were trying to do for Miss Pussy.

Well, that Widow was a caution. She rattled the jay so, by leaping up in the air and cutting at him with her switch, that he only gave one feeble squawk and scuttled away.

The eagle did better. He lighted beside Pussy, and just as we steamed up to the Widow, he tried to raise the unconscious Cat. She was, however, heavier than he thought, and the Widow came down on him like a thousand of bricks.

He gave one noisy yell, and mounted in the air.

"Palo Alto," I said, " stop! —wheel! "

The beauty did as I told him. " Can you face that music again? " I asked, just throwing the words at him.

" Yes," he breathed, " if you do it quick."

" Come on, then," I shouted. " Here, eagle, snatch the Widow's bonnet, and we'll see to Pussy."

The eagle, who was circling round in the air, did as I told him. He lighted on the bonnet and tugged at it, with the Widow whipping his legs, while Palo Alto and I dashed up to the Cat.

" Seize her in your teeth," I said; " very gently, boy — now, fly for it."

He did fly — oh, this was fun! — much better fun than the tiger-in-the-marsh affair.

He held Pussy just as gently as he could with his powerful teeth, and, in the twinkling of an eye, he had laid her down on the wet sand in the midst oi the crowd of animals.

They all pressed round her. " Stand back! giv< her air! " I cried. " Bring some fresh water, som(one."

Jumbo squirted a little from his trunk on her! " Now, Pussy, wake up," I said; " wake up. One^ mortal put you to sleep, another says for you to rouse yourself. Wake, I say," and I shook her gently.

A very aristocratic-looking macaw flew to my

"PALO ALTO AND I DASHED UP TO THE CAT

loulder. " When my dear mistress on earth used
have hysterics," he said, " nothing would bring iier to but for the doctor to say, * Well, there is no lelp for it, we must cut off all her beautiful hair,
id put ice on her head.' "

I looked at him. Then I said, addressing the mimals, " You see that there is no help for it, we lust shave Pussy. Give me some of your stone knives."

" There, you see she does not move," I went on to the macaw. " This is genuine. Our friend, the Widow, has hypnotised her. Here, you, orangoutang, take her very carefully, and put her on the bed in my cabin. She will come to in time."

" Must I stay and watch her ? " he asked, anxiously.

" No, come back and see the fun. Mousie here will stay with her mistress. I will soon be home. You'll go, won't you, mousie?"

" Indeed I will," she exclaimed, her little face in a smile as broad as she could make it. " Oh, I am so glad to get my dear mistress, my darling mistress. Let me on your shoulder, orang-outang?"

" Go through the woods to avoid the Widow," I called after the big ape.

" No fear of my not doing that," he cried, looking over his shoulder, and off he went with big strides, yet sometimes glancing behind, for a cry had been raised, " The President! the President! "

CHAPTER XXIII.

THE ROUT OF THE ANIMALS

Dear old Joe was indeed coming, his face all in a wrinkle.

After him trotted Jess, the pups, Malta^ Toby, Brisk, Jenkins's former cows, with Fleetfoot, carrying Davy and Bella on his back.

" This bringing of mortals to the Island is a complicated business; I must stop it," said Joe, anxiously. Then he addressed the crowd: " Brothers, I have no power to subdue the Widow, except that of brute force. We must gently crowd her to the air-ship. Is it ready?"

" Yes, sir," exclaimed a hundred voices. " It is over behind the Hill of Arrival."

" Bring it round the Point," said Joe, " and have it all ready for starting. We will get the Widow in, and then it must leave immediately for earth. Where is Soko?"

" With the air-ship, sir."

"Let him remain with it. Jumbo, you marshal the elephants in front of those blue gums. Central

Park, you go with them. Bengal, you and the panthers, zebras, leopards, hyenas, and other wild animals, except the bears, station yourselves directly behind the Widow. Close in on her, and try to drive her gently toward the apes and monkeys, who will surround her in an inner ring, and always gently, tnind you, urge her toward the air-ship. I want the bears to be in the front row of this inner circle, because they have weight, but mind, bears, do not be aggressive. Be kind but persistent, and, no matter how provoking the Widow is, you are on no account to hug her."

Joe broke off, and thought deeply for a few minutes. Then he asked: " Has the Widow eaten anything to-day ? "

" No, sir," said a hyena, showing his teeth, * that's why she's so cross."

Joe sighed. " And I dare say she*s tired, as well IS hungry. Jumbo, how would it do for you to seize ler by your trunk and lift her to your back ? "

" I'd do it, sir, in a minute," said Jumbo, anx-ously, " if she wouldn't stick a pin in my trunk. If)he did, I might get crazy, and step on her."

" Did you know Mike McGarvie was dead ? '* jvhispered the Central Park elephant, putting his lead down to mine.

" Yes," I whispered back.

" I'm not going to take any part in this," he said,

with a glance toward the Widow. " Maybe the Widow is some relation to Mike. Good-bye, boy, I'm thinking of my keeper all the time," and he tramped off to the woods.

" Let all the birds gently swoop down over our guest, and drive her on," old Joe was continuing in his deep voice, " and the farm animals, the horses, cattle, sheep, pigs, goats, calves, and so on, will march round that belt of trees, get between her and the woods, and, seconding the wild beasts, will firmly press down this way toward the air-ship. There is no need of closing retreat to the sea. She would not want to wet her feet."

Joe had spoken, but there were a great many details to arrange. Who were to lead the various divisions, and who was to decide upon cases where animals did not wish to be separated.

" YouVe classed me with the wild animals, sir," said old Grayskull, coming up to Joe, " and little Billy with the domestic ones, but we're not used to being separated. I'd like to have little Billy with me. If the Widow got at him, I'd like to be near."

" Well, Grayskull," said Joe, kindly, " you and Billy run with the goats."

" If little Billy could go with me, sir, Stars-and-Stripes says she would take him on her back, while I ran alongside and told her which way to go. Her back's better than mine."

" I should think it is," I said, and I looked at old smirking Stars-and-Stripes, — an enormous leopard, with a back like a sofa.

t" Very well," said Joe, and it was as good as a ay to see Stars-and-Stripes start off, little Billy ith his soulful eyes balancing himself on her back. The apes and monkeys didn't like their leader. Oh, yes, Ponto's a good ape," they said to Joe, " but he's apt to get rattled. We'd rather have Bunker Hill."

Ponto stood looking on with a silly smile. " Yes, Joe," he said, " I'm easy shaken. I'd rather have Bunker Hill."

Bunker Hill, who appeared to be as solemn and steady as the monument, came near, and at a word from Joe, walked off with his detachment.

" Poor soldiers, going off to war without any arms," I said. " The Widow has the only weapon on the beach."

Joe looked more worried. " Jess, you stay with me," he said. " Now let us go up on that sand-hill and watch the affair."

I tried not to laugh, for Joe was dead serious. However, at last I had to get behind him and snicker. The walk of his soldiers was the funniest thing. There was no " Up, guards, and at her! " about them. They were all beaten before they began. Well, first the wild animals ranged into line. It didn't take long to rout them.

The Widow just charged up the sand-banks with her bonnet-pin and her switch; then there was nothing but squeals and tails. You see, they were handicapped. They couldn't hurt her. However, they could form again, and when she descended to her shrub cave, the lions, and panthers, and wolves, and tigers, and poor little Billy tumbling from the leopard's back, and limping beside Grayskull, formed in another row, but this time further back among the tree-trunks, where Joe had intended them to go.

The elephants never budged. They stood like rocks, but then the Widow took no notice of them, beyond throwing a few stones and trying to hit their small eyes, a thing she couldn't have done in a hundred years, for I never saw a girl or a woman yet that could throw a stone straight. They just shut their eyes, and curled up their trunks, and they were in a fortress.

Well, the fun began when the monkeys came tiptoeing down the beach. Some were on their hind legs, some on their fore legs. Old Bunker Hill marched in front with a banana skin hanging out of his mouth. I don't know what his idea was in chewing it, unless it was to terrify the Widow. It certainly didn't improve his looks.

Behind his troop of monkeys, little and big, marched the farmyard battalions — such an army of !• them. A red bull was leading them, and was |

i

making awful sounds away down in his throat to give himself courage. A dark cloud of birds hovered over the monkeys and farm animals. When Bunker Hill came within a few rods of the Widow, who was saying nothing, but just resting easily on her switch and bonnet-pin, he stopped and put up his paw.

It must have been an agreed signal, for the most awful uproar burst forth. It deafened us where we stood, and the Widow was much nearer.

However, she was plucky. She just stood out, settled the dirty cuffs of her wrapper, fixed her bonnet, and waved her stick.

Then they tried their gently crowding business. For a few minutes we saw nothing but dust, and feet going round and round, with a red wrapper in the middle.

" Fm afraid it's the Widow that's doing the crowding, Joe," I said.

" Oh, I hope my pups are in the rear," said Jess, in distress. " If she hurts one of those pups, I shall want to bite her."

"Don't be afraid, Mother," said Joe. "Look there," and he pointed to six specks in the far distance, scuttling in and out the breakers, and making a wild dash for home.

"Oh, I'm so thankful," said Jess, "so thankful. My darling pups, I must run after them, and see if they are hurt."

" Mother, there are other pups in the skirmish," said Joe; "some who have not a mother."

She did not hear him.

" Joe," I said, " we've been beaten."

" I fear we have," he repHed, with a troubled air. " The monkeys are retreating."

At that instant, my friend, the jay, flew over our heads.

" Oh, it's fearful," he screamed, excitedly. " That lady seems to have as many legs and arms as a centipede. Bunker Hill's face is laid open, Ponto's wrist is dislocated, and no end of sheep have their eyes closed. They got frightened and tried to run home, but instead they ran right up to the Widow. The ram Portland has his fleece covered with red spots. Whenever the Widow has nothing else to do, she runs her bonnet-pin into him as if he were a pincushion, and he trots round and round her as if she were a fence post. I tried to show him a way out, but he couldn't understand. Oh, it's fearful! " and he flew away.

" Blue jay is a great exaggerator," muttered Joe.

" The wild beasts are out of it, though," I said. " They are breaking, breaking. The farm animals can't get away. Law me, she's after the goats — poor goats! "

" Apes and monkeys," cried Joe, loudly, and he ran to meet a flying group coming toward us, " run

|» gi^e Mont of tfie ^nlm^ln asi

^Kthe desert, scour the wood. Find the goat, and ^Kng him here."

1^" He won't come, sir," said a big chimpanzee, whose eyes were half starting from his head.

" Force him to come," said Joe. " Quick, quick, don't you see how your brothers the farm animals are being hurt? "

The apes ran away, thankful to turn their backs on the rout.

Other fleeing animals kept arriving. A hyena, with his lips curled back over his teeth, said: " It's no use, sir, she's bewitched. Poor Billy is laid out, his back is 'most broken. The wolf is up among the japonicas licking him."

" Go back," said Joe, " gather your brothers, try to surround the farm animals and press them away. The Widow is simply torturing them. As soon as you accomplish this, I will try to entice her here by means of the goat."

The hyena turned and went back, but not as fast as he had come.

Presently we saw him rallying the dispersing wild animals, who formed a wedge, and with lowered heads slipped in between the Widow and the unfortunate domestic creatures. We saw the hyena take the ram by the ear, and pull him out of the crowd, then pell-mell, higgledy-piggledy, hurly-burly, the animals came galloping in a disordered mass down the beach.

" She's a regular Napoleon," said Joe, " just loot at her."

As cool as a cucumber, she was sitting down, taking off her carpet slippers, and shaking the sand oul of them. Then she fanned herself with her apron, and stared out at sea.

Joe looked round on the panting, heaving crowd. " Did any one tell her that we wished to put her ini an air-ship to take her home? "

" Yes, sir," said a shout of voices, " and she said I she'd air us, and ship us, and wreck us, till therej wasn't anything left."

"Where is Bunker Hill?" asked Joe.

" Gone home, sir. His face doesn't look pretty. He says he believes in letting women have their own way."

Joe sighed. " Well, lie down, all of you, and rest yourselves. We may have to make another attack."

He walked up and down restlessly, until there was a great bawling heard in the distance.

The apes were dragging the goat along, and he didn't want to come.

" Oh, mercy, mercy, mercy, sirs," we heard him cry.

" My heart it beats, it stops, it stirs, My mistress will my flesh annoy. My liberty's my only joy."

■

I

gfie JSiout of tfft Mnimulu 283

" Come on," we heard the apes say, " and stop that back scratching. It's no good — the President wants you."

" The President wants me! " the simpleton called,

" The humblest beast, That on this Island makes a feast. You surely are mistaken friends, You wish to serve some low-down ends."

*' No, we don't," said the apes. *' Come on," and they dragged him to the President. The goat fell on his knees before Joe.

" Oh, hide me, hide me, hide me, sire, I fear my mistress' dreadful ire. She'll pick my flesh from off my bones, She'll throw my remnants on those stones.'*

" Yes, she'll hide you," said Rag, " you needn't bother the President."

The goat was crying.

" Jerry, I thought your tears were over," said Joe, sternly.

" I-I-Fm just like human beings, Mr. President," blubbered the goat. " I-I cry for things I haven't got, and when I get them, I cry because I have. Let me run back to the desert, the sweet desert. It's very lovely and lonely there."

" Jerry," said Joe, " you once liked your mistress. Now do her a kindness. You needn't let her catch

you, but just go over there a little way. Show yourself, and such is her attachment for you, that I have no doubt she will come running this way, so that we can coax her into the air-ship. By the way, has it come round the Point ? "

" Yes, sir," said the golden eagle, who was sitting on Jumbo's back, " it's close by, behind the magnolias."

" I didn't want her to see Soko till the last moment," said Joe, " for, unfortunately, she has taken a prejudice against him. Now, Jerry, start."

" I won't," said the goat.

" Come, that's treachery to the State," said a rhinoceros, prodding him with his horn.

" Hold your tongue," said Jerry.

" Seize him, apes," said Joe, " walk him down the beach toward the Widow. If she sallies out, don't loose him, but guide him this way."

The apes and the goat began their cake-walk, and in spite of the solemnity of the occasion, we all burst into a roar of laughter.

Such cross-legging it, such nipping and pinching, such cries from the goat, and butts, such beautiful butts — there was an ape bowled over on his back all the time.

There were four apes, and they had a great time to find holding places. There wasn't much of a tail, there wasn't much of a beard, for it had got thin

^vom wagging and crying, his ears didn't amount to ^Huch, his horns were small and broken, and he had ^aTpoor, wiry crop of hair. However, the apes managed to hang on, and after a time the Widow began to prick up her ears.

Then she hailed them. " Hello, is that me goat you're bringin' to me, me own sweet goat that loves me so. Just bring him, just let me love him. Oh, me beautiful, friendly goat," and she rose and clutched her switch and her bonnet-pin.

The goat's struggles were awful, and one time, he had all the four apes down on the sand.

However, they were good wrestlers, and they hauled him further. When they got quite near the Widow, and saw that she was crouched for a spring, they suddenly turned his head, and started off toward us.

The Widow gave chase, and they let her come near enough to give the poor goat one clout. Then they let him run.

There was an awful consternation among the animals, and Joe was afraid there would be a stampede, and they would get hurt.

" Turn tail, everybody," he said. " Turn your heads from her. A few cuts behind won't hurt you. ni confront her."

This was noble in the President, and a low roar of applause went round.

Then the goat came dashing in, pressed among the animals, and hid himself in the thickest of them, between the knees of a giraffe with a rampart of elephants behind him.

Joe stood right out in front of the crush, and Rag and I stood beside him.

" Madam," he said, when the red cyclone hauled up in front of us, " what do you wish? "

" I'd thank ye for me goat, ye low-down, impident beggar of a dog," she said, shaking the switch at him.

"Very well, madam, go get him," said Joe, politely stepping aside.

The Widow drew back. She didn't want to get into that press of animals.

" Bring him out," she said, waving her switch, " bring him out, or I'll be the death of some of yees."

It was fun to see the animals trying to look at her. They had all done as Joe said, and turned their backs to her, but they were dying to see what was going on, and couldn't help turning and twisting their heads and shoulders.

" Madam," began Joe, but he got no further. That dreadful woman was clipping him over the legs with her switch.

I was sorry for Joe. Only that morning he had been thinking such deep thoughts about the World of the Blessed, and now he was being cut over the legs just like a common dog.

m

gfir JSiont of ttie Mnimalu 287

He was very forgiving about it. " Madam," he said, " we wish you well. You do not understand us. I should like to see you eat and drink something. You act so disturbed that I think you must be hungry."

" I'll drink you, I'll eat you," she screamed, and she sprang at the whole three of us.

" Run, Joe," I said, " we can't strike her, as she as a woman."

i The old dog didn't lose his head, and trying to get j round the crowd of animals, headed for the air-ship, [hoping that she would follow us.

Unfortunately, the others didn't understand him. Like crazy creatures, they broke for shelter, and x>lted toward the woods.

The Widow had a beautiful time. She was right hmong us. On account of numbers, no one could -un very fast, and she could skip here, there, and everywhere, pinning and switching, touching up a ion, a donkey, a sheep, a calf, a fox, a wolf, a horse,)r a slow-going cow. Some of the animals vowed :hat she rode for some distance on the back of a iger, but I didn't see that.

I couldn't see much that was going on, for some >f those blessed animals, in spite of their fright, re-nembered me, and kept a close guard round me, md when we got a little free from the crowd, a mung Indian pony told me to spring on his back.

I did so, then I had time to look round. I just roared. Everywhere were animals with tails between their legs. Joe was riding off royally on the back of a lion into the depths of the wood. Our party followed him, and soon we were having a council of war in the depths of the forest.

It was a lovely place. I stooped down and took a drink from a little brook where there were rows of thirsty animals.

Joe sat on a bed of ferns. He panted for awhile, then he looked up at some crows who had followed us. " Go find out where she is now."

The crows flew away. Presently they came back screaming, " She's caught him."

"Him?" said Joe.

" Yes, the goat — she's taken off her apron, she's tied him to the string, she's dragging him toward that place on the beach where she was sitting. He's pleading for mercy, and she's grinning."

Joe got up, stopped panting, and looked desperate. "Oh, this is awful!"

" Can't you do something ? " I said, impatiently.

He stretched out his paw. " Be quiet a minute, please. I am thinking. Is there nothing that would terrify that woman? "

Suddenly he flung up his head. His face was calm and resolved. " Crows," he said, quickly, " I did not see a mouse in the late contest, did you ? "

K " Not one, sir," they all croaked, hoarsely.

" Fly to the other side of the Island, to Mouseville. Tell every mouse there to come to me as
speedily as possible. Tell them it is a case of
life and death — to come all, and leave only the
; young ones and the very old ones at home. Fly
i now! "

The crows set off without a sound. They were on business and would not chatter.

" What are you going to do now, Joe? " I asked, curiously.

" To prove whether she is a woman or a witch. If she is a real woman, she will be afraid of a mouse."

"Afraid of a mouse, Joe, when she wouldn't run from a lion? "

" You will see, my dear boy," said the good old fellow. " In the course of a long life, I remarked something that always struck me with surprise. There were good and bad women in the world. They didn't look alike, or think alike, or act alike. They had only one thing in common. Every single woman I ever saw would run from a mouse."

" That's funny," I said. " I know my mother is afraid of them, but I didn't know other women were."

" Just wait, my dear boy, you will see," and he sank back on the ferns.

CHAPTER XXIV.

THE CAPTAIN OF THE MOUSE BRIGADE

"Poor goat!" I said, "I wonder how he is getting on ? "

A carrier-pigeon obHgingly went to find out.

" He is down on his knees to the Widow," he said, when he flew back, " and she is telHng him how she is going to torture him when she gets rested."

" Wh\'7d^ doesn't he run away? "

" She has him tied to a rock."

" Poor goat! " I said again.

" She must not be allowed to torture him," said Joe, firmly. " Pigeon, you watch her. Call some of your brothers, and if she starts up to beat him, you must fly in her face and confuse her."

The pigeon shuddered. " She'll likely catch some of us, still, we're ready to help — But I don't think she'll begin yet, for she's pretty well tired out — and she's extravagant, too, in her language. She's telling the goat that she's going to push him in a well of boiling oil. Now, we haven't any such well on this Island, so how could she do it ? "

" She is a woman of great imagination," said Joe, but he looked uneasy, and turned his head toward Mouseville.

" In plain words, a story-teller," said Rag.

We all had a nice little rest before the mice came, but they weren't long in arriving. Such businesslike little animals! I was delighted with them.

The crows did their work well, for the first mice arrived on their backs. They flew low, and the mice held on their feathers with their tiny, sharp teeth.

" Now, Mr. President," said the first mouse to arrive, " what is your will ? "

I looked at him. He was just a common gray little fellow, but he was standing up to the President like an elephant.

" Captain," said Joe, " I want you to speed our parting guest. You have heard of her."

" The Widow, yes," said the mouse, briskly, " but we mice are busy people, you know. We have to do our work first, then play afterwards."

" Don't work too hard, Captain," said Joe. " You are getting very intense. Well, I want you to surround the Widow and urge her toward the air-ship by Point Expectation. Don't run up on her dress, or annoy her. Just firmly close round her, and head her toward the boat. You think she will mind you ? "

"Oh, bless you, Mr. President, yes," said the

mouse. " We can do anything with women. I don't need to wait for the rest of my connection to arrive, I can start with what I have," and he gazed round on the few hundreds of mice that had dropped in by dozens on the backs of larger animals or of birds of different kinds.

" Very well," said Joe, " shall I command, or will you?"

" 1*11 do it myself," said the mouse, sharply. " Here, tame mice, you white fellows, form on this side, single file. Halt! "

A thin, white line immediately drew out before him.

" Spotted half-breeds to the left," said the Captain. "Halt!"

The spotted line drew out, and then came the turn of the gray mousies.

" Gray mice, follow me," said the little Captain, " here, dog, you be Widow."

This to Rag, who looked rattled, and was aboi to slink among the ferns with his tail between legs.

"Stand still," squealed the Captain. " Noi gentlemen," and he addressed the mJce, " this whi^ dog is the Widow. Surround her in good styli urge her toward that bay yonder. Steady, march!

Rag acted like a simpleton, and shivered, as tl circle of tiny creatures, all with eyes shining, heac

lowered, and a fixed purpose in their eyes, dosed round him.

Then, not thinking of what he was doing, he slowly advanced.

" That will do," said the Captain. " Break ranks, follow me, snake fashion, not a head showing, not a tail raised."

Sure enough, they went off like little snakes through the moss and ferns.

Joe heaved a great sigh. " They'll accomplish their mission. I wish I had thought of them before. Now let us go watch the Widow. Don't show yourselves, brothers. She might charge us. I want the ! mice to stalk her."

We crept like another band of mice down through
I the forest to the edge of the beach. There were some
i thick clumps of shrubs here, and we posted ourselves
among them — Joe, Rag, I, Dandy, who had just
joined us, the Indian pony, and some foxes, wolves,
panthers, and monkeys.

The most of the farm animals had gone home. They were tired of being chased. Only the sharper ones remained with the wild animals, who were all intensely interested.

The Widow sat with her hands crossed over her knees, only turning once in awhile to threaten the goat, who was the silliest picture of distress that 1 ever saw.
;

The Widow remained for some time, now looking at the goat, now at the sea, till suddenly she gave a shriek, and drew in her feet.

" What is the matter, mistress ? " asked the goat, cringing to her.

** Matter — it's a mouse," she said, " as sure as I'm a living sinner. Yow — there's another! " and she skipped on to her feet,

Joe's face was radiant. " Poor woman, we'll get her home now, and we shall be happy, and she will be happy. Good little mice! "

" Rats! Murder! Help! " screamed the Widow, and now she was dancing up and down on the sand, holding the old red wrapper tight about her.

" Poor thing," said Joe, " I'm sorry to have her disturbed, but it won't last long — boys, boys — "

This was to Rag and Dandy, who were almost killing themselves laughing.

•* In whatsoever clime we be, Mirth springs from some one*s misery!"
said Jce, under his breath.

" Oh, law me, I'm dead! I'm killed! I'm m\ir\ dered before me own eyes — " yelled the WidoT " Help! help! " and didn't she throw one arm roun(Jerry's neck?

He looked like a ninny. He wasn't afraid of th< mice, and he didn't know how to help her. I gues

he didn't want to, for we suddenly heard him roar, " Untie that apron string."

" Oh, my! oh, me! oh, my, oh, me! " gasped the Widow, and her fingers trembled like leaves, but still she managed to untie the knots that she had made.

" Well, I'm blest if that goat isn't deserting her," said Dandy.

He was — he was running down the beach, shaking his head, and leaping for joy.

Nov/ the Widow was undone. She was carrying on a dreadful dance, and the mice were closing in on her. We could see them now. Their little heads were all up, and their tails were slipping about like tiny snakes.

"March, lady!" cried the little Captain mouse. *' Don't dance, march! "

" Tell her to drop her switch," called Joe, standing up and showing himself, " likewise her bonnet-pin."

The poor Widow, even in the height of her distress, had held on to her instruments of torture, but now she dropped them pretty quick.

** March, lady," said the mouse again, and he went closer. " Ouch! " she cried with a leap and a spring, and she went tearing up the beach with all the mice scuttling behind her.

They were splendid little soldiers, and as brave as lions. Though there was danger of their getting

stepped on in her wild springs, they formed a half-moon around her, and urged her on till they got close up to the air-ship.

We kept abreast of them under the trees, until they got to Point Expectation. Then, headed by Joe, we ran down to the beach.

The Widow had taken no pains to learn anything about the Island, still she had an idea that Joe had most authority, so when she saw him coming she screamed, " Call them off — the dirty-smelling beasts! "

Dandy curled his lip. " Smelling! — Just look at the clean little things. Not one of them would touch her ragged, untidy dress. Go home and put yourself into your tubs, Mrs. Washerwoman."

" Brothers," called the little mouse Captain, " wash yourselves."

In a trice, every small mouse was on his hind legs. His fore legs went like lightning over his face, ears, and back, and his little tongue licked so fast that I could not see it. Last of all, each tiny fellow took his tail under his arm, or his leg, and polished that off.

" Now my army is clean," said the mouse Captain, dryly, " if it wasn't clean before."

The Widow wasn't paying any attention to him. " I want to go home," she was shrieking. " I hate this nasty place. When does the next steamer call here, ye scalpeens ? "

" THEY FORMED A HALF-MOON AROUND HER, AND URGED HER ON "

" Madam, here is your air-ship," said Joe, running forward. " Captain, this way, please."

" And I'm not going up in the air again in no clothes basket," screamed the Widow, ** I sha'n't go one step," but even as she spoke, she had to go forward, for the Captain of the Mouse Brigade, in obedience to Joe's orders, was urging her on.

"Have you got any stones in your pockets?" asked Joe.

" None of your business, you unclean beast," she shrieked.

Captain Mouse approached her.

" Oh, keep your distance, keep your distance," she begged, " yes, here they be, I'll heave them out," and she threw out about a dozen good-sized stones.

" Step into the ship," said Joe.

At that instant, Soko, grinning at her antics, stuck his head out of the car.

She fell back when she saw him. " I'm not goin* with that dowdy reptile."

" Captain," said Joe.

The Widow went into the wicker car.

" Now, fly, sweet birds," called Soko, to Duke and her mate, as they sat watching from a rubber-tree.

Soko loved the swans, and always wanted them beside the air-ship.

The beauties spread their wings. Soko's young ape helped pull in the anchor, and they were off.

" Keep in the car," we heard Soko roar, " keep in the car, or you will fall into the water."

The Widow was fighting him. We could see her body half out of the car.

" Back, back to the Island," ordered Soko, then a rope came flying out, and we all clutched it.

Soko had the washerwoman by the arm when they came down, and he was breathing hard and fast. " I can do nothing with her, sir," he said to Joe. " You must let me have some mice."

" Will you go, Captain ? " asked Joe.

" Yes, sir," said the plucky little fellow, " and I'll take one of my sons. He's got an eye like a needle. Come, Corporal," and he jumped into the car.

" Murder!" bawled the Widow, crouching in a corner.

" Now, madam," said Soko, rubbing his arm, " every time you spring at me, I'll set a mouse on you. I won't molest you if you are good, but if you make any more of those cat springs, you know what to expect."

The Widow looked thoughtful, and didn't say anything.

Captain Mouse was sitting on his hind legs nibbling a morsel of cake he had found in the car. " She looks hungry," he said. " Give her something to eat."

" I sha'n't eat," piped the Widow, " ye'd poison me.

" Wouldn't do anything of the sort," said the Captain. " Give her a cake, Soko. If you don*t eat it, madam, I'll run over your ankles and tickle you."

She screeched, and held out her hand for the cake, and our last view of the Widow, was of a woman eating and drinking, and having a good time looking at the scenery.

" I'm glad she is afraid of the mice," said Joe, in satisfaction. " I was afraid she was a witch, and not a woman."

CHAPTER XXV.

TRANSPORTING THE ANARCHIST

Joe went home, and Rag, Dandy, Jumbo, Blue jay, and some other of my particular friends among the animals went with me to my cabin.

For awhile, we all sat on the grass, talking about the Widow and the mice, then at supper-time we had a lovely meal together, eating cakes and drinking brook water that the monkeys brought to us in gourds.

I could never get enough of those Island cakes. They weren't rich enough to hurt any one, and yet they were rich enough to make you feel glad that you were eating cake all the time.

I must not forget to say that we had some honey, too. Honey sent to me by some bees across the Island. It was made from wild thyme and orange-blossoms, and it was good, I can tell you.

Well, as we all sat there talking, and the dusk came on, a long trail of animals passed by. I think whenever it was possible they took a turn round my way, to say good night to me.

They nearly all had something to say about the races. Now that the Widow was gone, they were to be our next excitement.

" By the way, Bluejay," I said, " you were going to tell me about them, and we were interrupted."

" Well, I was only going to talk things over," he said, " and mention probable entries. I have nothing official to say. Soko was to attend to all that. I don't know who will take his place now that he has gone to the earth."

" The jay is a great gossip," said Dandy in my ear.

He and Rag were lying beside each other on the bank just above my head. I was so glad the two dogs had got to be like brothers. Now, Rag would not miss me so much when I went.

" Let's go over the list," said Bluejay. " First, there are the regular racing horses. I can tell you we have some here that made records on earth, and they can run even faster in this world."

" Don't forget the dogs, Jay," said Dandy, " the coursing dogs."

" Oh, yes, the greyhounds," said the Jay, carelessly. " They will want to enter, I suppose, but, of course, they are not big, and noble, and swift, like horses."

" Nor calm, and conservative, and reposeful in manner, and quiet, and conscientious, like bluejays," said Dandy, ironically.

The Jay went on quickly, " Then there are zebras, and deer, and ostriches."

" Wait a minute, Bluejay," I said, " Httle Steal-Away wants to speak to me," and I held up my hand to a small owl, with big, beautiful eyes that had perched near me.

She flew to my wrist. " Master Sam," she whispered, " they are going to ship the Anarchist this evening. Don't you want to see him go ? "

Steal-Away had a queer, ghostly little voice, and she kept looking over her shoulder, as if she expected some one to pounce on her.

I sprang up. " Boys, let's go to see the Anarchist."

The dogs sprang, too, and Jumbo, who was lying down, began to get up.

" Are you going on the word of that young night gossip ? " said the Jay, angrily.

" Brother," said the owl, mildly, " you'd better go home. Every jay has his day, and every owl has his prowl."

" Good for you, owlie," I said, patting her. " You're equal to the goat. Go home, friend jay, while you can still see to fly."

" May I come back in the morning? '* he asked.

" Yes, brother, come to breakfast," I said.

" Good night, friends," he chattered, and in quite good humour flew away, but had the misfortune to

bump his head against a tree branch, whereupon the owl laughed, softly.

" Brothers," I said, " is it true that I can see and hear better here than on earth, or do I only imagine it?"

" It is true," rumbled Jumbo. " Our senses, blunted on earth by toil, and care, and worry, and the dreadful noises of civilisation, are all quickened here — now don't you want to come up on my back, dear boy? Your young limbs must be tired of scampering away from that Widow."

" All right. Jumbo," I said, and he put his trunk round me, and swung me up.

" Master Sam," said Dandy, as he ran along by my side, "do you know we always take away bad animals by night ? " - "Do you," I said, "and why?" Wr " It makes such a scandal and such a commotion in the daytime," said Dandy, " and some of the animals fuss so — the ladies especially. Would you believe it, Master Sam, this Anarchist elephant has been as ugly right straight along as he was the day you came, yet some of the animals have been petting him, and sending him fruit and flowers and cake."

" To that old brute," I said, " that wanted to kill Joe?"

"Yes, to that brute — and do you know," and fie lowered his voice, " Jay says Jess sent something. I won't say ifs true, but the news has gone round."

" I don't believe she is so silly," I replied.

" No, she is not," said a deep voice near us.

It was Joe speaking, and Dandy slunk behind Jumbo.

"Jess is sorry for the elephant," Joe went on, "but she believes in the wholesome effect of discipline. When the elephant comes back from the Isle of Probation, my mother will be as kind to him as any one. Just now she is too much grieved and shocked at his wish to take my life, to do anything for him."

"But isn't that the highest nobility, Joe?" I said, "to do good to your enemies?"

" Yes, brother," replied Joe (I noticed, that although I had requested many animals to call me brother, Joe was the only one who would do it). "' Love your enemies is a sublime commandment, but when your enemy has gone crazy, and can't distinguish love from hatred, you must try first of all to get some sense into his maddened brain. If we loved the Anarchist too hard just now, we'd let him loose on this Island, where he would probably blind and confuse all the young animals by his peculiar logic, and attempt to murder half the old ones. No, I think we are doing right to transport him for awhile, but he will be carefully watched, and at the first sign of repentance, back he comes."

"What is the Isle of Probation like?" I asked Joe.

" Very like this, only smaller, and with only a few animals on it, and they have no President and no government. They roam from one place to another. They never work. They rage and idle and fight each other. When this elephant arrives, they will gather round him, and listen to all he has to say, probably make a fuss over him. Each animal will relate his grievance, and for awhile he will be lionised. In a short time, they will likely all turn against him, and give him a terrible thrashing."

"But they can't kill him?"

" Oh, no, but they can make him suffer. Imagine being wounded and miserable — it is worse than death."

" How will you know when he wants to come back?"

" By our bird telegraphy. We always have a lookout of birds on the Isle of Probation."

" Are there ever any bird Anarchists ? "

" Very seldom; birds, as a rule, believe in good government. I remember a vulture that gave us some trouble, but he only stayed one day on the Isle of Probation. He made such an uproar that the lookout sent an urgent message for his return."

" That bird was fun," said Dandy, snickering softly, and running forward beside Joe. " I can recall his coming back. He yelled, * Monarchy! Constitutionalism! Conservatism! Absolutism! Im-

perialism! Turkism! Police! Military!' and so on for a week. He's the most conservative bird we have now. He says those Anarchists anarchised him out of all nonsense. They were awful, and beat each other all the time when they weren't asleep or feeding."

" Here we are at the corral," said Jumbo, " but you'd better stay on my back, Master Sam.

The Anarchist might break loose."

It was queer to see the animals moving about softly in the dark. I could make out three or four elephants, a number of old monkeys and tigers, leopards, and ever so many bears.

" Come up here, Dandy and Rag," I said, " I want to keep you beside me," so Jumbo lifted them up.

I put an arm round each, while Jumbo stood like a tower.

" The last Anarchist we had," whispered Dandy, " was a weasel. He gave no end of trouble, for he was so small that we couldn't lock him up. He'd crawl out of every place we put him in, and he vowed he'd taste all our brains from Joe down."

" How did you transport him ? "

" Oh, we didn't bother about the air-ship for that little nuisance. An eagle just gripped him in his talons, and flew off with him. None too gently, I fear, for Weasel yelled all the way to Probation.

He told the eagle he'd have the blood of all his young ones, and his uncles, and aunts, and cousins, and relatives to the fiftieth degree, and the eagle only squeezed him harder."

" And what became of him? "

" Oh, he came back, of course. They all do, and mighty glad we are to see them, for they are our brothers even before the scales drop off their eyes. Weasel now lives in the eagle's nest, and keeps his young ones warm at night if the eagle is out to a party."

" I'd like to send HilUngton to Probation," I said, « thoughtfully.

B " What are you laughing at? " I asked. B He wouldn't tell me.

B " I know," said Rag. " He's thinking that maybe if you took a turn of the Isle of Probation yourself, you would forgive Hillington."

" I wouldn't forgive him for fifty Islands," I said.

" Oh, come out of your air-ship. Master Sam," said Dandy, impatiently, " or you'll have to be probated yourself when you die."

" When I die, I'm going to the World of the Blessed," I said, proudly. " Joe told me I would."

" But not if there is hatred in your heart," said Dandy, anxiously. " They have an Isle of Probation, too, in the World of the Blessed. I've heard of

it from the birds. Come, Master Sam, forgive Hill-ington. I want to be your dog in the next Paradise. Who knows, I may have a golden tail,"

Rag began to laugh.

" Oh, hush up," said Dandy. " A very well-known man, called Luther, promised his dog a golden tail in the resurrection, and if his dog got one, Master Sam might get me one."

" I'd like one, too," said Rag, getting interested.

" Whist, boys," I said, " they're going to edge the Anarchist out. Steal-Away, where are you ? "

The little owl flew down from a tree branch to my shoulder.

" Tell us what is going on," I said, " I can't see distinctly."

Steal-Away's eyes were like saucers. " The big animals are lined up each side of the corral gate," she said. " Silvertip is just taking down the bars. The elephants and other bears stand ready — there he comes — you hear him ? "

" Oh, gracious, yes," I said, " he's trumpeting like a good fellow."

" He's prancing in his walk," whispered Steal-Away. " His stomach is full of good food, and he is proud. Now the animals are closing in round him. He has just given Bengal a thwack."

" Poor Bengal! " I said.

" He has retired limping," Steal-Away went on, " the elephants are crowding now."

I

" Crowding? " I repeated.

" Making a push, you know," interrupted Dandy, " that is a great word on the Island. Instead of clawing, and tearing, and biting, they push and press a fellow till he gets sense."

" The African elephants are each side of him," Steal-Away continued. "He is banging them, but they don't care. They are pressing him this way. Jumbo, you would better march on."

" I will turn aside," replied Jumbo, and he stepped under an oak-tree.

The procession passed us. We could dimly see and perfectly hear the unhappy Anarchist, raving, trampling, trying to bolt, and always being headed off.

" Now, we'll make a detour, and get to the boat rst," said Jumbo, and he tramped along under the ak-trees, until he got more out in the open.

Steal-Away flew ahead, telling him which way to go, though he could see pretty well himself — much better than I could."

When we got on the beach, he rolled along in his funny run. It seemed to me the Island must be shaking under him, he was so big.

" What kind of a boat are they going to take him in? " I asked.

" A whale-boat," said Jumbo, " it is drawn up in a bay yonder."

Soon I could see dimly ahead in the darkness a huge boat, almost filling a pretty little bay. " Of course, you could not take an elephant in an air-ship," I said.

When we got nearer, I saw that it was a huge, flat affair, with neither sails nor machinery. " What makes it go? " I asked.

" Rockaway is waiting outside," said Jumbo, " our big, faithful blue whale. He is enormously stfong. He will take them flying through the water."

I gravitated down one of Jumbo's legs, and ran up to examine the boat. It was big enough to hold three or four elephants. While I was leaning over it, I heard a tremendous trumpeting behind us, and scuttled back to Jumbo. " What's up, old fellow ? "

" They are binding him," said Jumbo, " with grass ropes. It would not do to have him go unfettered in the boat. He might plunge overboard. Here they come."

I could see through the soft darkness that the Anarchist wasn't quite as lively as he came hobbling over the beach. His trunk was lashed to his body. There was a long trail of rope on one of his hind legs, and he was holding his tongue.

The bears seemed to have him in charge now. They were walking on their hind legs, and if he paused, one of them would give him a tap with hi? paw enough to stagger a church.

I leaned up against Jumbo, and watched them. "Where is Joe?" I asked.

" Gone home, probably," said Dandy. " That is one thing I like about Joe. He is master here, and yet if he gives any one a piece of work to do, he doesn't stand over and nag all the time. He can trust his animals. Soko is just the same, but some of the animals are horribly fussy. A few of the cat tribe, tigers and such like, most drive me crazy."

The Anarchist was now close by. Some apes and the elephant steadied the boat, while Silvertip gener-alled.

"Isn't he masterly?" remarked Jumbo; "he lasn't been rolling grindstones for nothing."

Almost single-handed, Silvertip was pushing the 'elephant in the big boat, and quite single-handed, he jeized the dangling rope, wound it all round the ^Anarchist's fore legs, tied it in a knot, fastened it by means of paw and teeth, then sat down in the stern.

Kern stepped to the bow, a few young monkeys skipped in as aids-de-camp, the bears on shore waded out, gave the boat a push, and off it went.

" That will be a nice little pull for Rockaway," observed Jumbo.

We saw the boat pause at a short distance from the shore, where Rockaway was waiting for it in deep water.

Kern leaned forward. We knew he was throwing out to Rockaway the rope that lay coiled in the bow, then we all called out to the Anarchist, " Goodbye, brother, come back soon," and then turned away.

" They shipped him darkly," said Dandy. " Hello — what's that?"

We were all strolling up the beach. It was a lovely night, if it was dark.

" It's the swans singing, maybe," said Rag.

Oh, I forgot to say that a pair of black swans went with the whale-boat. Never any sort of a craft started out from the Island without an escort of these birds. The animals all loved them, and were almost superstitious about them, for Dandy told me that they all had an idea that they couldn't go or come safely without their beloved birds.

Well, when Rag said that maybe the swans were singing, Dandy began to laugh.

" The swans never sing when they are leaving the Island, you stupid, only when they are coming home, and, moreover, that noise never came out of a swan's smooth throat."

CHAPTER XXVI.

THE DANCE ON THE BEACH

"Well, I vow it's that goat," said Rag, disgustedly, " isn't he enough to make you sick ? " Away down the breeze, the noise was coming.

I

She's gone, she's gone, the cause of all my grief. Now I'm a happy goat, now I have found relief. I'm putting on my glorious freedom suit, It fits me well — now that you can't dispute."

" Yes, I can," bawled Dandy, " I wish you'd go put your head in soak again."

The goat ran up to us. " Do you know how to dance the Lancers ? " he asked, eagerly.

"Yes, I do, but I won't dance with you," said Dandy.

" Why, you're a poet, like this dear go-at," said Jerry, admiringly. " Now do let us have a dance."

" No," said Dandy, decidedly.

" Why not? " teased the goat.

" Because it isn't proper," said Dandy, with mock bashfulness, " it puts silly thoughts into one's head."

" It wouldn't in mine," said the goat, earnestly.

" No, 'cause you're so chock full now that another couldn't get in," said Dandy.

" Will you have a round dance, if you won't have a square one? " begged the goat.

" Not a round one, nor a square one, nor a pentagonal one, nor a heptagonal one, nor an octagonal one, nor a duodecimal one, nor a triangular one, nor a bisected one," said Dandy, stubbornly, '* nor any kind of a one."

" Why, you love dancing," observed the goat.

" Yes, but I like to choose my partner."

" You needn't dance with me," said the goat, humbly.

Dandy began to give way.

" The animals all love dancing," whispered Steal-Away, in my ear. " Look at old Jumbo there, how he's listening."

I stuffed my fist in my mouth to keep from laughing.

" Come on, then," said Dandy, making three or four bounds in the air, " call up some of the animals. Mr. Sam, may I have the pleasure of the first two-step?"

" But it's dark," I said, staring round about me.

" Oh, not so very," said Dandy, " it's fun to have a little darkness. You go bumping against each other, and everybody laughs."

I

" I t-t-tell you, there's a moon," said the goat, stuttering, excitedly, " a nice, steady, old moon, she'll soon be up."

" Run — fly — call some animals," said Dandy, giving him a push, " and a few birds to whistle for us. Mind don't invite too many. It's no honour to be asked to a crush."

" Oh, help me, some one," said the goat, piteously. *' The notice is so short. Steal-Away, you come," and kicking and throwing out his hoofs, he made off like a streak.

Steal-Away didn't look very anxious to go. " We birds have all the work, and none of the fun," she said. " They won't let us dance, and we have to sing to beat the band." K " Can you sing? " I asked.

" Not sing exactly, but there are hooting parts where I can help. Dear me, I have no pleasant task. The robins and larks are always mad in their first sleep."

" Tell them I want them to come," I said.

" Oh, that alters matters," she observed, in a changed voice, and she flew away.

The guests weren't long in arriving, and very soon big forms and little forms came trotting, galloping, and scampering down the beach.

The birds were slower, but presently they arrived; Steal-Away flying behind and driving them on.

They did look sleepy, but they were good-natured, and perching on one of the sand-hills, they put themselves under the leadership of a nightingale.

It was fun to see the tiny creature stand on one claw, and mark time with the other.

That was a dance, and I doubt if any one ever saw another like it. It seemed to make all the animals crazy. Perhaps they can't stand the going round and round motion as well as we can.

I opened the affair with Dandy for my partner. First we marched up and down the beach two and two, then we broke ranks and waltzed. This was the serpent dance.

Then we had sets of Lancers up and down the firm, hard sand floor. Mind this was all in half darkness, but just as we were at the second figure, a big moon poked her head above the sea, and stared at us as if to say, " What on earth are you doing over there, boys ? "

I just shouted. I hadn't been able to see well before, I only felt that things were funny. Now I made every one out quite plainly, and there were some daisy surprises.

The elephant Borneo was dancing with a tigress, and the bears, who had all run back when they had heard there was to be a party, for the bears are very fond of dancing, were hugging tiny atoms of creatures that they could scarcely get hold of. One old

"ONE OLD GRIZZLY HAD A RABBIT"

grizzly had a rabbit, a brown bear had a beaver — I could not for the life of me see how they held on to each other, and indeed, during the latter part of the dance, the grizzly and the brown bear both took iir partners under their arms, and spun round alone.

The foxes were mostly dancing with sheep. Some)od on their hind legs, some kept on all fours, and irtners were always losing each other. That was a reat feature — to lose your partner and wander round searching for him or her, getting cuffed id banged by the others who weren't lost. I thought I should die laughing. I threw myself own on the sand by the birds, who never stopped laugh, but went on with the most beautiful whis-ing imaginable. I rolled and tumbled over and rtr, but the animals never minded a bit. The kangaroos alone were enough to choke you. |uch gamboling, such wobbling, and they chose ich queer partners. One Mr. Kangaroo had a Miss Giraffe, a Mrs. Kangaroo had a wolf who grinned feverishly at her all the time.

I tried not to laugh at Jumbo. I turned my back on him a dozen times, but he always veered round in front. He had a lamb for a partner — a little, sleepy lamb that had come with its gay mamma. There was no use in Jumbo's trying to take the lamb round the waist, or the lamb to get his little hoof on

Jumbo's shoulder, so lammie just ran round and round under Jumbo's huge hulk. Jumbo danced, and lammie tried to keep from being trodden on. His little face was very anxious. I think he was glad when the dance was over.

I must not forget the goat. He lost what little head he had at the beginning, and kept missing his partner, and running round and round, snatching others, and getting smacked and bowled over, and rising again, and dancing a little bit by himself, and going after other animals' partners again, and getting whacked, and so on, through the whole programme.

Really, I thought I'd have to go home, I was so weak from laughing, and then when they had all danced till they were tired, didn't they propose having a cake-walk ?

That finished me. The animals were most awfully funny without trying to be funny, but when they set themselves in dead earnest to be clownish and comical, I just lay on the ground and gave little gasps. I hadn't any breath left.

Imagine Jumbo and the lamb coming by. Jumbo ogling and lammie twisting his little head, and trying to look coy.

Then a grizzly and a rabbit, and Rag and a coon.

Rag was delicious. There wasn't an animal there that enjoyed himself half as much.

Just when the cake-walk was in full swing, some monkeys came running down the beach. I had wondered where they were when all this fun was going on that would be so much to their liking.

Bless me! hadn't they stopped to dress? There

Kas a shout when they appeared in the moonlight, Dlding up shawjs and skirts, and clutching their bats and bonnets to keep them on.

The other animals with one accord gave up the beach to them.

" Where did they get those clothes ? " muttered ^^ag, who had come to sit beside me. m " Vegetable fibre," replied Dandy. " The monkeys often make them just for fun. The hats and bonnets are of leaves and flowers. Now look, you'll see some life. They're going to have the Backwards."

"The What?" I asked.

" The Backward Quadrilles. Don't you see, they are all dressed backward. The most of their faces are so hairy, that under their hat brims you can't tell which is front and which is back."

Sure enough, their dresses all fastened the wrong way, their head-gear was trimmed to make the backs of their heads look like their faces, so we had the curious sight of a lot of animals dancing backward.

I couldn't laugh. Something inside me just made

a gasp or a squeak once in awhile. I had used my laughing apparatus so hard, that it was all out of gear, and I felt sore.

I was glad they hadn't come first. Those fluttering rags of clothes, those humanlike actions, were perfectly killing. When they stopped dancing, and I heard they were going to have a cake-walk, I roared for Jumbo.

" Come, old man, pick me up and take me home. I'm played out. If I laugh another bit, I'll die. Lay me carefully on my bed. Don't any one speak to me. Maybe I'll get this kink out of me by morning."

The animals all gathered round, but when I saw the monkeys' anxious faces under the backs of their bonnets and hat brims, I collapsed, and Rag drove them back to their dancing.

I heard next day that they kept it up till Joe sent all the cocks on the Island to crow them home.

The good old Puritan dog didn't approve of dancing, unless they would have their parties by sunlight.

He said he didn't see what made them like to get down on the dark beach, and hustle each other about, when they ought to be in bed and sleeping.

None of his family were at the dance, and the great question agitating the Island when I woke up the next morning was, " Would the President

artie Burnt on ttie 3Beact| 3^1

allow the races to come off at ten sharp as had been arranged ? " No, he would not. " You can't play all night and all day, too," he said, so the races were postponed till the next day, and the animals were all given a half day for rest, and a half day for work.

CHAPTER XXVII. joe's departure

I HAVE just been looking at the pile of paper I laid out to write this story on. I took so many sheets, and said, " When I fill them up, I'll stop, for I don't want to be prosy."

The sheets are most gone, and I have to shorten up. I've been wondering what I'll leave out, for I do believe I have enough to fill seven books.

It isn't so hard to write a story, if you've got anything to say. I used to wonder how folks did it, but I see now you just take your paper, make up your mind what to leave out, and start in.

I guess I'll have to give my tour round the Island the go-by, and I'm mighty sorry, too, for I saw some pretty queer animals, some I didn't know were in the world.

Do you know what a panda is, and a cacomixle, and a coati, and a kinkajou, and a sambur, and a muntjac, and the ghostly-looking tarsier? I didn't till I went round the Island.

But I must say a word about the races that pr 322

1

ceded the tour. We had them, and I never again expect to see such races.

Greyhounds, deer, some wild cattle, a couple of ostriches, and more horses than I could count, took part.

Palo Alto won, though an ostrich pressed him sore, and it was on his back that I went round the sland. Rag and Dandy were my only followers. !lag because he would not be separated from me, and Dandy because he was such a tramp that he knew all the animals.

I keep saying that we went round the long narrow Island, but we didn't. We only got part way. Palo Alto galloped quickly through woods and fields, md only stopped when we came to settlements of mimals.

There we paused, because I wanted to talk to the nimals. They all had such interesting stories to ell. Each creature could have written a story of is or her life. I would sit listening, till Dandy ould urge me on, saying that we hadn't seen a six-nth part of the Island yet.

It was on our second day out that the interruption
e. We were in a lair of pumas in a thicket. We
t up late at night telling stories, or rather the
as told the stories, and I listened. Listened
rd, for I never knew before how kind to the
iman race those savage creatures could be.
lends 6i mankind they call themselves.

One of them told us how he came to die. One time when he was out hunting lambs, a farmer and a dog tracked him. He killed the dog, for he just hated every canine he saw. But he wouldn't touch the man. He sat perfectly still, with his back against a fence, while the farmer approached with his knife. The puma said he just stared at the man, and tears ran down his cheeks. But the farmer didn't care for his tears, and soon killed him.

I felt sorry for the pumas, and I wish you could have seen the good bed they made me in the thicket. I just wallowed among the rose and poppy leaves they had strewn over it, and slept like a dead boy till I was roused enough from my deadness to know what an extra good time I was having.

Some one was trying to wake me, but I made up my mind that I wouldn't wake. I had spent the most of the day before on Palo Alto's back, and I deserved a rest, so I just went on having an uncommonly good time. Still the whispering and fluttering in one ear kept up, and the soft nosing and pushing of the other.

I wouldn't wake, oh, no, not I, and I didn't, till, something took me softly by the shirt and shook ' me.

Then I flew up. " Let me alone, can't you? "

Palo Alto was on one side of me, and a swallow on the other.

'* Oh, come, come," said Palo Alto, trembling with excitement. " Something wonderful has happened. The swallow says that he has been sent after us to say the bird telegraphers report that a beautiful air-ship is to come from the World of the Blessed to our Island, and they think it is for Joe."

They didn't need to say anything more. I flung on my coat. The swallow flew ahead, and I sprang on Palo Alto's back, and with Rag and Dandy tearing after, we called a hasty " Good-bye," and ** Thank you," to the pumas, and turned our faces homeward.

kPalo Alto just flew. Rag and Dandy could not sp up with him, but came pegging along with a lole bunch of pumas who had wanted to come as soon as they heard the news.

" Swallow," I called, to the little skimming morsel, as he flew over me, " where shall we find the air-ship ? "

He dropped to my shoulder. " In the Vale of Smiles, Mr. Sam."

I knew it well. It was a beautiful, cup-shaped valley, green and smooth, and located beyond Point Expectation and the Hill of Arrival.

"Do you think we can get there to-day?" I asked, anxiously.

" Oh, certainly," the swallow said, " at the rate

:

Palo Alto is going. He is like a winged horse. I will not add a feather weight to his burden," and he flew up into the air.

At noon we stopped for a rest, and I can tell you Palo Alto got a good rubbing down.

He lay on a grassy bank by a stream, and with the help of a near-by colony of monkeys I manipulated him.

Then he drank a little water, and started again.

Early in the afternoon we began to be in familiar surroundings; then the old points came into view, and now we began to go slowly. There was a great press of animals ahead of us. Thousands and thousands of them, and flocks of birds hovering in the air were all massed round the brim of the cup-shaped valley.

There was perfect silence. I began to greet my animal friends in a loud way, but soon held my tongue.

Down in that glorious afternoon sunshine was something as glorious and as beautiful as the sunshine. The air-ship had arrived.

I slipped from Palo Alto's back, and surveyed it curiously. It was different in make from the airships in ordinary use about the Island, but it must have come from the same place.

The animals never made their air-ships. They could not. If one wore out, or got out of order,

fl

they always found a new one in its place, put there by some kind Higher Power for their convenience and use.

Well, this air-ship was not balloon-shaped like the ordinary ones. This was long, and instead of a gas bag, it had revolving fans or wings or arms — I don't know what to call them.

Anyway, they were soft and white, but firm-looking, and they just fluttered gently in the little breeze blowing through the valley.

It wasn't very close to us, and I couldn't see very well, but on board the long, canoe-shaped wicker car below the wings of the air-ship, I could make out animals with white skins.

" What are they ? " I whispered to Palo Alto.

" Two snow-white fawns," he said, " the most gentle and beautiful of creatures. They were once on the Island, but they look different now — so different."

" Different — in what way? "

*' Oh, more lovely, more gentle. Can't you see their graceful, beautiful movements, and the look in their eyes ? "

" No, I can't," I said, impatiently. " I haven't your long sight." Then I turned to a shepherd dog at my side. " When did the air-ship arrive? "

" Only a few minutes ago," he said, in a low voice. " As soon as it came, a beautiful dove flew away in the direction of Joe's home."

" Then you are sure it is Joe that is sent for? " " Sure — he is the best animal on the Island." While we were talking in a low voice, more animals and birds kept arriving and surrounding the Vale of Smiles. They looked over each other's shoulders, the birds perched on the trees, but without a chirp or a twitter. No one spoke. They all looked down into the Valley at the beautiful white creatures who lay in the wicker car. Presently they got up. I could see them do that, and both looked our way.

The animals were falling back and making an opening. Good old Joe was coming, followed by his whole household. On the brink of the Valley he stopped. The sun shone all round him. His dear old head was yellow and glorious. He pressed up to Jess, and put his muzzle close down to her face.

She did not look sad. No one did. I never saw such a collection of beaming faces. Those that hadn't hair on them just shone, and some that had hair were so joyful that even their fur seemed shining.

Well, the animals didn't all crowd round him to say good-bye. A few near him did go up and touch him, or gently lick him, but they mostly stood off, and looked as if they were saying, " Well, dear old Joe, you are off for a grand trip, but we will join you some day."

I

He spoke to some of them. Jess and her pups, and the rest of her family, remained standing near le, while Joe went quietly up to a few to whom he rished to say some last words.

First he beckoned to the black Cat. She went

him, and hung her head while he spoke to her. [o one heard what he said, but every one noticed fow sad the Cat looked, and now we knew that she really cared for Joe.

After she crept away, he asked the goat to come forward. Jerry came hopping along with a silly grin that died away when Joe begged him to be more serious.

After he skipped out of sight, Joe went up to a group of tigers and implored them to coax Tammany from the marsh. He also asked them to pay a little more attention to their neighbours, the snakes, for they felt themselves neglected.

Then he asked for Soko. The good old ape was hiding himself away among a crowd of his relatives.

Joe made him come to him; then he led him to the edge of the Valley. He said nothing, but after looking all round to see that every animal and every bird saw him, he gently touched him with his paw.

" What does that mean ? " I whispered to Palo Alto.

" It means that Joe wishes specially to show his approbation of Soko."

" Is he making him President? "

" Oh, no, he has not the power. The animals as a whole must elect Joe's successor. However, the departing President knows better than any one the duties and responsibilities of the position, and he often in some way expresses his opinion as to which animal is best qualified to fill the place."

" The animals will appoint Soko, I am sure," I said, positively.

" Yes, I think they will," replied Palo Alto.

" Then why don't they give him a cheer now ? "

" It would not be seemly," replied Palo Alto, " not in the presence of messengers from the World of the Blessed."

Joe was standing beside his mother. " Brothers," he said, " there is one other called with me. Where is Ruth Alden, the rabbit?"

A whisper of " Ruth Alden " passed all round the brim of the green cup, and soon a very sur-prised-looking white animal came hopping along around the green edge.

Joe looked at her kindly. " Did any one ever hear any evil of our little sister? "

No one ever had. She was a model rabbit.

" Dear friend, come with me," said Joe, kindly, " but first I must speak to the boy."

I ran forward and, kneeling down, threw m>j arms round him. " You sha'n't go, Joe. I war you."

" But I am called, dear boy. Some day we shall meet again."

" I'm homesick," I said, " and miserable. I want you to stay. I don't like this."

Joe's old face beamed. " To you this is like death. To us it is new life. There is no death, dear boy. It is but passing on from one stage of existence to another — do remember this, my beloved earth friend, and brother, and when you go back to your home, do not forget the animals."

I sprang up. " If I forget them, may I die a sudden death, and spend all my years in the

Isle of Probation."

" Gently, dear brother," said Joe. " You will not forget them. I should not have spoken."

" And I am going to tell everybody what I have seen here," I cried. " I will make them believe me."

" They will not," said Joe, sadly. " There are some people on earth who would not be converted to kindness to animals, if all of us were to rise from the dead to visit them — now, boy, I want to ask a last favour of you. Will you forgive Hillington when you return home? "

" Now, Joe," I said, " you know I can't do that. It isn't in my heart."

He said nothing, but of the two of us, dog and boy, there was more angel about his face than there was about mine.

He skilfully changed the subject. " Where is Rag?" he asked, kindly.

I was just beginning to explain, when my old beauty arrived. Tongue out, body on fire, but his manner calm. Dandy lagged behind him. They were nearly dead from running.

Joe's eye ran over them both, in a curious, understanding way. Then he said, " Rag, don't sorrow too much when your master goes away from you — "

Rag stopped panting for an instant, set his teeth, and looked up at me.

" And Dandy," said Joe, " my last request of you is that you stand by Rag. Don't let him feel lonely and miserable — and now I must go — Mother — "

Jess stepped forward and they put their heads together for a minute.

I have said that everybody was joyful, but Jess was joyful and sorrowful, too, if that is possible.

She looked proud, and yet her face was all wrinkled, and there were tears in her eyes.

" It won't be for long. Mother," said Joe; then he turned and paused on the descent to the Valley.

I ran up to him. " Joe, I'll think that matter over. It isn't worth while to vex a good dog like you, for the sake of a miserable cur like Hillington."

He shook his head, " Brother, do you think that is the right spirit in which to forgive? No, don't

speak, please. Turn it over in your mind. I leave it to your generosity. Good-bye, dear friends, good-bye, one and all," and he turned and went down, down the winding path.

The little rabbit crept after him, and we watched them, oh, how we watched them!

Half-way down, he stopped for the rabbit to v/alk beside him, then when they got near the airship the fawns came out to meet them.

That was a meeting — and yet there was no fuss about it. Joe knew the fawns. Palo Alto whispered that he had been very fond of them when they were on this Island.

The two big, white, perfect creatures bent over Joe, touched him lovingly, then stepped into the car with him.

As soon as they all lay down, the white wings of the air-ship began to flutter, then to spread out firmly, then it rose from the ground.

Oh, how we stared at it as it slowly mounted.

" Why, that is more like a flying-machine than an air-ship," I said to Palo Alto.

" It is a flying-machine, I think," said Palo Alto.

" And who manages it ? " I asked. " Those fawns are doing nothing."

" I have heard," replied Palo Alto, in an awed voice, " that behind those white screens is a human being — one from the World of the Blessed. You

can imagine what pleasure it would be to an immortal fond of animals, to manipulate a ship to and from from this Island."

The swallow who sat on my shoulder whispered in my ear, " Just now when the rabbit got near that pearly white thing, I saw an arm stretched out, a white, glistening arm. It took the rabbit so gently, so very gently, and drew it in, and the rabbit nestled down. Ruth Alden was very fond of human beings. If she found one in the air-ship, she would go to him rather than to the fawns."

" Oh, why can't I see, why can't I see? " I muttered to myself. But I saw nothing beyond the whiteness of the winged ship, and the blueness of the sky. The machine went very slowly at first.

" That is done on purpose," murmured Palo Alto, " for it can fly like the wind. It is to give us as long a view as possible."

The great throng of animals stood motionless with upturned faces. There was a hush in the air. This white mystery made a queer feeling come over me.

Then suddenly, as we looked, the broad wings seemed to spread themselves more, one minute we saw them, the next they had melted into the sky. Joe was gone.

The animals still stood for a long time staring up into the air.

Then they looked at each other with quiet, dazed Faces, as if to say, " Well, we have lost him," and then with one accord they began to gather round Soko.

The old fellow was soon hidden in the multitude of animals.

* What does this mean ?" I asked Palo Alto again.

" It means that Soko is going in as President by acclamation," he replied, with satisfaction. " There will be no vote taken — I am very glad," and he, too, pressed forward and left me.

The congratulations were very sober, and soon the animals quietly dispersed and went to their homes.

Jess led all her family back to her house on the hill. Bella, perched on old Jim's back, rode beside her, saying comforting things, " Don't fret. Mother, Joe is better off. Who knows — maybe he'll be a President over there."

Soko, too, went home with Jess.

" I wouldn't be surprised if he leaves the other apes and monkeys and lives with Jess," said Palo Alto. " It will make her miss Joe less, and if he is to be President, it will be better for him to live away from his own people. Some of the young monkeys are apt to get too familiar."

" Take me home, Palo Alto," I said, " take me

home. I've got the awful feeling inside me that I had when Rag died. If I don't feel better soon, I'll have to go home."

I had to go, anyway. Two hours later, Soko came to my cabin. I think he knew I would be feeling badly, and after comforting Jess, he came to comfort me.

We were sitting talking, when suddenly he put up one of his hairy arms, " Listen."

I did listen, but heard nothing but some birds singing.

" Come this way," he said, and he led me to a little hillock.

I did as he bade me. At a short distance from us was a clump of magnificent, California redwood trees. In their tall tops were the birds whose sweet voices I had heard.

" You said you wished to hear some bird telegraphy going on," he whispered. " Now is your chance."

" I didn't know there was a station so near," I said, in surprise.

The birds were trilling again. There were three or four of them — thrushes and robins.

They would sing in a short, sharp way, as if asking questions, and then put their pretty heads on one side as if to get answers.

Soko looked at me, sorrowfully. " Do you understand them ? " I asked.

a^Oe^g BtpUVtnVt 337

" Yes," he replied.

"What do they say?"

" Your mother is becoming ill and worried over the trancelike condition of her son."

"That settles it," I cried, "I must go home." Then I checked myself. " How do they know ? They are not telegraphing directly to earth."

'* No, they are only receiving the message transmitted by another group of birds. Your earth birds fly up as high as they can, and sing the news to our outposts."

" Oh," I said, and I drew a deep breath. Then I asked, " How soon can I leave? "

" As soon as you like," said Soko.

" Give me half a day to say good-bye," I exclaimed. Then I changed my mind. " No, if my mother is suffering, I must go at once — but Rag — I can't leave him."

Soko said nothing.

" Rag," I called, " come here."

He ran up from the beach where he and Dandy were resting.

" Rag, Fve got to go home. I can't shirk it any longer, and I can't take you — oh, what shall I do? "

" Master," he said, " I'm going back with you."

" You can't. Rag, you're dead. They won't let you go."

" Would you take him ? " asked Soko; " come, now, would you take him if you could ? " Yes, I would, if I could always have him with me.

" Suppose he should be stolen from you ? Suppose you should die and leave him? He might be cold and hungry; he might be ill-treated. Could you stand that ? "

" Oh, no," I cried; " no, no. It kills me to think of Rag suffering. I'll leave him, but — "

I couldn't talk any more. I went and rolled on my bed, while Soko left to get the air-ship ready.

It was a special honour to me that he went. The President was not supposed to do such work, but good old Soko was fond of boys.

CHAPTER XXVIII.

II COME BACK TO EARTH K My leaving was different from Joe's. In his case, Si was joy. Everybody knew that he was going to be perfectly happy, more happy than he had ever been before. They knew that he had no trials before him, while, in my case, I felt that the old animals especially were sorry for me. I was only a boy. I might have a troubled life. I still had to die, and they pitied me.

" On the other hand," said Soko, cheerfully, " you may die before you get to be a man."

"I don't want to die, Soko," I said; "I want to live."

"That is all right," he replied; "that is the sounder philosophy. Fight your battle bravely. Don't shirk life's troubles, and you will get some pleasure as you go along. I would not wish to have you morbid, and feel that there is no pleasure in life, and that death is the only thing to look forward to. That is wrong. No, when I spoke, I meant that, if death should happen to come to you by the order of the Great Ruler of all Things, you would meet it as serenely as you will undertake living again, and that, moreover, it would be a blessed thing for us to know you were safe in the World of the Blessed."

" I understand, Soko," I said. " Oh, dear, I wish this day were over."

Word had gone round the Island that I was to leave — the birds took care of that, and the bakeries, the fields, the roads, and the woods were deserted. Nearly every bird and every animal on the Island, lined up on the beach to see me go. Many of them, indeed, had not reached their homes after seeing dear old Joe leave, before they heard of my approaching departure.

The Hill of Arrival was black with my special friends. I had begged for some of them to go in the car with me, but Soko was firm. Only the Cat could accompany me. Therefore, without any leave-taking, she sprang into the car and sat down.

I hugged Jumbo, and he rubbed me with his trunk. I took little Billy, who, by the way, had quite recovered from the Widow's drubbing, up into my arms and squeezed him hard. I stroked my mother's Angora, and took a dozen messages from her and Taffy to their mistress.

" But she won't believe a word of them," wailed, the Angora, dismally, " she will say you have beei dreaming, my dear boy."

" Yes, be prepared to hear that, Master Sam," said Palo Alto, gravely. " They always say it on earth, when the specially favoured try to reveal after-death mysteries."

I threw my arms round his neck. " You are almost human," I said, " you are better and nobler than some human beings."

He shook his beautiful head. " Not as good as I ought to be. Not good enough yet for the World of the Blessed. Oh, I want to go there so much and see my dear master."

I turned away. He almost made me cry. I must talk to some one ridiculous. " Bella," I said, " where are you, girl ? "

" Here, boy," she cried, " coming, coming. Bella's heart is most broke."

" Broken," said Davy, running up my leg and into my pocket out of reach of her beak.

She forgot her sorrow and began to look for him. " Oh, the odious rat, to interrupt Bella, when she was having such a good cry — such a lovely cry — such a comforting cry."

" Comforting, Bella," I said; " well, I like that."

" Comforting, yes," she snapped; " when I am just bursting, it does me good to cry. Oh, I'm sorry you're going. Bella loves you, boy, she'll be your pet bird in the next Paradise."

" What about the Morrises, Bella? " I said, mischievously.

" Oh, I forgot," she said, suddenly composing herself. " First come, first served, and Bella was their bird first. Well, Master Sam, can't you keep near the Beautiful Joe animals and birds in the World of the Blessed?"

" I don't know, Bella, but if I get there myself, I'll make a try for it — where's Jess ? '*

" Here I am," said a meek little voice, and out of the jam of lions, horses, sheep, tigers, and other big animals, good little Jess ran up to me with every pup following her.

" This is a dreadful day for me," she said. " Two blows — I do not know how to stand it."

I stooped down and patted her. I patted every one of the pups, who for once were looking serious.

She didn't want to see me go. " I can't endure it," she said. " If you will excuse me, I will go home. Wrap yourself up, dear boy, so you won't take cold in the car, and don't forget to be kind to the mother dogs on earth," and with drooping head and tail, and every pup filing after her in the same sad manner, she walked slowly home.

After she left, there was dreadful confusion. The animals all kept crowding forward, till they almost pushed us up into the air from the Hill of Arrival.

Soko looked at the sun. " This will never do. We are wasting time. Every creature wants to say

good-bye to you, and is afraid he will get left. Brothers! " and he shouted to them, " stand back, form in a line down the Hill. Pass rapidly before the boy. Just touch his hand as you go by, and if he wants to single any one out for conversation, he can do so. Bears and wolves, act as marshals."

This plan worked well. The marshals urged the animals on, till at last they got them going by on a trot.

It was astonishing how many I had got to know in the short time I had been on the Island. And their faces were all different to me. No two sheep looked alike. Every animal, even down to a mouse, had his own expression.

Some of the mice broke ranks, and ran up my legs to sit on my shoulder and gently bite my hair, and I wouldn't have them disturbed. They were so small, they could see nothing from the ground.

" Make way for the snakes," I cried, when they came along, for I remembered what Joe had said.

They were very grateful, and do you know, a snake is not very bad to feel, if you do it under-standingly. They are certainly graceful creatures.

Jumbo stood one side. He did not join the procession of animals. Dandy and Rag sat beside him, and when I had said good-bye to about a quarter of the animals, I had to stop.

" Halt! " cried Soko, " time is up. The boy will simply wave his hand at the rest."

" Except the goat," I said, staring at him, as he came running up.

Upon my word, he was crying again. Tears were actually pouring down his old beard.

" I am just beginning to feel," he said, chokingly, " how much indebted I am to you, the author of my happiness, and now you are going to leave me."

" Well, don't take it so hard," I said. " Try to make some poetry — come now."

" I can't poetize," he said, " and at the same time lachrymatize."

"What's lachrymatize?" I said to Soko.

" Cry — pure and simple."

" Well, Goat," I said, " do whatever makes you feel happier, but don't cry for me after I've gone back to earth, for I sha'n't probably think of you."

He dried his tears at that, then I began to think I'd told a story.

" Of course, I'll think of you," I said, " and every animal on the Island. YouVe given me a fine time. I sha'n't forget one of you, and I hope we shall meet again."

" Now you've done for him with that touch of sentiment," said Soko, in a low voice.

I was dismayed. Hadn't that old goat of a goat gone back to his former place on the beach, where he was running up and down, and crying for me just as he had cried for the Widow.

Can any one give me a stick ? " I said, des-;rately. * Oh, let him alone," said Soko, " he'll get over and, anyway, it's no worse to have him crying lere, than it is to have him careering about the jland making poetry. He is enjoying this, too — lere is a luxury in his grief."

Oh, yes, it is worse," I said. " Here, help me, animals and birds, all that have sharp beaks, or horns and claws."

Some of the large birds obligingly flew down, and followed by many former beasts of prey, I set out for the goat.

He was sobbing, and stamping, and crying. " Oh, Master Sam, oh, sweet and gentle Master Sam, oH, darling Master Sam, how I shall miss you!"

" I'll darling you," I said, and with the help of my allies, I pinched, and pulled, and yanked, and spanked him, but finally overcame him by tickling him under the ribs.

This set him to laughing, and we ran up into the woods.

" Now if I hear of you crying for me again," I said, shaking my fist at him, " I'll come back from earth and punish you so much worse than this, that the Widow's treatment will be ball play beside it."

He sat and looked silly, with one hoof over his hairy chest. Then to my joy, he began to make doggerel again.

" Hearts are aching, brows are sad, Souls are bursting, minds are mad — "

I just dashed away. " Soko, let's get off," I said,! " before he has a relapse. Now, Rag, Rag, I say, if s your turn."

I was pretending to be cheerful. Goodness knows — my heart was like lead.

The old fellow twitched himself up to me, and put his head between my knees.

" Dandy," I said, trying to be light and airy, ** will you do one last favour for me?"

" Yes, boy," he said, in a dull voice.

"Will you stand by Rag?" '

" I will."

I turned away. The two dogs almost finished !' me.

" And wild animals," I said, lifting up my voice so I could get at all of them, " a favour from you. Will you all try to get the tiger out of the marsh, and be good to him for my sake? Tell him I left him a new name — Tiger Sunshine, and that I shall think of him very often when I get back to earth."

Such a roaring, and squeaking, and calling, from the animals — they would do what I asked them, and my mind was at rest.

Ik " Now, birds," I said, looking up into the air, Inhere there was a thick, dark cloud of moving feathers, " how can I shake a claw with all of you ? " " You can't," said Soko. " They are to escort us fifty miles out. Come, are you ready ? "

" Yes, all ready, except saying good-bye to Rag. Rag, old fellow, look up."

He could not. His tail just barely moved. I saw a tear on each of my dirty shoes.

" Rag," I said, " you don't care."

He gave a kind of groan, and I dropped down and took him in my arms. Then I bawled — bawled like the goat, only worse, for 1 had more sense.

Well, it had to be got over with, and presently I pushed him aside and stepped into the car.

** Let go," said Soko, and one of his young nephews sprang to the anchor.

The whole flock of swans from Swan Lake rose with us. They had all begged to escort me home, and as a special honour I had not the usual two, but some hundreds of the beautiful birds to accompany me right to my mother's house.

It was a wonderful sight to see them and the other winged creatures — birds, birds everywhere. The magnificent swans near at hand, and every other sort and kind known in the Union, and manv foreign birds, flying on either side of us, and above us, and below us.

But I only looked hastily at them. They were careful to leave an opening in their ranks, and what I looked hard at, was my dog — my friend — more brother than dog — the little pup I had raised, the friend of my older years.

His face was dreadful. Even Paradise didn't make up for me — Sam Emerson, only a common sort of a boy in a baseball suit, to most people, but to that dog — well, I don't know what I wasn't. I was a prince, a king in gorgeous clothing. I was the whole world with Paradise thrown in.

" Good-bye, Rag," I called, " good-bye, goodbye!"

He raised his head once, then it dropped like lead. I saw Dandy run up to him, but Rag pushed him aside. Then leaving the other animals, he went off by himself, and the last view I had of him was of his dear old head hidden in a clump of bushes.

" Soko," I said, " I'll remember anything you can do for that dog."

Soko smiled, gravely. " He'll be the most petted animal on the Island. I can promise you that — and who knows, perhaps in years to come he may be President."

Rag a President! — my heart began to feel

MORE BROTHER THAN DOG"

lihter. A President on the Island of Brotherly
love! That was better than being a common dog California.

" I will take him under my especial tuition," said
soko, " and as your dog, he will have great prestige Imong the animals."

And if I took him back to earth, he would soon fet old," I said. '* He would lose his teeth,
and lis hearing, and his eyesight would go. He would suffer."

" It is better as it is," said Soko.

" Oh, it is much better," I replied, and my spirits began to rise with the balloon.

We were out of sight of the Island now, but away out here in this glorious air, I carried
with me that last picture — the long beach, the sorrowing animals massed together, and looking
up into the sky; and my own white beauty apart from them, his head run into that clump of
shrubbery.

" Look down," said Soko, suddenly, " there is a flying-fish speaking."

I leaned over the side of the car. A slim and graceful flying-fish — a swallow of the deep — was skimming the crest of the waves. His pectoral fins were slightly quivering, his head was upraised, he was saying something to Soko.

" He says the fishes want to say good-bye to you," remarked Soko. " They are all down below, and as

many of them as can, will make leaps into the air. They wish you a pleasant journey."

" Thank you, fish," I called down. " How did you know about my leaving?"

" Oh, we hear everything," replied the flying-fish in a watery kind of a voice. " We have air scouts. Yankee Tom sends you his best respects."

" Give mine to him," I said, " and tell him I'll never eat another codfish as long as I live."

The fish darted below into the deep, blue water, then we began to see more fins, and tails, and inquisitive noses. I distinguished ever so many fishes that I knew, and that I had heard about during my talks with animals on the Island — Big Nose whale, Sharkies, Primus and Secundus, Yankee Tom, Old Rockaway and all his family, pikes, perches, salmon, sea trout, and others too numerous to mention. Some of them in their excitement made beautiful leaps, and, forgetting my sorrow, I began to laugh, and hung out of the car so far that plump down among my friends I went.

I wasn't a bit frightened. The fishes were so thick that I felt as if I couldn't sink, and, anyway, old Rockaway caught me on his back, and humping himself, sent me flying into the air to Soko's outstretched paws.

The balloon had made a beautiful swoop, just like a bird. The fishes nearly killed themselves laughing

at my mishap, but Soko didn't laugh. He just tore

I my clothes, and began to rub me down. ' You might take cold, boy," he said, rebukingly. '* But I couldn't die while I am with you, could — come now, Soko, tell me," He wouldn't. I think he thought they had told . enough about the mysteries of life after death,

and the immortality of inhabitants of the Island.

' It was fine down there," I said, stretching out my arms to the water, " so cool and fresh. I would like to take off my coat and trousers, and put on a tail and fins."

Soko said nothing at first, but after awhile I heard him muttering to himself as he rubbed me. " Joe was right. This mixing of mortals and immortals is risky. I'll have no more of it in my regime."

I gave a howl. " Soko, I want to visit the Island again."

" Wait till you die," he said, shortly. " I don't want to wait till I die." He said nothing, and I began to be thoughtful. Then, for we were rapidly ascending, I leaned over the side of the car. " Good-bye, brother fishes, good-bye."

" Higher, Bonn," said Soko, to his nephew, and up we spun through the air. The fishes were frantically waving fins and leap-

ing, but they soon faded away, and I saw only a plain, blue sheet of water below, and above us the slowly leaving crowd of birds.

Their heads were all pointed toward the Island. " They will take back the latest news of us," I said, half aloud.

" The latest news," said Soko, " they know on the Island now that you fell into the sea."

"They know!" I exclaimed, "how do they know?"

" You had no sooner touched the water than the birds were telegraphing from above. Do you suppose they would send out such an army of birds without some reporters among them ? "

" I never thought about it," I said, and quite quiet from surprise, I stared hard at the big, slowly moving flock above.

I kept waving my hand at them, and I saw many a flutter from wings and heads and tails that I knew were meant for good-byes. Then, just as we were getting out of sight, they began to sing — that is, all the birds that could sing.

That was a song — sweet, and mournful, and yet cheerful. First it made me want to cry like a baby, then I smiled, and then it was so stirring that I felt my fists balling up as if they wanted to fight some one.

" Good-bye, dear birds," I just yelled after them,

" good-bye, good-bye! " then I sank back in the car, and muttered to myself, " I suppose they won't hear a word of it."

Soko was looking at me curiously. " Boy, you have a good deal yet to learn, about sound waves."

" A good deal," I repeated, with a kind of scorn of myself, " I have everything to learn. I am an ignorant empty-brain. When I get home I'm going to study — you just see, and if I can't catch up to some of you animals in knowledge, I'll be jiggered."

Soko laughed, and I began to look round for something to do, for whenever the excitement stopped, I had that awful feeling in the pit of my stomach that I had when Rag died.

Pussy was looking rather peaked, so I thought I would have a little talk with her, and holding my blanket well around me, I hitched myself over to the side of the car where she sat.

" Pussy," I said, " I wish I could take you to earth with me."

" Meow," she said, just like a common cat.

"But, Pussy," I said, "as I can't do that, try to get to the World of the Blessed before I do. I should like to have you there to meet me."

" I'll try. Master Sam," she said, pitifully. Then she went on in a low voice, " Those animals made a great fuss over your leaving."

"Yes," I said, "they did."

" But not one of them feels as badly as I do," said the Cat. " I am so dismal, so hopeless. Those animals like each other, and I hate them all."

" Suppose you begin by trying to like them, Pussy," I said. " That may hasten your getting away."

" Well, I'll try," she said in a miserable voice, *' but it will be hard work. Not one of them ever did as much for me as you did. I might have been lying there on that beach yet in a dead hypnotic state, if it hadn't been for you."

" Pussy," I said, " if you want to make the animals like you, like them — and like them hard. Make friends with Rag. He will advise you. He is a noble dog. Stay, haven't I some token to send him by you ? "

I examined my clothes. My handkerchief was gone long ago. I hardly ever keep one. My necktie was lost, but there were some buttons on my coat.

I wrenched one off. I tore a strip from my shirt, and passing it through the button, tied it round j Pussy's neck. " Show this to Rag," I said. " Tell ' him that he is to be chummy with you and help you in any way he can."

The Cat licked my hand. " Oh, thank you, thank j you."

I amused myself for a time by watching some , other distant air-ships, then I snuggled down beside j her, and went to sleep.

《

W 1^ (S^omt 3Batft to IBarti^ 355

Several hours went by, though they only seemed like minutes, when I felt her pushing me and whispering, " Wake up, boy, we are nearing San Francisco." ^H I sat up and rubbed my eyes. " We have had a ^■endid trip," old Soko was muttering to himself. ^■The young monkey was holding out my clothes ' to me. Long ago they had dried in the cool, dry air. It was damper now that we were dropping down over the Golden Gate, so while Pussy politely turned aside her head, I slipped off my blankets, and got into my garments.

It was very, very early in the morning. A sick, damp-looking sun was just dragging himself into : sight from behind the hills.

We sailed in over the narrow entrance to the i grand old Bay. Some early birds of Italian fishing-boats and some larger vessels were just making their way out to the Pacific.

Cliff House, the Park, Fort Point — there they were just the same as when I left.

" I feel as if I had been away for years instead of days," I said.

Soko was speaking to our escort of swans. I forgot to say how quietly and gracefully they had kept beside us all the way. Dulce, as my chief pet, flying so near the car that I could touch her sometimes with my outstretched hand.

For some reason or other Soko would not take them all into the city with us. All but Dulce and her mate were told to go perch on trees in the Park, till they saw the air-ship coming back.

Here were more farewells, and when they were over, we soared up to the top of one of the highest hills. The cable-cars were gliding up and down just the same as when I left, though they seemed smaller now than they were before.

I stared at the house, the garden — the Hilling-ton's house and their garden. Just the same, nothing had changed.

Soko sent Dulce ahead to investigate. She reported the coast clear, so we anchored the air-ship to the balcony.

Pussy crept out. " Your nurse has left the room," she whispered. " She took a pitcher in her hand, and has probably gone to get fresh water. Your mother is dozing in her bedroom with her door open."

" Say farewell now," said Soko, " we must leave at once."

I gave him an awful hug. I patted his young ape helper. I kissed Dulce — I am not ashamed to say so, and rubbed her mate's neck. He was an old beauty, but not as bright as Dulce; then I waited for Pussy, who was waving her paw at the false image on the bed.

g a^omt jgaefe to iSartfi 357

It faded — faded, then disappeared, and I caught Pussy up in my arms and squeezed her, and she lever squealed.

Be a good Pussy," I said; then I lifted her into
le car, raised the anchor, and watched my friends
i disappearing into the damp moist gray of the sky.
Oh, how lonely I felt. I heaved an awful sigh,
id went into my room. I crept to mother's door.

was dying to wake her, but it might frighten her

death. I would better get into bed, so I stripped

my clothes, put on my pajamas, and in five

linutes, wasn't I asleep again? I am a fearful

leeper, can drop my head, and go off at any time.

CHAPTER XXIX.

MOTHER GETS A START

"Well, Mother!" I said.

It was a few hours later, and I was sitting up in bed.

Mother gave a great gasp, and cried, " Nurse, come here quick."

A young woman in a white cap came into the room.

" Good morning," I said.

" My darling! " shrieked mother.

" Hush," said the nurse, " don't excite him."

" Don't excite me," I said, " just wait, and I'll excite you. Please get out of my way, will you, till I get on my clothes? I'm starving."

" My darling! " said mother again.

" My darling! " I said, hugging her. " I'm mighty glad to see you again."

" Sweet child — I've been seeing you every day for the last week, but you haven't known me."

" Oh, no, no, you haven't, Mother," I said, " that's where you're mistaken."

" Oh, nurse, isn't he bright this morning? " said mother. " Can this be my sick boy ? "

" No, it isn't," I said, " the Cat took that one."

" The Cat!" cried mother, " oh, nurse, he has not recovered."

" Will you kindly get out of the room? " I said, staring at the young woman, " I want to dress."

She ran like a rabbit to the telephone. I could hear her calling up the doctor. K I got up.

^m " Oh, come back, come back to bed, my dear one," ^■pleaded mother, trembling with fright. " You are ^"'weak and exhausted. The doctor said that if you woke we must send for him, and we must on no account allow you to move — oh, is it possible — is it true that you are yourself again? I was afraid that you would sleep yourself out of that long trance into eternity."

" Mother," I said, giving her another bear hug to restore her spirits, " I have been in eternity. I haven't been in that bed all this time. Didn't I tell you that that thing was a false image the Cat made? "

" The Cat again," she shrieked, " oh, my darling, my darling — get into bed."

I was standing in the middle of the floor with my arms round her,

"Why should I get into bed, little Mother? I feel as strong as a horse."

" Oh, just to please me," she said, " do He down. Mother is going to faint, Sam."

I had to go back into bed, not very well pleased. " Well, will you let me have some breakfast up here?"

" Certainly, certainly, darling, but wait a minute, till nurse comes. Oh, it is so lovely to have you better. This slight delirium will pass away. Does your head feel hot, Sam ? Do you see specks in the air?"

" Mother," I said, drawing her down to a chair beside my bed, "you just listen to me. I haven't been home for a week — do you understand ? "

Mother nodded her head like a Chinese doll. ** For a week — yes, exactly."

"I — I've been away in an air-ship," I said, and for the first time I began to think that my adventures would sound funny to any one that didn't know of the World of Floating Islands.

" In an air-ship, yes," said mother, nodding again.

" And that false thing in this bed," I said, " was just put there to keep you from feeling uneasy."

" From feeling uneasy," she repeated.

" Mother," I said, anxiously, " I don't like your expression. You're not feeling well."

" Well, oh, yes, Sam, very well."

I went on. " The Cat made you believe that was me."

I

" Was me, that is, was I," said mother. " Oh, yes, the Cat, certainly."

" And the ape Soko took me to the Island of Brotherly Love."

" He did," said mother, with a choke and a shudder; " how kind! "

" And I had a great time, Mother," I said, and I proceeded to tell her.

That dear little woman sat there for ten mortal minutes, and I talked, and she didn't believe a word I said.

Then I gave up, and asked her to please order my breakfast.

She went into the hall, and I stuffed my face in the pillow to keep from laughing as I heard her talking to the nurse.

" Don't excite him," said the young woman, " and don't for anything encourage him to take anything but barley water and gruel."

" Mother," I roared, " please bring me up fruit, and biscuits, and eggs, no meat nor fish, mind, and hot cakes and syrup.'*

Mother tiptoed away, and presently came back with a compromise breakfast.

I grumbled, but I swept everything off the tray.

" Poor boy! how good to see you eat again,'* she said, watching me.

" Why, Mother, I've been eating like a pig the last week."

She wouldn't say anything.

" Oh, Mother, I wish you would believe me."

" I wish I could, Sam," she said, pitifully.

" But, Mother, suppose it was all made up. How could I, Sam Emerson, a stupid kind of a boy in school, no good at composition or that sort of thing — how could I make up those animals ? Why, lots of them, I had never seen before, and how could I make such a queer goat. Mother, and an awful Widow — not a bit like you — and monkeys and apes and bears — oh. Mother, you just ought to see those bears grinding corn."

Mother began to calm down, and get used to my animals, and now she just looked plain puzzled. Then suddenly a light broke over her face. " Sam, I believe you are calling up the old stories in that Natural History I used to read to you when you were a child."

" Mother, I don't remember a word of it," I said.

" Still you might have called it up. The brain does extraordinary things in delirium, or when the body is in a state of coma. And nothing is lost. All our apparently forgotten knowledge is stored away somewhere — now, dear boy, don't talk any more about your Island."

" Mother, I've got to or burst. It is going to be my business in life to talk about animals."

Like a good mother, she didn't argue, and presently she said: " Sam, I hope you won't blame me, but I knew how fend you were of your dog, and I couldn't bear to have him buried in case you asked for him, so I had him embalmed, but I think he'd better be put in the ground now."

" That's all right. Mother," I said.

" Don't you want to see him ? "

" Oh, yes, but I left Rag alive and well. This is only his false body."

" His what ? " and she looked frightened again.

I began to explain to her what I meant, but the more I talked, the more frightened she got, so at last I dried up.

Then I began to kick about, and said I must get up.

She managed to keep me in bed till the doctor came. He felt my pulse, and put a glass thing in my mouth, and just once I saw a queer look in his eye — a look that said, " Why, you don't seem like the same boy that I was attending yesterday." However, when I laughed and taxed him with it, he said I was mistaken.

I told him he had been fooled by a false body, and he smiled, a kind of down-to-the-ground smile, and said he was glad to see me in such good spirits.

He represented the medical profession. Mother had the law and the Church to argue with me, and an editor friend of hers published a very good story

in his paper, called " The Strange Hallucination of a Boy."

I laugh in my sleeve at all these people. They don't understand. The animals do. Every little while when some one has been laughing at me, I put my mouth down to my new dog's ear and say, " Have you ever heard of the Island of Brotherly Love?"

He gives me an understanding glance, and upon m.y word I believe the animals can look into the future better than we can.

However, I'm not talking so much about the Island now. I had to stop it because the fellows at school joshed me so. But I don't forget it, and I just stick up for animals all I can. I know they're watching me, and sending news to the Island of what I am doing, and it's queer how much comfort I get out of that knowledge.

The bird telegraphy is still working. Sometimes, when no one is near, and I see a bird singing away up in a tree, I shout a message to him. He understands, but he never gives me a message back.

I do wish the animals would communicate witl me, but they never do.

I must not forget to say that Hillington and had a grand make-up. He met me more than half^ way. He was afraid I was going to die. I tol(him about the Island. He looked queer, but h(didn't laugh; then he advised me to write it dowi

" Your head's full of it," he said, " and if you go chin-chinning with everybody, they'll only jolly you."

So I've tried to do as he said, and write down the affair for myself, and for old Joe's friends. I've rtried to do it, but haven't got on so very well, what with my trying to keep slang out, and fit nice-sounding words in; but I've got down what I wanted to say, Hillington tells me, for I've read it to him. So here goes for another good-bye.

Believe me if you can, some of you fellows that read this; and if you can't, when you come to San Francisco, ask for Sam Emerson, one of the junior members of the San Francisco Society for the Prevention of Cruelty to Animals, and he'll have a good talk with you about dream versus reality, and if he doesn't convince you, I don't know who can.